Trumpet

Jackie Kay

W F HOWES LTD

This large print edition published in 2012 by
W F Howes Ltd
Unit 4, Rearsby Business Park, Gaddesby Lane,
Rearsby, Leicester LE7 4YH

1 3 5 7 9 10 8 6 4 2

First published in the United Kingdom in 1998
by Picador

A CIP catalogue record for this book is available
from the British Library

ISBN 978 1 47121 321 2

Typeset by Palimpsest Book Production Limited,
Falkirk, Stirlingshire
Printed and bound in Great Britain
by MPG Books Ltd, Bodmin, Cornwall

For Carol Ann Duffy

The way you wear your hat;
The way you sip your tea,
The memory of all that –
No, no! They can't take that away from me!

George Gershwin

HOUSE AND HOME

I pull back the curtain an inch and see their heads bent together. I have no idea how long they have been there. It is getting dark. I keep expecting them to vanish; then I would know that they were all in my mind. I would know that I imagined them just as surely as I imagined my life. But they are still there, wearing real clothes, looking as conspicuous as they please. Each time I look at the photographs in the papers, I look unreal. I look unlike the memory of myself. I feel strange now. It used to be such a certain thing, just being myself. It was so easy, so painless.

I have to get back to our den, and hide myself away from it all. Animals are luckier; they can bury their heads in sand, hide their heads under their coats, pretend they have no head at all. I feel pain in the exact place Joss complained of for months. A stabbing pain on my left side. We couldn't die of the same thing?

There's a film I watched once, *Double Indemnity*, where the guy is telling his story into a tape, dying and breathless. I feel like him. I haven't killed

1

anyone. I haven't done anything wrong. If I was going to make a tape, I'd make it for Colman.

I crept out of my house in the middle of the night with a thief's racing heart. Nobody watching. I drove into dawn. Relief as I crossed the border into Scotland. I let down the windows to sniff the different air. I am exhausted. Every morning for the past ten days, someone has been waiting outside my house with cameras and questions. I have seen the most awful looking pictures of myself in the newspapers looking deranged and shocked. Of course you are going to look demented if some hack hides behind your hedge, snaps and flashes the moment you appear. How else are you going to look?

Even here now the sound of cameras, like the assault of a machine-gun, is still playing inside my head. I can't get the noise to go no matter what I do. I hear it over music, over the sound of a tap running, over the kettle's whistle – the cameras' rapid bullets. Their fingers on the triggers, they don't take them off till they finish the film, till I've been shot over and over again. They stop for the briefest of frantic seconds, reload the cartridge and then start up again. What can they want with all those pictures? With every snap and flash and whirr, I felt myself, the core of myself, being eaten away. My soul. I met a man once who wouldn't let me take his picture with Joss. He said it would be stealing his soul. I remember thinking, how

2

ridiculous, a soul cannot be stolen. Strange how things like that stay with you as if life is waiting for a chance to prove you wrong. Joss's soul has gone and mine has been stolen. It is as simple and as true as that.

Once, I came out of my house and at least ten of them were waiting, two days after Joss's funeral. I was still in a daze. I didn't react quickly enough. I couldn't find cover. I couldn't hide. They took me walking towards my car, entering my car, wild behind the steering wheel. I looked like an actress in an old black and white movie who has just bumped off her husband and is escaping. The wipers on, the rain on the windowscreen, my face, crazy, at the wheel. The blinding white light, flashing and illuminating me. I could barely see to drive off. Of course, the minute I am placed in front of that raging white light, I am not myself any longer. I am no more myself than a rabbit is itself trapped in front of glaring headlights. The rabbit freezes and what you see most on the road is fear itself, not a furry rabbit, fear flashed up before you for a second until your brakes screech to a halt. I have stared at the woman who was captured by the light for ages and ages to try to find myself in her. I have never seen my own fear. Most people don't get a chance to see what they look like terrified. If I had died they would have continued shooting, one shot after another. They would have taken me dead. The next day I was splattered all over the paper's again, more lies, more lurid headlines.

I had to get away. So I drove here. I've been here a million times and never noticed that left turn at Kepper. I threw a bag together and chucked it in the boot and took off. I've no idea how long it took me to get here. Time feels as if it is on the other side of me now, way over, out across the sea, like another country. I don't live inside it any more and it doesn't rule me.

I have a fire going. It is working itself up into a state of survival. The only noise inside here. Dry cackle, sputtering and spitting. It sounds possessed. It seems a strange fickle, flickering company to begin with, as if at any moment it might just die out, the flames pale and uncertain, but after a while it has transformed into my loyal, dependable friend. I sit here like this for an age admiring the full colours, looking right into the wild soul of the fire to try to find myself. I can see Joss bending down to light the fire, making his base with newspapers rolled and then tied to precision, then kindling. 'There's quite an art to building a fire,' he says, lighting it, smug, satisfied.

Colman is the only one who knows I am here. I left him a message on his machine. I think I didn't say much except that I was going to Torr. He can get hold of me if he wants, though I doubt he will. I don't know if he'll ever speak to me again. Bruce, the butcher, would always take a message. I won't hold my breath.

4

From the small sitting-room window, way down below, I can see the waves in the damaged light, lashing out at the rocks. My eyes follow the waves backwards out to where the sea is suddenly deep. It seems as if Joss has been dead for the longest time now. Every day feels like a week. I am awake for much of the time, staring out into the dark or the day; it doesn't make much difference.

My hand was shaking when I lit the fire. That's how absurd I've become. I can't even light a tiny cottage fire without shaking. It might be the beginning. Animals do that, don't they, when one goes first, the other follows later, often of the very same thing. I don't know what is real and what is not, whether the pain in my side is real or imagined. The terrible thing about pain is that it doesn't matter, it still hurts. It hurts like hell.

They will never find me here. Torr is off the beaten track. We never mentioned the existence of this placc to any of the media through the years. We kept it private. Colman is the only one and he won't be speaking to any of them. He told me he was too ashamed to go out. I never imagined that people could make such a fuss. I know now why they call reporters hounds. I feel hounded, hunted. Pity the fox.

Joss's holiday clothes are all here. Colman's model aeroplanes, fishing rods, old green bottles dug up from the sea. Colman's little antique collection. His coins. Joss's records. A box of his mild cigars. Everything that mattered to us, we celebrated here.

5

When we first adopted Colman we brought him here, not long after. We chose his name here too. Joss and I nearly divorced when it came to naming Colman. Joss wanted Miles; I wanted Campbell. Joss wanted Louis; I wanted Alastair. Joss wanted a jazz or a blues name. What about Jelly Roll, I laughed. Or Howling Wolf, Bird, Muggsy, Fats, Leadbelly. I was bent over double: Pee Wee. Joss slapped me across my face. 'That's enough,' he said. 'White people always laugh at black names.' I rubbed my cheek. I couldn't believe it. I just gave him a look until I saw the first bloom of shame appear on his. We gave up on names and went to bed. Sex is always better if you argue before. After, we compromised on Colman spelt the Irish way and not like Coleman Hawkins. That way we could get an Irish name and a jazz name rolled into one. Colman comes from the Latin meaning dove, I told Joss, pleased with myself. 'Is that right?' he said. 'Well, I hope to Christ he brings us peace.'

I must go out. It is a terrible day, the sky all gloomy and bad-tempered. It could turn sour. It could pour. But I need to get out. I put on my old mackintosh and sniff the salt in the air outside. I lock my door, just in case. I take a couple of steps down the road and realize I just can't do it. There are people here who will nod and say hello and ask me how I am. It's been four months or so since we were last here. I can't face them. Not today. Maybe later when it's dark I'll go out. I unlock my door. Take off my coat and sit down by the fire. It is still there, glowing. I feed it an extra log, the long red fingers snap it up with great gusto.

Most people here are oblivious to the happenings in the jazz world. Never heard of Joss Moody, Britain's legendary trumpet player. Some of them might have seen the papers. There's one thing: most people here just read the local paper. That was what we loved about coming here, the complete anonymity. Not a dicky bird out of anybody until the day that Joss told Angus, the fisherman, about himself. Angus came off his old leaking boat one day, reeking of fish. 'What's this I hear, eh? You didn't tell me your husband played the trumpet. Why the big secret. Can we no have a wee shindig?' Before the week was out I was showing Angus the trumpet: the big jewel in the huge jewellery box. I'd sometimes catch Joss stroking the velvet insides of that box with the same tender concentration that he stroked cats.

I first brought Joss to Torr in the middle of the winter. 1956. Our tyres skidded in the black ice on the road up here. When we finally arrived Torr was thick in snow and Joss was for turning back. The cottage seemed as if it possessed a memory of its own, one of those memories that remembers the distant past better than the recent. It clung to smells of people who'd lived here years ago. The rug was worn down to the bone. The paintings on

7

the walls were old oils by local artists with plain titles. Fishing Nets. Mist on Sea. Early morning, Kepper. Only one title disturbed me, Skeleton. A watercolour of an abandoned fish on the beach. I remembered it from when I was a child. I stared at the shape of the bones. I could see how simple it would be to choke to death. There were large cobwebs everywhere, hanging from corner to corner like fishing nets. Two mouldy coffee cups sat on the table. Duncan was last here. I was feeling the old excitement I've felt since I was a girl coming here on holiday, arriving to the smell of the past. The past had lived on in those small airless rooms whilst we had been away living our life. The past had been here all the time, waiting. It was wonderful. The dank musty smells of last summer. Punching the old spicy pillows. Sleeping in the noisy, creaking beds, the smell of rust and old blankets, the smell of damp walls. By the time we left after our fortnight's holiday, the cottage smelt different again, as if it had suddenly come into the present.

'Is this it?' he said. 'Right, the only way I'm going to get to like this place is if we christen it right now.' And we did. I slid down the wall and knocked a few cobwebs off when I came.

Once I was a fearless girl. I came to Torr every summer, climbed rocks, ran down the hills, dug graves for my brothers till the tide came in. Combed the beach for strange shells. It feels so

8

long ago, it is as if it was somebody else who lived that part of my life. Not me. The girl I was has been swept out to sea. She is another tide entirely. Way back in the distance. I can't imagine what she'd think of my life now, whether she'd think it was the life she was expecting to have or not. She always wanted marriage, I remember. Marriage, children. She wouldn't have been surprised at that. I married a man who became famous. He died before me. He died recently. Now what am I? Can I remember? Joss Moody's widow. That's what I am, Joss Moody's widow. She never imagined being a widow, did she? Of course she didn't. What little girl ever imagines becoming a widow?

Tonight, after dusk, I go out into the half-dark, wearing my bottle-green windcheater with the hood over my hair. Joss used to comb my hair every night. It was one of the few feminine things he did. I loved it. Him sitting behind me, pressing against me, combing my thick dark hair in firm downward strokes.

I follow the road down to the sea. This walk is so familiar the memory of it is in my feet. I don't even need to look. So many times with Joss, down the steep hill from Torr, round the corner of the harbour and up the other side towards the cliffs. Arm in the crook of arm down the hill, then when we came to the cliff path we'd separate, single file, Joss always behind me. It is muddy with all the rain. Slippy, dangerous. I keep on, taking one step up the cliff path at a time. The sea is moaning like a sick person. I can't take my eyes off it. No matter how many times I am near it, it never ceases to frighten me. I stand and watch the sea's wild movements, the huge awesome leaps. I can hear Joss saying, 'The great beast.' Down below, the upturned fishing boats look lifeless, lonely. I know which boat belongs to which man. Their oars, like long sad arms waiting to be lifted and brought to life. I am tense; afraid somebody is going to pounce on me. I shouldn't have come out. I'll need to head back. It is even harder coming down. I must be mad. I could tumble and fall into the sea. The idea is strangely attractive to me. There is nothing behind or in front of me: just me and the wind and the sea. Everything is so familiar it is terrifying. I try to hush my breathing. I break into a run. My legs are shorter. Grief is making me shrink.

I unlock my door and rush inside the house. My heart is in my mouth. It feels wrong; there is something the matter with this place. I listen for noises. It is as if somebody else is here or has been here. I go from room to room looking. My own coat hanging on a door hook startles me. The sudden flashlight of a car sweeping past outside. Nothing. This fear is taking me over. If they are not stalking me, I am doing it to myself. I try to make light of my fears. It was our secret. That's all it was. Lots of people have secrets, don't they? The world runs on secrets. What kind of place would the world be without them? Our secret was harmless. It did not hurt anybody.

There must be a mistake we made. A big mistake; hiding somewhere that I somehow missed.

I sit down on Joss's armchair. I am not sure what to do with myself. I find myself getting agitated, now wondering what to do with my hands. I pick up a book and try to read a paragraph but it doesn't go in. The words spill and lurch in front of me making no sense. I close the book and turn on the television. But the sound of the chat-show host's voice, the speed of his talk, distresses me. I turn it off. I put on some music. I can listen to music. I try and breathe with it because my breathing still isn't right. It is still too fast. Joss's breathing became very fast in the end. Fast and shallow. When I think of the breath he used to take in and out to blow that trumpet! When he was dying, I thought if only he could have one big trumpet breath, he'd get some relief.

The summer before I met Joss, I was here at Torr with my brother and his family. I felt restless, discontented with my life. I wanted a passion, somebody to speed up time with a fast ferocious love. We didn't have hot water then. At night, I'd sing in the freezing cold bathroom whilst I washed myself with the pot full of hot water in the old cracked sink, *Some day he'll come along, the man I love; And he'll be big and strong. The man I love . . . Maybe I shall meet him Sunday, Maybe Monday – maybe not; Still I'm sure to meet him one day – Maybe Tuesday will be my good news day.* Then I'd lie on my thin hard bed

11

trying to paint him in watercolours. I gave him a strong jaw.

I can still picture him the day we met in that blood donors' hall in Glasgow. How could I have known then? He was well dressed, astonishingly handsome, high cheekbones that gave him a sculpted proud look; his eyes darker than any I'd ever seen. Thick black curly hair, the tightest possible curls, sitting on top of his head, like a bed of springy bracken. Neat nails, beautiful hands. I took him all in as if I had a premonition, as if I knew what would happen. His skin was the colour of Highland toffee. His mouth was a beautiful shape. I had this feeling of being pulled along by a pack of horses. In my mind's eye I could see them, galloping along until they came to the narrow path that led to the big house. The huge dark gates. It was as if I had no say in what was going to happen to me, just this giddy sick excitement, this terrible sense of fate. We both give blood, I thought to myself. I wondered what made him give blood, what family accident, what trauma. We didn't speak that first time, though I could feel him looking at me.

The fire is shrinking too. Collapsing in on itself, turning to ash. I get up and put the guard over the fire and go into the kitchen. I stand next to the kettle for an age, rubbing my hands till the shrill whistle pierces through me as if I wasn't expecting it. I make myself a cup of tea to take to bed. Sleeping in our bed here is so terrible, I considered sleeping in Colman's old room, or sleeping on the couch downstairs, or sleeping on the floor. I felt as if I'd be deserting Joss though. I climb into our old bed and place my cup of tea at my side. The space next to me bristles with silence. The emptiness is palpable. Loss isn't an absence after all. It is a presence. A strong presence here next to me. I sip my tea and look at it. It doesn't look like anything, that's what is so strange. It just fits in. Last night I was certain it was a definite shape. I bashed the sheets about to see if it would declare itself. It won't let me alone and it won't let me sleep. I try to find sleep. Sleep is out there where Joss is, isn't it? That's what the headstones tell you. Who Fell Asleep On. Sleeping. Fell Asleep on Jesus. Joss is out there sleeping behind the sea wall. I can't sleep any more. Not properly. Sleep scratches at me then wakes me up. I dip down for a moment then surface again, my eyes peeling the darkness away. I don't know how many hours I have had of it since he died. It can't be many. It was a form of torture, wasn't it, sleep deprivation?

If I don't try to sleep, it might sneak up on me, capture me. I won't try to sleep. I will try to remember. The next time is six months later. We are back giving blood on the same day, Tuesday. I am brazen, full of knowledge. I approach him and ask him out. It is 1955. Women don't do this sort of thing. I don't care. I am certain this man is going to be my lover. When you are certain of something, you must take your chance; you mustn't miss your opportunity or life is lost. I remember my grandfather telling me that; how he knew with my grandmother, how he courted her until he had her. I tell him I've noticed him here before. We talk about giving blood, how we both hate it, but like clenching our fist and the biscuit afterwards. I ask him if he watches the blood being drained out of himself. He says he looks away at anything else. He says he is quite squeamish. What about you, he asks me, what do you do? I tell him I like to watch the blood filling up, the wonderful rich colour of it. He laughs as if he suddenly likes me. Then we both fall silent and he stares at me awkwardly, puzzled by me just coming up to him like this. But he isn't trying to get rid of me. He is looking me up and down as if appraising me. I am glad that I am wearing my good dress, with the polka dots and the straps. I know I look good.

We go for a drink in Lauder's bar. He tells me his name is Joss Moody and I ask him if that is his real name. He is offended. I see a look cross his face that I haven't seen before. Of course it is his real name, what am I talking about. I tell him it sounds like a stage name, like a name that someone would make up in anticipation of being famous. He laughs at that and tells me he is going to be famous. I laugh too, nervously. I know he's going to be famous also. I could have noticed then, I suppose. The way he was so irritated with me asking him about his name. I say, 'My name is

14

Millie MacFarlane,' as if I'd just heard it for the first time, as if my own name was miles away from who I am. I say, 'Millicent MacFarlane, but my friends call me Millie,' suddenly shy. We talk about anything. He tells me he plays the trumpet. He is so pleased with himself for playing the trumpet, I can see that. He says the word, 'trumpet', and his eyes shine. 'Would you like one for the road, Millie?' he asks. Him saying my name makes me weak. I hold onto the table and watch him go to the bar for his whisky and my gin.

He walks me to my flat in Rose Street, Number 14. And leaves me. 'I know where you are now,' he says. A little kiss on my cheek. I get in and throw myself on my bed, punch my pillow. Then I stroke the side of my cheek Joss Moody kissed and say, courting to myself, courting, courting, 'courting' until it sounds like a beautiful piece of music.

We court for three months. A kiss on the cheek at the end of the date. Meeting at Boots' Corner, at The Shell in Central Station, or below the Hielan' Man's umbrella under where the trains come out of Central Station on Argyle Street, between Hope Street and Union Street. The times I've waited for Joss sheltered from the rain, under the Hielan' Man's umbrella, imagining the Highland men years ago, fresh down from the Highlands talking excited Gaelic to each other. Either we go drinking or we go dancing. Great dance halls in Glasgow. Dancing at the Playhouse, at Denniston

Palais, at the Locarno, the Astoria or the Plaza, it seemed nobody would ever get old. Nobody would ever die. Even the ugly looked beautiful. Joss was a wonderful dancer; he loved to strut his stuff on those dance floors. A hive of jive. He was showbiz itself already. They all were. I remember laughing till I cried, watching one man after another get up at the Locarno and imitate Frank Sinatra singing 'Dancing in the Park'. The Carswell Clothes' shop competition. I remember loving the names of those bands at the dance halls – Ray McVey Trio, Doctor Crock and the Crackpots, Joe Loss, Oscar Rabin, Carl Barritean, Harry Parry, Felix Mendelson, and, my favourite, the Hawain Serenaders. Dancing makes us both happy. Big steps. Quickstep. Dip. We dance at the Barrowland way into the early hours. The atmosphere, jumping. The dance style, gallus. There is no tomorrow. There is just the minute, the second, the dip. The heat and the sweat. That feeling of being your body. Body and soul.

We come out of the Playhouse full of the night. Joss takes me home and walks off again, hands in pocket. I watch him turn the corner of Rose Street into Sauchiehall Street before going in. He never looks back. Never waves. I begin to think that there is something wrong. Either Joss is terribly proper and old-fashioned or there is something wrong. He never tries to touch me. He holds my hand or we walk with our arms round each other. We kiss, short soft kisses. Three months of kisses

16

on my left cheek, soft timeless kisses that grow into buds and wait. Each night I go home madly in love with Joss and terribly frustrated. I am twenty and he is thirty; perhaps the age difference is making him shy. Still, I am not a schoolgirl any more.

At night, I watch Joss walk up the street, hands in his pockets. He has a slow deliberate walk, like he's practised it. I go into my small bedroom. I have a single bed in the room, a dresser and a small wardrobe. I stare at myself in the mirror. Rub night cream into my cheeks for a long time. Imagine Joss standing behind me. Undress. Drape my bathrobe over my shoulders. Rub more cream into my cheeks. Use a powder puff under my breasts. Joss, behind me. I sigh, put my white nightdress on and climb heavily into my bed. I can hear Helen, my flatmate, up and about. I listen to her noises and fall off asleep where I'll dream of Joss again and again and wake myself up in the middle of the night.

I know I am waiting for something to happen.

It is Friday. I am going to see Joss tonight. We are going to listen to some saxophone player, I forget his name. Joss knows it. I like the world of these jazz places he has been taking me to. I like the smoke, the drink, the belief. It is an 'in' world. I always feel like I've been taken somewhere out of myself. I have to finish filing for the doctor and then it will be time to go home. I'm thinking, what should I wear? All the time I'm thinking, Tonight is the night. I sing to myself. I look at the clock in the reception. It is a tease. It barely moves.

Joss is late to get me. Joss is always late. When he finally arrives, he is wearing a blue serge suit and white shirt and striped tie. I am stabbed by his good looks; his thick dark hair, his intense eyes. Tonight he is all worked up. He admires this saxophonist. We have to rush. Out in the streets people stare at us, particularly at Joss. He knows quite a few of the guys in this club. Some strangers know him. He is already building up a reputation for himself, playing a few jazz bars and pubs and clubs. It is early days, he says, full of excitement. Early days for jazz and early days for him, for his new life. During the day he works in the fishing-tackle shop in Renfield Street. He says that's his other interest. I say you're an unusual man: fish and jazz. 'Better than fish and chips any day,' he says. Already there is a buzz around him, a magnetic force that draws other people towards him. He looks the part. He is tall, coloured. His father was African, his mother Scottish. He doesn't know the exact country, just the continent, he laughs gamely. 'It's a big fucking continent, so it is.' His mother never remembered and she's dead now he says. When I ask him what his mother died of, he hesitates, then seems to pluck 'heart attack' out of the thin air. I can't read his expression. 'Did you not get on with her?' I ask him. 'Not exactly,' he says.

When the sax starts Joss closes his eyes and keeps

them closed for the longest time. I find this a bit embarrassing. I feel as if I've lost him, that he belongs to the music and not to me. Other people shout out, little words of intense pleasure – 'Yeah!' Clap their hands. Stomp their feet. Listen to the music as if they themselves were creating it, with a strange filmic pride on their faces. They shake their heads from side to side in perfect rhythm to the music. Some of their faces point downwards, chin resting on their chest; others have their heads tilted back. All heads shake and shudder from side to side. Some people simply move their chin out and in, jerky movements, eyes shut. But every single face in this place is prepared to go the distance. All attention rapt, euphoric, dedicated. They will follow the sax down to the deep dark place, wherever it leads them, disciples to the cool blue. It is almost holy. I feel like I am in a church and I am the only one who has got her eyes open whilst she prays. The man next to me moves his right hand to the music, small snappy movements, his private conducting. I wonder whether I will ever let myself go enough to put on that serious jazz face, pouting my lips and shaking my head in tight syncopated movements.

The music changes. The sax is all slow and sad, like it is trying to remember something lost. I try tapping my foot in time to the soft shoe shuffle of the drum. At first I feel self-conscious. I'm not sure that my foot tapping looks like the other tapping feet. I'm not sure I've got it right. I know

I can't risk shaking my head, twitching my face or conducting with my hand. But this quiet tapping feels fine. After a while I don't even notice myself doing it. I have gone inside the music. It's a strange feeling, but there it is waiting for me. I am sitting in the middle of the long slow moan of the sax, right inside it. I feel something in me go soft, give in. I look over at Joss and find him staring at me. He's seen it all happening. He looks right through me.

It is dark now outside. The streetlamps cast their yellow light on the streets. A lot of us leave The Wee Jazz Bar at the same time. We look like people that have just been created out of the night, people who have just landed on the planet all at once together with the same pioneering, fierce look on our faces. We move along in our long coats with the collars turned up. It is windy. The wind blows a can along the street. Tonight is *the night*. Joss holds my hand tight as if he's protecting me from something.

He walks me right to my door. He goes to kiss me on the cheek, but changes his mind and kisses me full on the mouth. He grabs me up in his arms, sweeping my face towards his. He pulls me closer against him till my feet almost rise from the ground. His breathing is fast, excited. I open my eyes and stare at him whilst he is kissing me. His eyes are tight shut. He says my name as he kisses me, over and over again. I feel like I am dying. I take his hand and lead him up the stairs to my small flat. I hope Helen is sound asleep, tucked up in her little bed.

But when we get up the stairs, everything changes. Joss doesn't throw me on my bed like I am expecting. He paces the room. 'Sit down,' I say. 'Make yourself at home.' I've gone all shy. The intimacy of my own bedroom has made strangers of both of us. He sits down on the edge of my bed looking terrible, troubled. 'What is it, Joss, what's the matter?' There is something he has to tell me. Something he should have told me ages ago, months ago, but couldn't. He was afraid that if I knew I would stop seeing him. I feel sick. 'Knew what?' My mind is racing. Maybe he's married; maybe he's got one of those men's diseases; maybe he's committed a crime. I don't know what it can be. I catch myself in the mirror. My hair is all out of place; my eyes look as wild as his. I can tell it is something serious, but I try to laugh it off. I ruffle my hands through his hair and kiss his cheek. 'It can't be that bad,' I say. 'Nothing is when you are in love.' It is the first time I have ever told him this. It makes him more unhappy. He actually looks like he is going to cry. He tells me he can't see me any more, just like that. I don't believe this is happening. The moon is full outside the window, gaping in. The night is a lie. I want to go to sleep. I want to stop him talking and climb into my bed with him and fall asleep in his arms. I don't care what he has done. I don't want to know what he has done. He is saying he is sorry. The big moon gawps at me. It is strangely excited. I feel as if my world is turning mad.

I knock my night cream off my dresser. Something in me just blows. 'You can't do that,' I tell him and I find myself hitting him on the chest, crying. He gets angry with himself. I can hear him swearing under his breath. Then I hear him saying, 'Forgive me.' And he gets up to go. But I can't have that. I grab him and pull him back. He is taller than me. I can't shake him with my full force. So I shout instead. I don't care about waking anybody up. I scream at him, 'An explanation, you owe me an explanation. What's the matter with you? Are you sick? Have you killed somebody?' The strange thing is he already feels like he belongs to me. My anger makes him mine. 'You really want to know, don't you,' he says in a voice I can't quite recognize. 'You really want to know. I'll show you then,' he says. 'I'll show you what is the matter.' He has a strange expression on his face, as if for a moment he is suspended, not quite himself.

He takes off his blue jacket and throws it on my floor. He takes off his tie and throws that down too. His hands are trembling. I am trembling. I think maybe he's changed his mind and he wants to make love. I think, shouldn't he undress me first? I'm not sure. I try to remember what the couple of other boyfriends I've had have done. My mind goes blank. He is undoing the buttons of his shirt. He slows down now. Each button is

22

undone so terribly slowly. Underneath the shirt is a T-shirt. He takes that off slowly too, lifting his arms up and pulling it from his waist over his head. He discards it. His eyes are determined. He looks at me the whole time. An odd look, challenging, almost aggressive – as if he is saying, 'I told you so. I told you so.' He pulls the next T-shirt over his head and throws that away too. He has another layer on underneath, a vest. His clothes are spreadeagled on my floor like the outline of a corpse in a movie. The vest is stripped off as well. He looks a lot thinner now with all that off him. I'm excited watching this man undress for me. Underneath his vest are lots of bandages wrapped round and round his chest. He starts to undo them. I feel a wave of relief: to think all he is worried about is some scar he has. He should know my love goes deeper than a wound. 'You don't have to show me,' I say. I feel suddenly full of compassion. 'Did you have an accident? I don't care about superficial things like that.' I go towards him to embrace him. 'I'm not finished,' he says. He keeps unwrapping endless rolls of bandage. I am still holding out my hands when the first of his breasts reveals itself to me. Small, firm.

It is light outside now, a frail beginning light. I can see it from my window, tap dancing on the sea, on the rough scrubby hills. The sea is calmer today, shamed by last night's excesses. It is lying low, all blue and growling innocence. I am safe. I will go down to the shops. I have an appetite for the first time in days. I will go and buy a fresh loaf, some mature cheddar, some ripe tomatoes, some ham off the bone. I won't buy a newspaper.

Why go back now, ever? The people are kinder here and, strangely enough, more real. The people up here are more real. I could move up those belongings I want and throw the rest away. Our friends in London have turned sour or too curious. I don't want to see anyone. Except Colman. I wish I could see Colman. What could I tell him – that his father and I were in love, that it didn't matter to us, that we didn't even think about it after a while? I didn't think about it so how could I have kept it from him if it wasn't in my mind to keep?

I wash my face with cold water. I am so tired I have become a different person. The way I think is different. I know this; I can remember that I used to have more space inside my head. Now it is crammed full with worries. I flit about from one to the other like a nervous bird. I tell myself not to. If I was going to worry, I should have worried years ago. Perhaps it is me getting older. My grandmother used to worry that she was going to forget what she wanted to say. She'd write down notes and then forget where she put the notes. Sometimes, she'd seize upon the wrong note and end up telling you something that was out of date. I put on a pair of trousers, my cashmere jumper. A cameo brooch. I can at least look presentable to the world. I cannot have it said that Joss

Moody's widow has gone to the dogs. Joss liked to 'keep me nice'. I put my coat on and go out. I don't lock the door. I've never locked the door here and I'm not starting now. I will walk for a while until the shops open, along the coast. 'You'll take the high road and I'll take the low road,' I sing to Joss. He always liked me singing to him even although I can't sing worth a damn. Already the day is different than it appeared from the window. The wind is bitter and howling. Weather here in this part of the world is just as moody, just as subjective and disloyal, as people.

So strong, the smell of the sea if you haven't been close to it for a while. I can taste the seaweed and the fish in my mouth. The salt in my hair, on my cheeks. The wind blows behind me, making a balloon of my coat, rushing me along faster than I want to go. The sea isn't so calm, close up. I can stare right into its heart. The waves leap over each other in a frenzy. Above the waves themselves are the shadows of ghost waves trying to speak. I can see them chasing the real waves, wanting their life back. I have hardly walked along this road alone for years. We always came out for our walks together here. It feels odd walking on my own. The wind could pick me up and carry me out to sea. There is nothing holding me down. I could float. I could fly.

The harbour has stayed the same since I was a girl and came up from England on holidays here with my family. The chippie is the same chippie.

The photography shop here that was established in 1886 is still standing – F. Futcher and Son. The Family Butcher, B. Savage, has been here since I was a girl. His son runs the shop now. He's also called Bruce, like his father. They both have butcher's red cheeks and hands. There's a little Italian café run by the Dalsassos that does the best ice-cream for miles around and sells sweets in those big plastic jars. Sweets that so inhabited my childhood holidays here, it makes me laugh to see that they are still in existence. Soor plooms. Tablet. Sherbet Fountains. Cinnamon balls. Aniseed balls. Lemon bon bons. Coconut mushrooms. Peppermint creams. The Italian café does a good breakfast too. On impulse I go in and sit down. Mrs Dalsasso is pleased to see me. 'The usual?' she asks. Scrambled eggs on toast. 'Where's Mr Moody this morning?' she asks. I say, 'Mr Moody died a few weeks ago.'

'Oh, I'm sorry,' she says and grips my hand tightly. 'A nice, nice man, Mr Moody. A nice man.' I nod, wondering what Mrs Dalsasso would say if she saw the papers. I have a lump in my throat now. Mrs Dalsasso has made me cry. She is the first person to make me feel like an ordinary widow, to give me respect, not prurience. I'd like to weep into her pinnie. I sip my tea. I spill some on my coat and then dab it with a tissue. Tiny bits of tissue stick to my coat. She brings the scrambled egg on toast. I make myself stay seated. She gives me another look, one of those intense sorrowful Italian looks that would make

26

the most noble of people pity themselves. 'I'll leave you to yourself. You won't want to talk,' she says, her cloth expertly wiping the bottom of my cup. 'I bring another cup for you.'

I make an attempt at the breakfast so as not to hurt Mrs Dalsasso's feelings. I really should eat. My body is getting thinner. My clothes are half falling off me. Just over a month ago, my life was full of certain things I was going to do. Joss had a new tour. We were going to go to Tobago for a holiday first. Now here I am, out in the elements of this most familiar place, uncertain about everything. Even my own life. Especially my own life.

I decide to walk down to Lair and do my bit of shopping on the way back. The red phone box is on the corner near the chippie. Pass it. Turn back. Go in. Call him. Nothing to lose. Go on. Call him. I go inside the old red box, preserved like an Egyptian mummy. It should be knocked over to the side with a body in it, holding the phone. I put in my loose change and dial his number. His machine again. I start saying something, 'Colman, if you are there can you pick up the phone?' knowing that he won't pick up the phone to me. There's a wee boy putting bait on the end of his fishing line at the harbour like Colman used to. Joss taught him to fish. They both loved fishing together. Angus often took them out on his boat. Colman had his own rod from the age of three. This boy casts out his line like an expert, with a quick switch, then sits down to wait. I hang up and try again. 'What can I say to you, Colman. I am your mother. I love you.' I hang up again and go out into the wind. It slaps me on the face, stinging my cheeks. The weather is changing again. It is supposed to be summer. The trees sway about like drunks in the wind, cursing.

The wind is intimate with me. Running its long, strong fingers through my hair. Slapping my face, pushing me about, screaming in my ears. It is better to be out than in. I hurry on to Lair, the wind snapping at my heels. I am almost flying. The harbour at Lair is deserted. One or two fishermen bend over their boats, bloated and swollen by the wind. One of them calls out and waves at me. The simplicity of the gesture cheers me, warms me. A stranger's love.

I go into the first pub I see, The Old Ship, and order a pub lunch. Suddenly hungry. Haddock, chips and peas. There are a few men having a pint and a couple of couples eating lunch. A table in the corner, opposite the bar. There's a juke box playing 'Boogie Woogie Bugle Boy of Company B': *There was a trumpet man from down Chicago way. He had a boogie style that no one else could play.* I lift my knife and fork and hold them over my plate, suspended like aircraft.

My four brothers are at my wedding. I have on a pale green slinky dress. Joss and I argued about what colour of dress I should wear. I said I am not a virgin and he stared for ages and then, 'Fair enough,' he said, looking quite proud of himself. My nerves are high and circling the room. At the Registrar's Office I kept thinking of that bit in *Jane Eyre* where the minister asks if anyone knows of any reason why Mr Rochester and Jane should not marry and the man from the Caribbean suddenly stands up and says, Yes. My dress shows my cleavage. I look sexy and my four brothers and Joss are all staring at me with similar expressions in their eyes. My mother is here too. My father would have loved to live to see this day. My family very nearly didn't come. I didn't want to believe it of them. I didn't want to believe my own mother could be prejudiced in that way. When I told her I was marrying Joss, she said she had nothing against them, but she didn't want her own daughter. People should keep to their own, she said. It wasn't prejudice, it was common sense, she said. Then she said the word, 'Darky'. 'I don't want you marrying a Darky.' I stopped her before she shamed me further. I told her she wouldn't be seeing me again and I left. My brother Duncan came round to Rose Street and said the whole family wanted to come to the wedding. It seems they have overcome their prejudice at least for today.

Green slinky dress. High stiletto heels, black suede. A green ribbon in my hair. I even had my make-up done in Frasers this morning, for the first time in my life. So nervous, I couldn't properly enjoy it. My eyelashes kept blinking when she wanted me to keep them still. My cheeks started twitching when she was applying the foundation. It was excruciating. I liked best making my mouth into a kiss-me shape when she put on the three layers of lipstick.

There are seventy people here, swinging and jiving. The atmosphere is jumping. Glasses fill with King Bomba, with Koodoo, South African fortified wine, with Australian sherry. Glasses seem to fill by themselves, congratulate themselves. Sláinte mhath. The Moody Men, minus Joss, are warming up at the other end of the hall. Joss is over there talking to them. I knew he couldn't stay out of it completely. The band starts playing 'Boogie Woogie Bugle Boy of Company B'. Johnnie is singing, looking straight at me, signalling to me to walk across the dance floor. Joss walks to meet me. I cross the floor like someone walking on water. Our eyes on each other, till we get there. Joss takes me up in his arms and kisses me. Everybody claps and hoots. Then we dance. A circle of people, a human wall, swiftly forms around us. All gamblers' eyes on us. Joss takes my hand and we spin. I twirl under his arm; swing under his legs. He lifts me high in the air. He jumps, enjoying himself now. It is the 28th of October 1955. Twenty-eight is my new lucky number. I can feel my eyes shining. Joss looks more handsome than I have ever seen him. 28th of October 1955. I have become Millicent Moody. Mrs Moody. Mrs Joss Moody.

When the band finishes everybody cheers us and

makes lewd noises. Joss throws his arms in the air, dramatically and then bows. The Moody Men start up again with 'Ain't Misbehavin'. I spot some people singing into their partner's shoulders. *No one to talk with, all by myself, No one to walk with but I'm happy on the shelf, Ain't misbehavin', I'm saving my love for you.* We dance for ages. We dance as if we are in a movie. Everyone grabs the limelight as if their dance was a solo spot. 'Shake, Rattle 'n' Roll'. 'Bill Bailey'. 'Take the A Train', 'Why Don't You Do Right?', 'Blues in the Night'. *My momma don tol' me when I was in knee pants.* 'In the Mood'. 'Tutti Frutti'. 'Rock Around the Clock'. 'Dancing Time'. The band won't stop. It plays a rumba, 'La Conga'. Maryland. The Moody Men are in their element, changing music all the time. *Well, all right, OK, you win. I'm in love with you. Well, all right, OK, you win, baby, what can I do?* My mother is dancing with my brother. Her eyes fill every time she looks at me. Her only daughter, married.

Bill Brady comes up and says to Joss, 'Can I dance with the bride?' Joss dances with Eileen, my old school friend. Joss has no old school friends here, no family, nobody from his past. Just the boys from his band and some other buddies on the jazz scene. Joss's mother is dead. He never really knew his father. I look over Bill Brady's shoulder to Joss; he looks over Eileen's to me. It doesn't look right, him dancing with Eileen; they don't make such a nice couple. They look all wrong. *Ev'ry honey bee fills with jealousy when they*

31

see you out with me, I don't blame them, goodness knows, honeysuckle rose. For a split second, I feel jealous, imagining what it would be like if Joss were ever unfaithful to me. Then I remember and feel safe. We have our love and we have our secret. I smile at him dancing with pretty Eileen Murray, raise my eyebrows, blow him a kiss over big Bill Brady's shoulder. *When I'm takin' sips from your tasty lips, seems the honey fairly drips, you're confection, goodness knows, honeysuckle rose.*

I walk towards Joss ready to dance with him again. 'I'm going to ask your mother to dance,' he says. 'Break the ice.' I stare at them for a second. I have to stop myself laughing. My mother dancing with Joss is quite a picture. If she only knew. The Moody Men start singing the songs that have just come in from America like new trains arriving, steaming at the station. Old Mason Dixie Line. It is not my mother's idea of wedding music. She stands listening, appalled. Robert Brown sweeps me off my feet. Breathless, I dash for the Ladies.

Do I look like a bride? Do I look freshly married? I stare at myself in the Ladies' mirror for a long moment. I feel famous. Being a bride has made me feel famous. My cheeks are all flushed with marriage. I touch up my lips. Give my hair a quick going over. Where are the tell-tale signs? My eyes are the eyes of the newly wed. My heartbeat is too fast; I can feel it under my dress. I am so excited and happy I can't eat any of the food.

I come out of the Ladies and bump into Joss

about to go into the Gents. I kiss him. He is a bit edgy. 'Is anything the matter?' 'No,' he says. 'Dancing with your mother's a nightmare. She was holding me at arms's length all the way through "Please don't talk about me when I'm gone" so's she didn't get too close.'

Joss and I have done it. We are married. A few guests at the registry office this afternoon: my brothers, my mother, Johnnie, Brett and Ragnail from the band, Eileen. And that was it. Now this, grand finale. My mother has probably spent all her savings on this. I said Joss and I could try to pay it back, but she wouldn't hear of it. 'It's not every day your only daughter gets married,' she said.

Everybody keeps coming up to congratulate me. Some of my old school friends have come up from England. Friends of mine who Joss has not yet met come up and say, 'Where did you find him? Quite a catch.' Another one says, 'I'd watch him. The handsome ones have roving eyes.' I laugh, 'You are just jealous, Agatha.' I laugh heartily to myself. Quite a catch.

At three in the morning we tumble out of the party and get driven to my flat. We don't have the money for a honeymoon. We didn't have the money to get a house together. My mother's given us her old double bed; it's time I had a single, she said. Helen my flatmate has moved out. Flatmates should all have a shelf life. We are both drunk and laughing. He starts to undo my green dress and we fall into bed, kissing. We go down into our other world, till we are both drowning in each other, coming up suddenly gasping for air and going back down again.

We are so hungover the next morning that the breakfast I'd thought of making I can't. Bacon, sausage, eggs would turn our stomach. I get up and get some coffee, some dry toast. Thank God we've at least taken some days off. I take it through on a tray. Joss groans, 'Good morning, Mrs Moody.' 'Good morning, Mr Moody,' I say back and snuggle into bed with him. He puts his arm around me and holds me close. 'My Millie,' he says to me. 'My Millie.' He kisses me. 'I just can't believe I've got you. Tell me it's real. Pinch me.' I pinch him. 'Not that hard,' he says.

Tonight, I am tired out from all the walking I have done, the fresh spirited sea air, seeing Mrs Dalsasso and hearing Colman's voice on his machine. I climb up the narrow, creaking staircase, round the corner at the top into our small bedroom here. I have just seized *Anna Karenina* from our shelf of books in the hall. Last night I woke up and reached out for Joss. Tonight I will put the spare pillows on Joss's side so that I need not wake up to that dizzy empty space; my legs scrambling about as if in mid air, trying to find the rung of the ladder. I stop at the first sentence: 'All happy families resemble one another, every unhappy family is unhappy after its own fashion.'

A postcard drops out of the book. It is not dated. Joss's small writing goes right through me. It is as if he has just written it for me because I have just found it. It is his latest communication. 'You'd have a ball here. It's terrific. The views are colossal. Miss you like mad. If you could only just get up in the air and come and see me right now, I'd tell you a thing or two. And make you mine.' I turn it round and there's a picture of the Golden Gate Bridge. Despite myself, I smile.

I can hear Joss saying, 'For Christ sake, Millie, don't mourn me, celebrate me.' Modest to the end. 'Have a wee shindig.' Shindig, the word we've used for every party since Angus said it that time. Shindig. Perhaps that is what I should do. Go back down to London and face them all and organize a memorial party for Joss, get all his friends to play, make Colman come. Get a Celtic band as well. Joss's funeral wasn't right. Maybe that's what I will do sometime, but not now. I can't face the people right now. I can't stand to see the look on their faces.

I read *Anna Karenina* until I feel the book drop out of my hands. I put the postcard in as a marker and go off to the place where I know I will find Joss. As I unlock the door of our house, I know we've been burgled. I can sense the presence of danger. Something is not right. The window in the kitchen is wide open and there are potted plants knocked over the floor. Joss isn't there. I look for a note. Nothing. All our drawers are hanging open – mouths spewing clothes. The sheets have been ripped off our bed and someone has written something horrible in the mirror. But I can't read it because it is written backwards in mirror writing. His trumpet is missing. I search frantically everywhere but his trumpet has gone. That is all I care about. The bit of money we'd saved for our marriage is gone from under the bed. Where is Joss? Has he been taken away?

A small black girl climbs in through the window. She takes my hand and we walk down the stairs, down Rose Street till we come to Renfield Street, round the corner till we come to 14 Abercromby Place. She stops. Waves goodbye to me. I go into the stranger's house and there is Joss sitting in front of the dresser mirror in somebody's bedroom playing his trumpet. The light in the room is beautiful, religious. Sudden last burst of late light. Joss looks like God with a trumpet. His face glows. The music makes him blush. He is playing Millie's Song. His trumpet burbles and moans. The heat comes off the music. The heat comes off Joss. The sweat pours down his face. Suddenly, we are in a different country. Outside the window there's a mosquito net. A table with two cold cocktails on it. The music of animals and insects in the bush. Joss turns towards me and half his face is missing.

I sit bolt upright on my bed. Heart racing. I gulp down my glass of bedside water. He's gone now. I have lost him. I have lost him twice. I will go out again today, buy some more shopping.

Somehow I have to find the strength in myself to keep going. Just keep going. That's all I need to do. Wash, eat, sleep. I go downstairs and put on 'Millie's Song'. Then I play 'Fantasy Africa'. That was Joss's first big hit. We never actually got to go to Africa. Joss had built up such a strong imaginary landscape within himself that he said it would affect his music to go to the real Africa. Every black person has a fantasy Africa, he'd say. Black British people, black Americans, Black Caribbeans, they all have a fantasy Africa. It is all in the head.

We went practically everywhere else: Russia, Scandinavia, Australia, New Zealand, Hong Kong, Japan, the Caribbean, the United States, Chile, Peru, Cuba, Argentina, Paris, Germany, Italy, Holland. Joss's trumpet was like a magician's hat. The minute we came back from one of those places, he somehow managed to capture the atmosphere of the place and slide that into his music. It is not yet dawn. I can see the darkness will soon open up. But for now the sun is in hiding. I make myself some toast and take it back to bed. I climb into my bed and go to eat my toast. I've got a plate of butter in my hand. I go back downstairs and search for my toast. I find it finally in the fridge. I am definitely losing it. There is no doubt about it. I have lost my grip. Coming upstairs with my cold buttered toast, I have the sensation that the stairs keep taking a step back from my foot. The carpet is going from under my feet. I feel myself sink and come back, sink and come back. Since Joss died, I have lost my sense of gravity. I get back into bed and lie flat on my back. I lie still like this for a few moments, staring up at the cracked white ceiling. There are some strange bumps in the plaster I've never noticed before. I try to focus on one of the bumps. It looks to me as if it is getting heavier, as if the ceiling could just give in any day now. I tell myself I am being ridiculous, but I get up again and go downstairs holding on to the side.

It is raining outside. Horizontal rain, slicing across the sky in sheets. I can't really go out in this. I pick up 'Fantasy Africa' and look at the picture of Joss on the back. Big Red McCall (Joss's drummer for ten years) was quoted in the newspaper as saying that some members of the audience would make jokes about Moody's baby face and high singing voice. Big Red flatly denied this. He said, 'I'd fight anybody who said that. I never suspected a thing.' I look at the picture on the album cover, but no matter how hard I try, I can't see him as anything other than him, my Joss, my husband. It has always been that way since the first day he told me. I can't remember what I thought the day he first told me. I remember feeling stupid, then angry. I remember the terrible shock of it all; how even after he told me I still couldn't quite believe it. I remember the expression on his face; the fear, that I would suddenly stop loving him. I remember covering his mouth with my hand and then kissing it. But

38

I don't think I ever thought he was wrong. I don't think so.

I kiss his picture on the cover. He looks suave, sophisticated. 'What do you think of it, Millie? Do you think it looks good. Do I look good?' He can't believe his luck. He has a wife and he has an album. He can't contain his excitement at his own success. He has got none of the blasé sophistication that he will acquire in years to come. He tells me it is all down to me, that I have created him, that I am responsible for his success.

He sings a Pearl Bailey song into my ear, changing the name to my own. *Oh, Millie had to go and lose it at the Astor / She wouldn't take her mother's good advice.* We dance around the room, Joss kissing me and singing at the same time. *Had to go and lose at the Astor, at the Astor last night.* We make love on the living-room floor. He pulls my hair and kisses me all over my face. He pushes himself into me. He mutters things in my ear. I am possessed.

When the love of your life dies, the problem is not that some part of you dies too, which it does, but that some part of you is still alive. Sitting here in our small living room at Torr, opposite his armchair, what hurts me most is the fact that I am still alive. If it weren't for Colman, I would not be sitting here feeling this strange sharp pain of the living. Every single tiny thing I do has an odd feeling to it. Stirring my cup of tea. Opening the curtains. Making my bed. I can't sit at peace.

I am up and down the stairs like a yo-yo. I don't know how to be myself any more. I don't even know if I am being genuine. I question my own actions as I might question the actions of an actress. The only thing that feels authentic to me is my past.

One day early in my marriage, I'm out walking and I see this beautiful baby. He smiles at me. I ask the mother his age. All the way home to Rose Street, I have that baby's smile in my head. That night I dream I am pregnant, standing in front of my mirror, turning this way and that, admiring my swollen belly, my heavy breasts, my dark nipples, like dark fruit. Joss lies sleeping next to me, his arm hanging over me. I take his hand and move it away. I feel furious with him. Why can't he give me a child? He can do everything else. Walk like a man, talk like a man, dress like a man, blow his horn like a man. Why can't he get me pregnant. My old autograph book from school haunts me. Margaret Baxter writing the daft ditty: 'First comes love, then comes marriage, then comes Millie pushing a baby carriage.' It's pathetic, I know, but here I am saying it in my head and bursting into tears. Will I ever get to push a baby carriage?

Weeks go by with me obsessing about babies. The very sight of them makes me want to cry. I feel jealous of mothers; spiteful. Joss pulled the wool over my eyes. He keeps asking me if something is the matter because I don't want to make love any more. I only want to make love if it can get me pregnant. One night we are in bed and Joss is drunk after a gig. He starts to climb on top of me. I push him off. He doesn't stop. I push him off again. And so I tell him. 'I want a baby.' The room goes quite still. I can hear the air outside listening to us. Joss is silent. He looks like I've slapped him in the face. Like I'm playing dirty. I tell him he tricked me, he made me fall in love with him, that I couldn't do anything else but marry him. He keeps saying, 'This is not fair, Millie. Don't be like this.' If he could, he tells me, he would love to get me pregnant. If he could he would love to watch a baby grow inside me. If he could, he'd love to get into bed at night and stroke my big belly and listen to our baby's heartbeat. If he could, he'd be a good daddy. A baby made out of both of us would be beautiful. I am crying. He's crying too. Everything comes crashing in. Miracles are not possible. He says, 'You never said I was expected to perform a fucking miracle, did you? Did you? Did you?' I can see his anger now, flaring suddenly out of his tears. His love for me is being shaved into small curls of wood on the floor. Sawdust. His heart is made of wood. 'If you want a baby that badly,' he says coldly, 'you'd better leave me while you are still young.' It is my turn. I pull his head towards me and kiss his face. I lay his head across my chest. Stroke his back. His back trembles like an injured animal. We listen to the night together, to the odd car rumbling past, to somebody whistling in the dark. Then sleep takes both of us and holds us too tightly.

When we finally wake up, it is as if we are waking in another time. Things are so different between us. I wish I hadn't said anything. Now this imaginary baby is in both of our heads, reeking havoc, having tantrums. Joss gives me a cold look that cuts through me. It is awful to see cold looks on your loved one's face. I feel like I'm in a nightmare. We have never rowed before. I thought we'd sorted it out last night, but he has woken this morning, sour. 'Joss?' I say, softly. 'Joss?' 'What!' he says roughly. On his face, underneath the coldness, I can see a bright fire blazing. Fury. I pluck up the courage to ask, 'Are you angry with me?'

'What do you think?' He's getting himself dressed violently, pulling on his trousers, tying the belt too tight.

'Where are you going, Joss?'

'Out. I'm going out.' I try to stop him. I tell him I'm sorry but none of it works. I have hurt his pride. I think I have hurt his manhood.

I will have to let it go, my image of the small baby in the Silver Cross pram with a navy hood, sleeping snug under a white blanket, oblivious to the world, like a dream. I will have to let go of her, my imaginary daughter. I feel like there is no tomorrow. If I can't have a baby, I can't have tomorrow. I'll be trapped in today and never have tomorrow. Joss doesn't understand. He doesn't want a baby. He wants me. That's all he wants.

42

Late afternoon, Joss returns and announces quite unexpectedly that if wanting a baby so badly is making me unhappy, I can have one. He says it as if it is a simple matter of going down to a shop and buying one, like you would a puppy. 'How can I have one?' You could sleep with someone else, he tells me. 'I'm sure it wouldn't be difficult. Go on holiday and get off with somebody. What about Brett? I'm sure he fancies you anyway. You needn't tell him what you're up to. You can just let him think you're being unfaithful to me.'

'I could never do that,' I say, shocked. 'What do you take me for? I could never sleep with anyone but you.' A big smile smudges Joss's face. 'Well,' he says, 'we could adopt a baby.'

'But we wouldn't know what we'd be getting,' I say.

'Don't be daft. We wouldn't know that anyway.'

'What would we say was our reason for adopting?' I ask.

'We'd say you've had a hysterectomy,' Joss says.

'No, we'll say your sperm count is too low!' The look on his face is a picture. I laugh so much my stomach hurts.

One of the bits in the papers said something like, 'Millie Moody must have felt lonely and frightened. Must have felt she was sitting on a time bomb.' But of course it didn't feel like that at all. I was never lonely, seldom frightened. I am frightened and lonely now. Our secretary said to me the

43

day before I left to come here, 'You'll get over it.' From the look in her eyes, even she didn't believe that. I miss Joss. All this fuss has made the missing worse. I am the only one who can remember him the way he wanted to be remembered.

When I came down the stairs this morning, there it was lying in wait for me. The letter.

Already lying there on the hall floor like that, it looked far from innocent. It looked culpable. Or am I going mad? I trust my instincts. I always have trusted my instincts. I had a bad feeling the moment I saw that letter lying there and I was right. I should have burned it. I should not have bothered to open it. It has this address on it. It hasn't been forwarded on. It is not Colman's writing. Somebody else knows I am here. Who else can know I'm here? I put the letter on the mantelpiece to play for time. It ticks beside the clock. I try to finish my breakfast.

I start lighting my fire. I snap the kindling and tear up the newspaper. I roll it and tie it. I take a match out of the large box of matches and light the fire. Then I bend down and light the letter, holding it in my fingers. I watch the ends of the paper curl and recoil, blackening first round the edges, until the whole thing is sucked into my fire. Now it is ashes. She is a liar. This Sophie Stones is a liar. There is no doubt about that. It is all I need at this moment in my life – a nasty liar. Colman would never talk to such a person let alone 'collaborate'. If she had talked to Colman, she would surely know how to spell his name. 'I am interviewing Coleman,' she writes, 'about Joss Moody. I'd like to talk to you about *her* too.' How vicious of her to try to pit my own son against me. She has the nerve to offer me money if I 'cooperate'. I mustn't even think about it. I must put the letter out of my mind.

But phrases from the letter flicker in my head. 'I'm not being funny but—' 'Both sides of things.'

PEOPLE: *THE DOCTOR*

Doctor Krishnamurty arrived at the house of Joss Moody at three in the morning. Weekend duty. As soon as she entered the house she smelt the unmistakable smell of death. From the smell of it, this man had been a long time dying. The doctor did not relish a home death. It was the only time when she wished she was a hospital doctor and could hide in the sanitized hygiene of hospital death.

The doctor asked the wife if she had noticed the exact time when her husband had drawn his last breath. Mrs Moody had. She said it was the first time she'd actually looked at the clock in what seemed like days. It had been 1.12 a.m. She had phoned some time later after she had sat with him alone for a while. She knew, she said, it was the last bit of peace she would get with him. Mrs Moody had the air of someone who has been coping for so long so well she didn't know how to stop. The look of someone who would not cry for some time, who would organize the funeral efficiently and then break down in a heap in six months. Doctor Krishnamurty patted Mrs Moody on the arm and said, 'You must be exhausted. Would you like me to prescribe a sleeping pill?' Mrs Moody didn't want a sleeping pill. She wanted the doctor to get on with it and leave her house. She wanted to be alone.

Doctor Krishnamurty was shown up the stairs and left in the room alone with Mr Moody. There is a strange quality to an ordinary room with a dead person in it. A new kind of silence. A stillness. It was not just a room with a body in it. Everyone called it 'the body', but for Doctor Krishnamurty, so soon after the death itself, it was not just a body to her. It was a man, a person. Even a soul. Perhaps that was what she could feel in the room, the tangible sense of the soul departing. Or perhaps it was to do with the company the dead keep. Not emptiness. Not nothing. But something.

Doctor Krishnamurty got out her medical certificate and started filling in the obvious, prior to her own examination. Time of death: 1.12. Date: 21 July 1997. Sex: Male. She then felt the pulse which was quite empty and listened to the heart which was silent. She undid the pyjamas to examine the body. There were many bandages wrapped around the chest of the deceased which she had to undo. The bandages were sticky and sweaty. They were very difficult to remove. Doctor Krishnamurty felt as if she was removing skin, each wrapping of bandage that she peeled off felt unmistakably like a layer of skin. So much so that

47

the doctor became quite apprehensive about what kind of injury the bandages could be hiding.

When she first saw the breasts (and she thought of them again driving home, how strange they looked, how preserved they looked) she thought that they weren't real breasts at all. At least not women's breasts. She thought Mr Moody must be one of those men that had extra flab on top – male breasts. But they really were too big for that. They were even a different colour slightly from the rest of the body. Also, the doctor was struck by how young these breasts looked compared to the rest of the body. They hadn't aged. It took her pulling down the pyjama bottoms for her to be quite certain. Doctor Krishnamurty wondered at the woman waiting for her downstairs.

She got her red pen out from her doctor's bag. What she thought of as her emergency red pen. She crossed 'male' out and wrote 'female' in her rather bad doctor's handwriting. She looked at the word 'female' and thought it wasn't quite clear enough. She crossed that out, tutting to herself, and printed 'female' in large childish letters. Then she put the medical certificate in the envelope, wondered what the registrar would make of it, sealed the envelope and closed the door on the dead woman. The last thing she saw before the door had closed completely was the bandage lying curled on the bed like a snake.

She handed Mrs Moody the medical certifcate certifying the death in an envelope. She gave

48

Mrs Moody a searching look, but found nothing in her face to indicate anything. She decided to say nothing except, 'You will need to take this envelope with you to the registrar when you go to register the death.' Mrs Moody nodded, said politely, 'Thank you, doctor,' and the doctor left. She drove off in her white car at quite a considerable speed.

The pale, bloodless light dawned on her.

COVER STORY

He never hit me. Never raised a hand or a fist. A belt, a buckle or a boot. I'll say that for him. Not once. Hardly ever raised his voice. Didn't need to. He'd hold my hand in the street. Liked that. Holding my hand in the street for people to see. Father and son out and about in the street. People that didn't know I was adopted said things like, 'You're your father's spitting image, you are.' What I wanted when I was a kid was to look like my father. You could write a list of things after his name. Good-looking. Talented. Charismatic. When I was little, I could coast, bask in his glory. 'Joss Moody's son.' It was all right, it was, being Joss Moody's son. Only when I became Colman Moody did everything start to become a total fucking drag. It's a tall order when you are expected to be somebody just because your father is somebody. The children of famous people aren't allowed to be talentless, ordinary fuckwits like me. It's the enhanced gene pool theory. Except I didn't have his genes which should have got me off the talent hook scot-free, but didn't somehow. I never figured that out. I mean, what am I? Colman

Moody the guy who tried to be an au pair in France and got knocked back. The guy who did two years of a four-year course. The bloke who hung out in India for a year taking people on trips on his rubber dinghy. The guy who flopped his A-levels first time round. Colman Moody, son of Joss Moody, the famous trumpet player. You know the one. The one who pretended to be a man and fetched up a woman at his death. Conned his own son. That boy must have been thick. Two planks. Colman Moody the guy who didn't do nothing.

I can tell you things. I'll tell you things, no problem, anything that interests you, right. But my life isn't all that eventful. Scandals don't make events happen, do they? I mean it has only become eventful now; after his death. Then the life, the one I thought I knew I'd lived, changed. Now I don't know what I lived. It suddenly isn't the same life. It's a whole different ball game. Know what I mean. I haven't got the same life.

When I'd tell people I was adopted they'd say things like, you could have been brought up in another part of the world, with rich parents, poor parents, Mormans, communists, fascists, bankers, Catholics, Methodists, zoo-keepers, serial killers. You could have gone straight to a cold old orphanage. Yes, Cole, you could have been a Barnado boy. Or one of them poor sods that's been abused by those psychos in care. Let's face it, a pal of mine said, adoption is a lucky dip. Lucky you ended up where you did. I'd like to find some of those fuckers now. Ask them what they think of this. The children of lovers are orphans anyway. I forget who it was that said that. Some bright spark. It about sums me up.

I was a traditional boy in an untraditional house. I was always going about the place freaked out and embarrassed. My parents were not like other people's parents. Whenever they came to my school they stuck out like a sore thumb. I don't know what it was. A different life makes people look different. Even their skin. Their clothes were more glamorous. They didn't look like they worked a nine to five. I wanted parents that looked like they worked a nine to five. It was bad enough with all that jazz never mind this. My life was unconventional. A lot of my childhood was spent on the road. Touring. Place to fucking place. I'd have been happier at home watching *Star Trek* with a bowl of cornflakes. Too much, it was. All that razzamatazz. Other kids envied me and I envied other kids. That's it. Grass always greener. Kids of bohemian parents long for a square meal on the table every night at five-thirty. My mate Sammy knew that Tuesday was fish pie day and Wednesday was steak and kidney. I'd have loved that. When I stayed in my mate Sammy's house, I loved everything being regulated. But Sammy hated it. I kept saying we could swop. I mean I'd already swopped from the mother who had me; so why not again. But Sammy lost his bottle and couldn't ask. I suppose I was boring as fuck. I'd have liked to have been made to have a bath every night in the same house in the same town. My mother was strict about my homework. Had to take it around with me wherever we went. I remember practising reading in dingy old jazz clubs before my father went on. I liked that. Sitting at a brown table with a Coke and a book. A lot of the time my mother would not want to go with my father on the road on account of my schooling. But he was unusual for a jazz man. He wanted his family with him. It's pretty ironic really. If we didn't go with him, he'd come back with a hangover and a hang-dog look on his chops. He got nervous or superstitious if we didn't go. And pissed.

I used to think he had affairs at times like those. All men are bastards, including myself. I used to think I was quite cool being able to think like that. Once, I even asked my mother how she'd feel. Just to stir things up a bit. Send the dust flying. She said he never would be unfaithful and gave me an odd smile that makes perfect fucking sense now. See that's what I mean. I'm going to have to go back over my whole life with a fine-tooth comb and look for signs like that. I've got to do it. Jesus. It's embarrassing, that's the worst of it. Pricks saying, Really, Cole, didn't you know? Bastards asking me questions. I'm so embarrassed I could emigrate. Just get the fuck out any fucking where. That's what I wanted to do when the shit first hit the fan. Just get the fuck out of this country.

I couldn't miss his funeral. No matter what he'd

done to me. Just couldn't miss it. I considered it. Kept me awake the whole night before the morning of his funeral. But I'm too superstitious.

I never liked jazz. Everybody who came to our house, all they ever talked about was jazz. I got so bored I could have bored a hole in my own skull. If I was a fanatic I'd have been over the moon. But I wasn't. Some of my father's friends suspected me. I don't know what of. Maybe they thought I didn't deserve him for a father. Probably they thought I was a sulky, yellow pain in the ass with no personality. Those guys liked personality. They liked people speaking out and being outrageous. I was not at all extrovert. I liked the dark corners of sulking. I liked sliding along the walls of our house in a state of chronic depression. I liked counting the blackheads of my acne. I didn't care. I was in my own world. I pretended I didn't give a flying fuck what my father thought of me. But I did. I suppose I wanted him to be proud of me as a man, as a black man. I fucking worshipped him.

I goes in my father's bedroom. I am six years old. I opens their wardrobe. My daddy keeps his trumpet in here. I opens the big silver box, and there it is, all shiny inside. I touched it. I did touch it. Then I strokes it like I've seen my father do and it purrs. I runs my fingers over the keys then along the fur, the purple fur in the box. My fingers are burning hot. I tells it a story about a magic trumpet like itself. Then my mum

54

*finded me. I can't make anything up. She says,
Colman, what are you doing? Get out of your father's
trumpet. So I close the silver lid and push it back into
the wardrobe. Daddy must have forgotten to take
his trumpet, I says. I hope it doesn't make him bad
luck, I says. As if I was worried about it.*

How did they pull it off? I mean you have to get
a marriage certificate and stuff like that. How did
they do it? I'm not sleeping nights trying to work
this one out. Part of me thinks, Chuck it in, Cole.
Give it up. But the other part of me is pure
obsessed with it. Every time I try to put it out of
my mind, some other fucking question pops up
like a fucking jack-in-the-box.

How did they get me? I mean no adoption
agency would have done that then, would they? I
mean they don't even do it now all that easily.
I was reading some rumpus about some couple
of blokes that wanted to adopt this little boy. I
mean fair enough; good luck to them, it's not my
problem.

There's nobody else. No brothers or sisters. Just
got me. They got me from the Scottish Adoption
Agency in Edinburgh. 1962. I was born in 1961
but they had to wait a few months.

They told me that agency was extremely pleased
with them given my colour. They said the agency
called them 'a find' as I remember. A find. I am
the same kind of colour as my father. We even
look alike. Pure fluke. Or maybe I copied his smile

55

so much I look like his carbon copy. Anyhow this was long before all this transracial adoption business. So it was an accident. Funny how bad luck can turn into good luck and then back to bad luck again. Story of my life. I've always been a self-pitying bastard. Now I've got good cause, I have. I'd rather have had some bod that was an army officer, some wanky accountant, some asshole businessman, man, any fucking ordinary man would have done. I think the agency must have thought they'd have had trouble placing me if Joss and Millicent Moody hadn't come along.

We moved from Glasgow to London when I was seven. I got rid of my Glasgow accent. Well, almost. Some people claim they can still hear strains of it. My father clung on to his. Determined that everyone would know he was Scottish. When I came home with my cockney accent, my father got all cut up. He'd shout, 'Speak properly!' Seriously. It was a fucking nightmare moving down here with that accent. I got ribbed. Non stop. Got it both ways. London was seething, racist. I don't remember much about Glasgow. I remember the inside of my gran's house in Kirkintilloch. All her ornaments. The smell of her mints on her breath. Her big high bed. I only had the one gran, my mum's mum. My dad's mum died before I was born. My memory's shit. I got a bike once for my birthday. Must have been six. It was bright green. Brand new. I thought I'd never learn to cycle, then one day I suddenly did. That's it. My father kept telling me I was Scottish. Born there. But I didn't feel Scottish. Didn't feel English either. Didn't feel anything. My heart is a fucking stone.

I'll go down their house and look for the important papers bag. My mother's not there now. She's gone to Torr. I've got keys. I've always had keys to their house. I'll let myself in and raid the bureau. My mother kept anything important in an old leather bag that looked like a doctor's bag. All the shit is in there. Do people get a marriage certificate? I fucking don't know. There must be a birth certificate though. I've got no idea what it says on my father's death certificate. I suppose it must say Joss Moody. I'll need to find that out too.

I've never been a nosey bastard in my life. I wasn't the sort of kid who hung about and earwigged at the door or at the top of the stairs. If something forced me to listen, I'd listen. But this. This is different. I've got a right now. It's my life. I can go and snoop and prowl and sneak about the place. I can take things out and not put them back. I will. I'll do any of it. I don't care who it upsets.

My father was nice to everybody. Even though he was famous. He was pleasant to people. Smiled and talked to fans. Wrote bits of letters to people. See, all those people, they'll be as flabbergasted as me. The fucking Joss Moody Fan Club will have to close down, man.

We were poor till I was ten. I didn't get hardly anything new. Well, except that new bike. Everything else had been worn by somebody. I wore other people's kids' clothes that my mum got at Oxfam. I used to imagine the boys that had worn the dufflecoat before I did. What their life was like. I used to imagine them as I was doing up the toggles. My dad hung out in those really grotty jazz bars. More dens than bars. I can still see myself sitting there, wrapping up my empty crisp packet into a fake cigar, puffing. Exciting, they were, when I was very little. He always practised in the top room of some pub because the Wee Jazz Band, or the Delta Dog Swingers, or the Jugg Stompers or the Joss Moody Dream Band or the Shoogie Woogie Boogie Men or whatever – I've lost count of all the weird names my father had for himself – couldn't afford a decent place to practise. He was always coming back then, looking deflated because some pub had turfed him out and said they needed the room for a function. That way of living seemed to go on for ages. We went to Torr every summer because it was cheaper. My dad was always counting his takings. He'd get me to sit on the floor, spread out a newspaper, and build pounds, towers of sixpences, threepenny bits, crowns. I liked doing that; it made me feel rich. I didn't like it when my father took all the money and put it in a plastic bag to be taken to the bank. I never understood why the bank deserved our money. I'd get a shilling for a pokey hat from the van.

When we moved down to London I still called an ice-cream a pokey hat when I was with my parents and called it an ice-cream with my mates. There were lots of words like that that I used because it cheered them up. I was practically schizophrenic. But now I come to think about it, I wasn't nearly as schizophrenic as him. Doing what he did is in a different league from saying mocket to one person and dirty to another.

If he was angry with you, you knew about it. It was worse than a slap or a slinging match. He'd just go all cold and quiet on you and it'd give you the creeps. He'd say things like, 'Colman, I'm disappointed in you.' Once he was really angry with my mother and my mother was all upset. She put a tea towel over her face and cried underneath it. I tried that. Put a tea towel over my face and cried when he was angry with me. I made big sighs behind it like I'd seen my mother do. Big sighs, made the cotton breathe with me. But my father never seemed to feel guilty like we wanted him to. If he was angry, he was justified. The tea towel never stopped him. Throwing the towel in. When he was seriously angry his face darkened like the sky when it's about to pour down. Heaveeee.

There's hardly any particular times I could talk about. Everything gets all jumbled up. I haven't got a fucking clue what happened when I was nine. Don't remember my ninth birthday. Not really. I do remember a few things. Like once I was on this bus with my mother and this black man got on. This was in Glasgow. So I'd be six or

59

something like that. And somebody said something horrible to him, called him a fucking ape or some shit like that. And my mother, in a fucking flash, was on her feet giving the guy dokey. Saying she was ashamed to come from the same country as him and that he was pig ignorant. Pig ignorant. I remember that expression because it made me laugh out loud. Then I remember him staring at me, the nasty man, and saying to my mum, 'No wonder,' or something. And the black man who had been called an ape, I couldn't take my eyes off him, was just sitting with his eyes low, looking at the bus floor. Embarrassed as fuck I expect. Then my mum grabbed my hand and we got off that bus and walked home. We'd got off too many stops early and I had to half-run to keep up with her rage. I don't think she told my dad about that one. Just as well it hadn't been him. I remember wishing my mum had just kept her mouth shut and not said anything. I was scared people were staring at me. It made me look at my own colour of skin when I got home. Maybe that was the first time I really noticed it. And I was sort of surprised by it. That's about the longest memory I've got and unfortunately it doesn't really involve my father, does it.

What gets me is why he didn't tell me. I can understand him keeping it from the rest of the world maybe, if he thought that was the key to his success, but why couldn't he tell his own son? Sometime or fucking other. I'm over thirty. I'm not some adolescent or some 'wee boy'. There was plenty of times he could have said something. I never had a bath with him or saw him or her naked. But then plenty kids never saw their parents naked. That isn't all that unusual. I mean some parents were just uptight. Kept their fucking privates to themselves. Sammy got to see his dad's willy. Sammy's family were dead casual about all that. Once I saw Sammy's mum's bra hanging on the back of a chair in their living room. I stared at it for fucking ages. Sammy said his dad's willy was so big it worried him. He didn't want one that big, he didn't think it looked nice. He made it sound really horrible. Said it was the size of a big carrot and had lots of dark hairs at the top. Wild. I was appalled and fascinated. I tried for a couple of weeks after Sammy saw his dad's 'wee man' to get to see my dad's, but it never happened. The door to their bedroom was always shut. Tight. And I was probably a bit relieved. I never pulled it off. Just as well. Imagine if I'd been confronted with a big frigging mound of venus.

My parents liked Sammy. He was the only one to get to come to Torr with us. I used to be convinced that my father liked Sammy better than me. It made me jealous. Sammy and my dad talked more, laughed more. Once my father even gave Sammy a shot of his trumpet which drove me mad. He told Sammy he'd got the hang of it really quickly.

Things are falling into place. He never taught

61

me to swim. No wonder. Where would he have got changed? Said he couldn't swim. He never went to the doctors, said he was terrified of them. Even the urinals. He never fucking used the urinals. Said they were common and you could catch things and there were unsavoury men who could be dangerous. When I stop to think about it; which is what I have done; stopped to think; stopped my whole life just to think about this, talk about this; stopped seeing my mates; stopped my job; stopped sleeping at night; when I stop to think about it, it is spilling out all over the place. Everywhere I look it rears its head. Waves a menacing hand, says Hello there, I'm over here. I've made a complete idiot of myself. I am what my father called an eedyit. *Eedyit.*

Before I became Colman Moody, I was William Dunsmore. If I'd stayed William Dunsmore all my life I'd have been a completely different man. Definitely. I mean a William Dunsmore's smile would be different from a Colman Moody's smile. All my facial expressions would have been different. I bet even my walk would have been heavier if I'd been William Dunsmore. Heavy-footed. Maybe a bit lopsided. One of my favourite things, when I was a kid, was imagining what I'd have been like if I'd kept that name. I remember the day she first said the name. It seemed incredible that I could have ever been William Dunsmore. I laughed and said the name again and again. 'William Dunsmore? Are you sure?' I asked her. I didn't like the name William or Willy or Bill. I was pleased to be called Colman, not William. But now I'm not pleased, not pleased at all. There's not that many Moodys around. You just need to mention Moody and people think of the trumpet man that turned out to be a woman.

In fact if my father had wanted immortality, he couldn't have connived a more cunning plan. This one puts the tin lid on it. If the jazz world was so 'anything goes' as my father claimed, then why didn't he come clean and spit it out, man? The 1960s were supposed to be cool. Flower people. Big joints. Afghans. Long hair. Peace. Why not a woman playing a fucking trumpet, man, what was wrong with that?

I never fancied boys; no. I've always been one hundred per cent heterosexual, except for those times when I was about sixteen and my mates and me would have a joint and a communal wank listening to *Todd* or *Genesis* or *Pink* Fucking *Floyd*. Or watching the *Old Grey Whistle Test* on the box. I don't like that hippy music any more. It was just a phase.

We didn't talk a lot about me being adopted. To tell you the truth, I didn't give a toss about my real parents. My thinking was if they weren't interested in me, then I wasn't interested in them. Simple as that. My mother would tell me that this other woman would have loved me and found it hard to give me up. I just said yeah, yeah, and privately thought, Bollocks. I mean, if you love a kid you keep them, if you don't, you give them up. Simple. Money don't matter, what people think don't matter. If you want a kid and you get a bun in your oven, you'll fucking cherish the whining squirming brat, or not. I mean you don't give your own kid the bum's rush when it is first born and call that love, do you? What caring mother chucks her baby out on its raw arse and calls it love?

If I'd got the chance I'd have probably liked to see a photograph of my mother and one of my father. I don't even know which one was black or where the black one came from. Haven't got a clue. People are always coming up to me and asking if I'm from Morocco, Trinidad, Tobago, Ghana, Nigeria, Sierra Leone, Jamaica. Some asshole the other week was convinced I came from Hawaii. You look identical to the people there, he said. Stopped me dead in the street and says, Hey, are you from Hawaii? I dunno, I says. Then I thought the next fucker that asks me where I come from, I'm going to say, yes, I come from Hawaii, Morocco, Trinidad, or any place they ask. What does it matter anyway?

My father always told me he and I were related the way it mattered. He felt that way too about the guys in his bands, that they were all part of some big family. Some of them were white, some black. He said they didn't belong anywhere but to each other. He said you make up your own bloodline, Colman. Make it up and trace it back.

64

Design your own family tree – what's the matter with you? Haven't you got an imagination? Tell me really, that's what I kept saying, tell me where your father was really from. Look, Colman, he said. Look, Colman, I could tell you a story about my father. I could say he came off a boat one day in the nineteen hundreds, say a winter day. All the way from the 'dark continent' on a cold winter day, a boat that stopped at Greenock. Greenock near the port of Glasgow when Glasgow was a place all the ships wanted to go. He came off that ship and although it was cold and grey, he liked it. He liked Greenock so he settled. Or I could say my father was a black American who left America because of segregation and managed to find his way to Scotland where he met my mother. Or I could say my father was a soldier or a sailor who was sent here by his army or his navy. Or I could say my father was from an island in the Caribbean whose name I don't know because my mother couldn't remember it. Or never bothered to ask. And any of these stories might be true, Colman.

It drove me mad. Which one? I said. Which one is true? Doesn't matter a damn, he said. You pick. You pick the one you like best and that one is true. It doesn't change me who my father was or where he came from and it certainly doesn't change you, he said.

He was wrong about that. He was wrong. The stupid bastard was wrong. I'm sure he used to be right. I'm sure when I was a little kid he was right about everything. He was so right his hair shone. His black skin glowed. Even his ears looked clever. He was so right then and I went about the place trying to remember all the things he told me and the way he told them. I'd copy some of his big words. Kidology, that was one. Or colossal, that was another. Facetious, he'd say, 'Don't be facetious.' And I'd say joking, 'What does that mean again?' And he'd say, 'A smartass. Don't be a smartass.'

My father didn't like discussing his family. He had no old photographs of himself when he was a kid, not one. I suppose if I look in their house I could find some photographs of Josephine Moore hiding somewhere. Unless he cut himself up or burnt himself to hide the evidence. I hope he didn't. I hope I can find some. If I saw a photograph of her, I could convince myself that I'm not living some weird Freudian dream, some fucked-up dream where I don't know my father, my mother or myself. I don't know any of us any more. He has made us all unreal. It doesn't matter where your father came from, Colman, he said. Like fuck it doesn't.

He was wrong. He was wrong about everything.

I'm not bothered about knowing about those blood parents of mine. My mother told me a few bits about what they did. All they do is cause pain – parents, blood parents or mickey mouse parents,

66

all they do is mess with your head. Not to be trusted, man. Shit, I wouldn't have kids. No way.

I came into this world weighing a modest 6lbs and 2ozs according to my mother. I've always remembered those numbers; I was a lightweight. But my mother told me there was a big fucking hurricane around the time I was born. Blew the trees in our street down and several slates off the roof. Made quite a commotion. The winds were stark mad when I arrived at the Elsie Ingles hospital in Edinburgh. When she came up to the hospital to see me for the first time, my mother said the nurses were full of the storm; how you could hardly tell the difference between the babies' high cries and the wind's.

I'm still skinny. No meat on me. Tall and skinny as fuck. When I went to India I looked like the walking dead, man. Got the runs and lost a stone and a half. My father said to me when I got back, you need to put on some weight, Cole. He called me Cole when he was being nice. My mother always called me Colman. I didn't ask to be adopted. Why should I be grateful to anybody. I was born under a sleeping star. Somebody wasn't paying no attention.

Some people get all the luck. There were guys like that at my school. They'd get chosen for the sports teams, they'd get the best-looking girls, they never wore glasses, especially not those extra-thick ones, or trouser patches, or naff shoes. They just looked cool. I wore glasses. Don't any more, as you can see. I'm vain as fuck now. Whoever invented contact lenses ought to be knighted.

My father had tits. My father didn't have a dick. My father had tits. My father had a pussy. My father didn't have any balls. How many people had fathers like mine? Which chat line could I ring up for this one? Imagine it flashing up on the screen after a programme about father/mothers, trani parents or whatever the fuck you'd call them: if any of this relates to you and you need someone to talk to, please ring blah, blah, blah. The line will be open for the next twenty-four hours. I could ring round the whole country and never find anybody that's gone through what I'm going through. I bet you.

I'm going to track him down. I'm going to trace him back to when he was a girl in Greenock, to when he lived under the name of Josephine Moore. Josey. Jose. Joss. But where did he get the Moody? Or was that just Moody blues? I'll write his fucking biography. I'll tell his whole story. I'll be his Judas. That's what Oscar Wilde said, isn't it. My dad often quoted it and laughed. 'Every man needs his disciples but it's Judas that writes the biography.' Frequently, he'd get pestered by would-be biographers: the impact he'd made on twentieth-century jazz demanded a biography, the letters would say. They'll be clamouring for it now. This is raw meat. And it won't be the music that will bother them now.

I used to be my father's disciple. Not any fucking more, mate. I've gone over to the other side.

I went into that funeral parlour and the man, the funeral director, takes me aside. He's got a look on his face I know I won't forget. Half awkward, half pure glee. Like things are suddenly looking up for him. He calls me Mr Moody. I think maybe he doesn't get all that many famous dead bodies and he's dead chuffed. Mr Moody, he says, I'm not quite sure how to put this but it had better be me who tells you rather than the death certificate. I am assuming of course that you don't know already? He waits. I see him reading my face. Know what already, I say, thinking the guy's a pillock. When I undressed your father to perform my routine duties, I discovered . . . I'm waiting for him. I think he's going to say he discovered my father had died of some other illness or that he discovered some weird mark on his body or that he discovered my father had committed suicide. I'm waiting. He's drawing it out. What the fuck has he discovered, that my father is still alive?

When I undressed your father, Mr Moody, I discovered that she is a woman. I was not told this. Your mother referred constantly to the deceased as her 'husband'. I thought the guy must be getting paid to perform some sick joke on me. Perhaps they have organizations where instead of sending a live kissogram to a birthday party, you send a weird deathogram to a funeral parlour. The man must not be the real man. I tell him I want to see the real undertaker, the mortician, whatever the fuck you call it, your boss. I said, is this your idea of a joke, you sick bastard? Who has put you up to this? I'm shaking him. Pulling his stupid thin lapels back and forth. This is all quite under-standable, he says. Don't fuck with me, I says. He takes me through to where the body is. Through to the cold parlour and shows me my father. I see him naked and it is only now that I realize that this is the first time in my life that I have seen my father naked. The funeral man shows me some surgical bandages that he says were wrapped tightly around my father's chest to cover his 'top'. I take a quick look. But that look is still in my head now. It has stayed in my head – the image of my father in a woman's body. Like some pervert. Some psycho. I imagine him now smearing lipstick on a mirror before he died.

I walked out of that place as fast as I could. I said thank you for letting me know to the funeral man. The sky was bright blue that day and it was sunny. Hot. I was sweating. Everyone was complaining about the weather. I remember wondering if I'd ever be able to talk about anything so ordinary ever again. What a fucking luxury it seemed to me to stand around and say, isn't it hot? A woman in a white top said to an old woman who was dressed for winter, 'Isn't this insufferable. Freak hot weather. Freak's the word.' I ran along repeating that to myself, 'Freak's the word.' I stopped and hung down to my toes and took a deep breath. My heart racing. Then I started up again. I was soaked. My hair was stuck to my head. My trousers were wet. The streets were on fire. Maybe I could just melt, I remember thinking, just melt away.

That's my daddy. The one with the orange tie. See. See, standing next to the man with the big drum. He is My Daddy. See his trumpet. That's his. His third trumpet. Slim Fingers, his friend, give it to him. That is his favourite. He looks smart, doesn't he. He is good to the trumpet. His eyes close like he sleeping.

My daddy finish and people clap. Clap, clap, clap. I stands on my chair and claps too. I have on a sailor suit. I just gets it. My mummy says, Sit down, Colman. But my daddy comes and picks me up, swings me in the air, high, high, through all the big smiles. Then sits me on his big shoulders. Says, All right, wee man. Everybodys crowds round us. Smacks my dad on the back. I'm going to fall off. I could. They could make me fall off doing that.

All right, wee man.

Yesterday I got rat-arsed. This morning I woke up with a disgusting taste in my mouth. Like that Billy Connolly joke: your mouth's like a badger's bum. Too many fags and pints, but it was the whisky that finished me off. I could never take whisky. I went into a pub I've never been into where I knew nobody and just sat myself down on a stool at the bar like I've seen depressed guys do in movies. I don't know how I got home. Woke with a fucking crashing headache, thumping, and

71

tightening the screws, going into my temples deep. Took a couple of Panadol. My stomach felt like a wobbly egg. Nothing in the cupboard. I went round the corner and bought some bread, but forgot to buy butter. Dry toast. Dry toast and tea. Hardly fucking breakfast at the Savoy, but there you go. I've always been a 'moany wee shite' – his words. Now he's given me something to moan about.

I went round to their house yesterday. It was strange. It felt like the whole house had died, not just my father. It gave me the spooks. The hall was all quiet and stealthy when it used to shake with music. The post was piled up on the floor. I had to move a mountain of the stuff before I could even get in. I went straight to the bureau in the hall and got out the old leather bag. I took the envelope marked certificates. I took all the adoption stuff about myself. I peeped in the envelope marked 'Colman'. Inside a white envelope fell out. A fresh envelope. My name on the envelope in my father's writing. You couldn't mistake his small, loopy writing. Under my name were the words, 'To be opened after my death.' Creepy.

But I couldn't open it. It'll just be a list of excuses and reasons. I'm not interested. I'm really not interested. I can't remember much of what I was saying yesterday. Sammy. I remember talking some crap about Sammy. You can run, but you can't hide. I'd discount a lot of that as junk. I think it's better to start all over again. From the top. When

72

I went to the shop this morning I saw the back of some woman that looked like my mother and she made me feel like shit. She had a scarf over her head and was hurrying because the rain just started coming down. I don't know where she was going, you never know where people are going, do you. All these people rushing about, they're all going somewhere. London's full of fuckers scurrying along. Even early in the morning, you can't avoid them. I can't get my head around it. Suddenly the rain was coming down vicious and I lost her, the woman that looked like my mother.

They kissed each other often enough. I'd catch them in the kitchen, or on the stairs, kissing. They had that special air of having something between them. I thought all parents had that. They passed looks. They said, 'Just a minute.' I always had to knock on their bedroom door. They taught me that from when I was small. My mother got into a double bed every night for the past thirty odd years and slept with my father, a woman. I am not being funny, right, but I think that's completely out of order. It's not because I hate gays or anything like that. If my mother had been a lesbian or my father a gay man, I don't think I would have got all het up about it.

What is it that is eating me? I'm not a bitter guy. Don't get me wrong. Please. It's probably the fact that my father didn't have a prick. Maybe it's just as simple as that. No man wants a fucking lesbian for his father. Maybe for his mother. But for his father! My father wasn't a man like myself, showing me the ropes and helping me through puberty when everything was mad and changed at the same time. The voice suddenly goes like something falling through a floor. The face gets itchy and rough. When you wake in the morning, rub the cheeks and get a shock at the stubble. A fright. So, fair enough you're going to be a man soon. These changes are normal. Everyone goes through it. My father went through it like his father before him. The shock of pubic hairs arriving unannounced, one at a time, then suddenly they've all sprouted like salad. The boy is gone. My father once said to me, I know what it's like, son, when I was going through some fucking teenage torment. I remember it myself. But he didn't, did he. That was an out and out lie.

What was his puberty like? I mean he'd have got his periods, wouldn't he? That's disgusting, isn't it? There's no way around it. The idea of my father getting periods makes me want to throw up.

My mother always told me it was all right for me to be naughty sometimes, but lying, lying was the scourge of the earth, the worst thing for a child to do. Own up, Colman. I think that was her expression. I am cut up. Since my father died I've been walking around, half alive myself, sleepwalking, with this pain chiselled into my chest. Jagged. Serated. Nothing makes it disappear. Not Milk of fucking Magnesia. Not Rennies.

A mate of mine's mother was carted off to the

74

loony bin when he was eleven. He wasn't told nothing. Your mum's gone off for a little holiday. He knew it was no fucking holiday from the wild look in her eyes.

Will I ever forgive them? No.

He is sitting on the edge of my bed, my daddy. He pulls my yellow blanket back. I am too hot. I am too hot and it is too early for bed. He gives me a spoon of medicine. I open my mouth wide and wait for the spoon to be put in my mouth and wait for my daddy to say, Brave boy. Because it is nasty horrible stuff. My daddy smells of his trumpet club. He takes my hand and sings, Dreams to sell / Fine dreams to sell / Angus is here / with dreams to sell. Then my daddy is sleeping. He does a loud snore. Then he catches his breath and suddenly wakes. He pats my head. Strokes my head. Hair just like mine, he says. Then he pulls my cover right up to my chin, says, Coorie in, son, coorie in. I am still not sleeping. I hear voices under the floor. My daddy is singing another song to my mummy. I hear next door's dog bark like he is angry. I hear children playing out in the street. I hear Sammy shouting. Then they drop their voices. Then I hear the house breathe.

My father had a lifelong terror, phobia whatever, about hospitals. Makes a lot of sense in hindsight. He was so scared of doctors, he passed that on to me. That's what parents exist for: to pass their phobias on generation to generation. Fuck, if I so

75

much as saw a white coat man, I'd wet myself and have a big Marks and Spencers. That was our family word for tantrum – I had my first big tantrum in Marks and Spencers apparently in the food bit. I went bananas because my mother wouldn't buy me some fancy chocolate bar. My mother said that her ears went bright red with shame. I was doing some high pitch scream and jumping up and down on her feet at the same time. So every time after that when I was about to lose it my mother would say, Don't you do a Marks and Spencers on me. My father thought of doctors as a whole breed apart; he had a million different words for them. And jokes. What's the difference between God and a doctor? God knows he isn't a doctor. Shit like that. If he wanted to insult somebody he'd say they wrote like a doctor, talked like a doctor, smiled like one. Needless to say, when he got ill, he just point blank refused to see one. This is 1997. I'm still not sure what he had wrong with him. Something to do with his liver. He said, the last time I saw him, My number's up, Cole. Like life was a fucking game of poker. I was destroyed. I tried to persuade him to see a doctor, but he was having none of it. I read somewhere that dying women are braver than dying men. He was definitely brave. But not brave enough to tell me the truth. And my mother didn't want me to stay the night, that night. She wanted to be on her own with my father.

So I went out with my mate Brady who has left

nine messages on my machine, man. The first one just said, Fucking hell, Cole. Ring me.

The day I went to the funeral parlour I still had the remains of a hangover. I puked in the toilet of the creepy place before I left. I puked everything up until I'd nothing left but bile. Bright yellow bad tasting bile. I'd never seen a dead person before. Never seen someone there and not there like that. Still and stiff. Unreal. The smell of disinfectant not the smell of people. The cold air spinning round the room. The sick noise of that big fan, its arm whirling around like some bad conductor.

My father looked fake. Everything about him. His skin looked like it was made of silicone. His eyes were closed, but I got the feeling that if someone opened them, the bright orange eyes of some huge doll would blare out at me. His hands looked like plastic gloves, as if they had never ever held a trumpet, as if the trumpet was just a dream the dead body had. I wanted to touch him to check he was real and not some waxwork, but I couldn't. I was too freaked out. I was scared shitless. I've never been so frightened. Someone had put powder on my father's cheeks. I don't know if it was the funeral man or someone else. The funeral man told me my mother was expected in later in the day and she was going to bring his suit, his best suit. That's what she wants her to wear, he said as if it was all beyond him. I'd forgotten my mother. I'd forgotten all about her. That meant she knew.

Well, of course she knew. I went to the toilet and then I ran and I kept on running through streets I didn't know in that cruel heat.

I phoned my mother and said things to her I can't now remember. She begged me to come round and see her. I told her she'd be lucky if I went to the funeral. I could feel how hollow her silence was, like I'd just scooped out her voice. But I couldn't stop. Ranting, man. Fucking ranting. Strung out, rattling. She said some balls like, Colman, try and understand. And she said sorry over and over again till that made me sick too. Colman, I'm sorry. Sorry, Colman. Colman. Colman. Colman. I started feeling dizzy at the sound of my own name.

I did go to the funeral, as you know. So did the jazzmen, all the old troopers from way back. Blokes I dimly remembered. Men from all the millions of bands my father formed before he stuck with *Joss Moody*. The Big Heads, The Expressos, Jazz Kiddin', The Earl of Hell's Waistcoat, Jazzin' It Up. I forget all the names. Anyhow. I never saw so many men cry in my life as at my father's funeral. Fucking Jesus. They all had huge big proper cloth hankerchiefs. I didn't cry. I just sat listening to them playing my mother's song.

I snatched a look at her. I wasn't sitting next to her, but I could see her from four rows behind. I knew she wanted me next to her, but I just couldn't. I was too mad. I sneaked a look at her when Tobias was playing her song and she was crying, not like how you'd expect, passive crying like the tears were something that was happening to her. Not big heaving sobs. Just futile little tears, man, going down her face slow. Seeing her like that, I half thought of going and standing next to her. That would have been enough for her. Just for me to have stood next to her. But then I remembered my father in that parlour, naked, and I thought, Nah, why should I?

When people left, my mother left too. She didn't stand shaking hands as they went out like she did for my grandmother's funeral. Then I saw her leave in her big black limo, alone.

She turned round and looked at me and tried to smile. I looked away. That's the closest I came to crying, man. Not managing to look at my mother. I was surprised at how many people turned up actually. Everyone in double fucking shock. Coat collars turned up and this is the summer. Looking like winter. Everybody looking like winter.

I wasn't going to bother with having a last look. But I told myself I needed to, just so that I could get it into my head that this whole thing wasn't a dream. The strange thing was it didn't help, because there was my father in the coffin back to wearing one of his suits. He looked normal again. He looked like himself, except for the fact he was dead and his skin looked odd and a different colour, but apart from that, he looked like my father. I could see other people staring at him longer than you'd think they needed to, thinking the same thing as me. He was wearing a blue serge suit and a white shirt and a stripey tie and black shiny shoes. I didn't know that you kept your shoes on in a coffin. It was the weirdest thing, but the man in the coffin and the woman that I saw in that funeral parlour really did seem to me to be two different people. My head was even more done in. He looked all right in that blue suit. He looked normal again. Dead; but normal. Better.

PEOPLE: *THE REGISTRAR*

The registrar had seen everything. Wild scenes of grief. People unable to write their own name. Trembling, blaming hands. People who seemed to think he was responsible for causing the death. That he somehow had attended the deaths of the anonymous, that he personally turned off the machines, pulled out drips, refused morphine; that he administered pain. There was nothing Mohammad Nassar Sharif could do to reverse the terrible finality of a death certificate. If he could hold the piece of paper between his fingers and shake it until it brought the dead back to life, he would. The certificates were not simply pieces of paper with names and numbers on them. There were people in there. Mohammad never let himself forget to imagine the dead person. He was not cynical, but the dead were easier to imagine than the living. Just one sentence, and Nassar Sharif could see them before him. 'He was a man who kept his thoughts to himself.'

When a person walked into Mr Sharif's office, he could tell whether that person was a death, a marriage or a birth. He could often be even more specific than that: quickly he could assess the type of death – old person, young person, sudden, slow. One swift look at the person entering his office was enough. He could predict what kind of marriage – first, second, third or fourth; first for the wife, third for the husband. He was never wrong. Four times in his entire career as registrar, Mr Sharif had presided over the sixth marriage certificate of some dandy. In all instances, he was a red-cheeked man with white hair, tall with cream trousers and a fairly modern sporty checked jacket. The wife was always thin, inevitably, unbearably young. Mohammad Nassar Sharif rarely read books any more. He preferred to remember the great books of his childhood, to reimagine himself reading them, when he thought the world was going to be bigger than it turned out to be.

Now, Mohammad read faces. The face of a pensioner coming in to register the death of a ninety-year-old parent was often elated. The pensioner might try to disguise her joy, but the minute she took up his beautiful marbled fountain pen to sign in the allotted place, her signature swept across the entry book with unmistakable pleasure. At last, the pen seemed to say, at last, a chance to enjoy retirement. The worst for the registrar was the death of children. He had children himself and worshipped them. To see the faces of those women was to see the worst sight in the world. Some of them forced themselves to come so that they could attempt to believe the unbelievable. He gave those women his pen gently, trying to pour as much love into the gesture as possible. Mr Sharif had kind eyes. His kind eyes and his elegant hands were all he had to offer the bereaved. He kept a tidy office. Every person was special to him; the crucial moments, a privilege. There surely can be few moments to compete with the awesome finality of Mohammad Nassar Sharif's birth, death and marriage certificates.

He had heard of registrars in other parts of the city that more or less had a factory going on in their office – in and out with conveyor belt brutality, cancer, divorce, stillbirth. With ferocious, unfeeling speed. Whirling the names down. Spinning with grief. Mohammad believed everyone in his office needed a moment of quiet. He sat with them for a moment of quiet after they had signed their names with his beautiful marble fountain pen.

Whatever the weather, whether it rained on the registrar's window, or whether the sun shone mercilessly through the registrar's window, Mr Sharif made sure everyone had their moment. As a consequence, people had to wait a little longer outside his office. Birth, death or marriage, the signature on paper was momentous. Some people were in a hurry. Perhaps it was their seventh birth or their seventh death. Mohammad tried to intervene with those

83

people. Gently, he asked them if they had given enough thought to the name, or if they were in possession of the deceased's medical card. Strictly speaking he did not need the medical card; but it was a way of getting them to slow down, to take a moment.

It was not fun for Nassar Sharif to see such emotion every working day of life, yet he enjoyed his job. He liked his splendid office. He loved the paper; it was of a fine quality. He knew his handwriting was elegiac; there could be no registrar anywhere in England with such perfect calligraphy. He had practised his writing since he was a boy in Bangladesh. His parents had told him if you write well you will go far. His parents would be proud of him having his own office now. Every name he wrote, even the most ordinary and banal of names, looked glamorous when Mohammad Nassar Sharif wrote it down with his fountain pen. He particularly enjoyed a long unusual name. A name that had some character. The stories that Mohammad had heard about names! The arguments he had witnessed about names! On one occasion there was even a fight between a man and woman in his office. A proper fight with slaps and punches. He had had to buzz his tough secretary that time to come and sort things out. The woman was a heavyweight. Mohammad loathed violence. He was talented at coaxing couples to avoid the violent outcome.

A couple would come in with a baby in one of those pouches that made the mothers look rather like kangaroos. The baby would often be crying. Mr Sharif's office had witnessed many a sore cry from a tiny outraged baby. The mother would spend a bit of her moment looking down at the soft hair on the baby's head. Then she would look up and say the name to Mr Sharif. At this point the father would suddenly intervene. The father would say something like, 'That is not what we agreed. I hate that name. I am not having it.' And so Mohammad, in these instances, would offer to choose the name himself. Both parents were usually so surprised at this that they would agree. Mohammad, delighted, would get to pick long or unusual names. You couldn't come from Bangladesh and not realize the significance of names, what they told you, the occupation they gave you. Sharif would not be a registrar today were it not for his name. He liked names of characters that had appeared in the novels he had read. Or names of the authors. He remembered some of his best choices: Thackeray Brown; Demetrius Duffy; Ayala Lucy Grey; Bovary Okafor. Once or twice, this intervention of Nassar Sharif's backfired on him. A couple of weeks later, the couple would return, united against the registrar, demanding that he made a new certificate, demanding that tiny Thackeray be renamed. This time the couple would be absolutely together in their choice; they would both want Nigel. Of

85

course changing a name is a complicated business and Mr Sharif would wisely advise the irate couple to keep the certificate the same, but simply call their child Nigel.

But Mohammad Nassar Sharif had never in his life seen a medical certificate where male was crossed out and female entered in red. On the grounds of pure aesthetics, Mohammad found the last minute change hurtful. The use of the red pen seemed unnecessarily violent. He knew of coroners and doctors who were overfond of the red pen. Compared to his beautiful black Indian ink, the red biro was a brash, loudmouthed, insensitive cousin who ought not to have received *anything* in the family fortune. Nassar Sharif would go further: the red biro should never have been born. It was a cheap impostor, an embarrassment to the fine quality paper used on such certificates.

Here was a woman sitting in his office whom Mohammad judged to be about sixty or so. A woman who seemed to him to be terribly efficient. She had come with all the necessary information and she had come within the time limit. A lot of people came after five days, traipsed down to the office ten days later, seemingly unaware that a death must be registered within five days. Goodness knew why the doctors and nurses don't inform these poor ignorant citizens of the correct procedure. Mr Sharif could only tell them, gently, that they should have come quite some time ago. He

86

would not reprimand the late death people, or, for that matter, the late birth people. Many mothers came well after the generous three weeks. Many mothers have lived with babies with ridiculous names for anything up to twelve weeks. Frog, Tumshie, Bellybutton, Chicken Pie, Poom, Bubba and Wean were amongst the catalogue of names that babies had suffered until the moment the mother arrived at Mr Sharif's office to transform Wean into Hamish, Bubba into Ella, Chicken Pie into Charlotte, Tumshie into Matthew and Frog into Aaron.

The woman sitting quietly in Mr Sharif's office had come on time with all the correct documents, with even more documents than she actually needed. She had a birth certificate for the deceased bearing the name Josephine Moore. A medical card for the deceased that is fifty-two years out of date under the name of Josephine Moore registered with one Doctor Miller in Greenock, Scotland. No pension book. Three rather lucrative insurance policies. A marriage certificate for the deceased bearing the name Joss Moody. It was all fascinating stuff for Nassar Sharif. She didn't say a word. She handed the documents over. Mr Sharif looked up at her from behind his half-moon spectacles. He couldn't read her face. He couldn't tell if she was embarrassed or not. She looked just like a widow to him. She had the widow's sad skin. A widow who had come to get the piece of paper that would tell her, because she still didn't believe it, that her husband had really died.

Nassar Sharif could not make head nor tail of all this information. It was as if she had brought to him the certificates and papers of two completely different people – a woman and a man. If it hadn't been for the fact that the sealed medical certificate contained that violent red pen, he would indeed have assumed he was dealing with two people, not one. Mr Sharif showed the woman the medical certificate. 'You were aware of the last minute change that the doctor has added here?' he asked, pointing to the large 'female'. The woman in front of him clearly was not. She asked Mr Sharif if he could be registered as a man. She said, rather enigmatically, it appeared to Mohammad, that this would have been important for her husband, to be registered in death as he was in life. Mohammad Nassar Sharif had never been shocked at anything he had seen in his years as a registrar, but something about the woman's fine composure shocked him. This woman had been married to the deceased for years. She had been married to someone who clearly had lived her life as a man, who had seen no doctor up until the moment of death, who had claimed no pension. Nassar Sharif was very curious. He wanted to ask the woman sitting quietly in his office how it was done. He wanted to ask her if she had found her spouse very attractive. Mohammad had learned never to indulge his curiosity. He told the woman

88

that he could not lie on a death certificate. He gave the woman a certificate for Burial; the deceased had a plot already saved, known commonly in his trade as The Green Form. This gave her permission to bury the body. He told her to take it to her funeral director.

Knowing what he knew, comparing the certificates of the life before him, Mr Sharif had a problem with names. He asked the woman if Joss Moody ever formally changed her name to Joss Moody. The woman told him she didn't think so. In other words, Mr Sharif concluded, one day Josephine Moore just plucked the name Joss Moody out of the sky and called himself this name and encouraged others to do likewise? The woman nodded, smiling shyly, proud of her spouse's achievement. The woman was an interesting person, Mohammad hadn't had anyone so interesting for some time. He had a problem, he confessed, in deciding what name to put on the death certificate, given the name Joss Moody was never officially sanctioned anywhere. The woman leaned forward towards Mr Sharif. She looked at his hands. She looked out of the window at the sun. A few drops of sweat appeared on her forehead. She didn't say anything for a moment. There was total silence between them. The silence had an unusual quality to it today because the woman's spirit was so fine. Mohammad could sit silent with this particular woman in his registrar office for a year, maybe two. One of his secretaries could simply come in and out with food and the two of them could sit there like this looking out of the window, watching the odd bird swoop and swoon before them, or the odd tree tremble.

Mohammad did not even have to impose his moment on this woman. The woman took it for herself, completely aware of the significance of the certificate. That woman would not take his lovely handwriting for granted. She would be happy she had a beautiful death certificate. He did not want it spoiled. He said nothing to her. He dipped his marbled fountain pen in the black Indian ink and wrote the name *Joss Moody* on the death certificate. He wrote the date. He paused before he ticked 'female' on the death certificate, then handed the pen to her; it was as if the pen was asking her to dance. She took the pen carefully and looked at it, twirling it around slowly as she did so. Then she wrote her name in the registrar's entries of deaths book on the anointed line. She looked as if she was praying as she wrote. He looked over to see if her writing was as lovely as he was expecting it to be. It was; she had a beautiful hand.

The woman smiled at him. The intimacy between them had been like love. Mohammad would miss her. She said, 'Thank you,' to him. She put her certificate and official papers in the Please Do Not Bend envelope that she had brought with her. She paid the fee for her own copy of the death certificate which she looked at before putting it away, as if to check that everything was all right. She picked up her brown leather handbag, putting the strap over her shoulder. She said, 'Thank you, thank you,' opened his door and closed it quietly behind her.

HOUSE AND HOME

The second letter has arrived in the same hand. Details only Colman could know. I've lost faith. Everything is out of focus. The sea is a blur. People pass by this window, fuzzy around the edges. The cobbles have no lines. There is nobody I can trust. When I go out I put my collar up. I have no idea how many people know. Someone came up to me yesterday and said she'd heard about Mr Moody and wanted to tell me she was sorry. I didn't recognize the face. It was a big round face, it looked scrubbed. Why can't I play the trumpet? I washed my hair this morning and clumps of it came out in my hand. I am moulting like an animal. 'My late husband,' I say to myself. 'My late husband,' to try to get used to the expression. If I could meet somebody like the woman with the scrubbed face and say, 'My late husband loved this kind of weather,' I'd feel better. I know I would. The sea is fog and mist and secrets and lies. It is all out there in the bad weather. I can feel myself coming down with something. Coming down a long way. It is like walking slowly down endless steps in a dark cellar, round and round. Dizzy. Out of kilter.

He has the key to this house at Torr. He has the key to our house in London. There is nothing to stop him from getting all our private papers, letters, photographs. No telling what he will do now. He is angry to do this. Consumed. I can see him as a wee boy, three or so, having a tantrum, screaming an ear-piercing, high-pitched scream, stamping on my feet, collapsing his legs like a peace protester. I can see myself dragging him along, rough with him, trying to get him back into our house to be safe from the stares, using all the force of a psychiatric nurse. The shame of it.

I was always afraid of him when he was that age. One day the tantrums just upped and left, away to torment some other former lovely baby. He is no longer within my control. I have no threats or bribes to make. He is too old for me now. His own man. There is nothing I can do. I can't quite believe it. You think you know somebody. You think you know your own son. You think you can always do something about your own child's behaviour, that it is down to you to guide him and correct him, even when he is a grown man. Your children never really properly grow up. Colman certainly hasn't. My skin looks tight in the mirror. More tiny veins have burst under my skin.

The rain has started down again. It has another voice. It is coming through the window, running along the edge of the window sill, blindly trying to find a river. I shut the window as tight as I can. The street is dark even though it can't be too late. The rain has changed the colour of the street and the time of the street. Everything outside looks dated, old-fashioned. I could go out and bump into somebody from the past, hurrying along with a hood up. On days like this when I was a girl, we could always bake, my mother and I. Light sponge. Shortcrust pastry, apple pie. Gooseberry crumble. Fairy cakes. Scones, plain and fruit. Fudge. Tablet.

I remember rubbing the butter into the flour for ages between my fingers and thumb. Let in as much air as you can. Dropping the flour through the sieve from a very great height. The rules of baking to my mother were more cherished than morals. There was something comforting about them. What advice would she give me now? I can imagine her: floury hands, pinnie tied behind her waist, hair tied back. But I can't imagine what she would say to me now. I can't hear a word.

At first, when I married Joss I became less close to my mother. I didn't want her to get too near. I visited her, took Colman up. She hardly saw Joss. He was on the road, I'd explain, always doing gigs to make ends meet. My mother didn't approve. Why can't he get a proper job? she'd say. This is no life for you. One time, out of the blue, my mother announced to us that she wanted to come down to London to visit us for a change. Colman was eight or so. I was so tense I couldn't sit down.

I cleaned everywhere: behind the bathroom pipes, skirting boards, underneath things. I washed doors and walls. I polished until my battered wood weakly smiled. I laid out a high tea: a cured ham, glistening with honey, waiting to be sliced, cheese, fresh soft bread, firm tomatoes, cakes. All ready and waiting. Then I paced the living room staring out into my street, waiting to see the dark green bonnet of Joss's Austin turn the corner. Colman paced with me, all excited.

Years of living in Scotland had made my mother believe she was Scottish. She spoke with a weird accent, quaint and unauthentic, the way you might expect a woman on a tin of shortbread to speak if she came to life. She said *Aye* a lot. And *dinny*. And *tatties*. Only she pronounced tatties 'tauties'. Put the tauties on to boil, she'd say.

She pats Colman's hair and says, 'My, my, what a thick head of hair. I think this hair could do with shearing.' Which immediately makes me irritated. Joss looks strange standing next to my mother. I hadn't realized I felt at all nervous about Joss till now. She is standing at too close a range. Firing range. I can have no privacy with my mother in my house. I feel as if the doors are open and the wind is coming in. Joss goes and puts the kettle on for tea. 'Lovely to have you here,' I say, putting my arm round her shoulder and squeezing her in an attempt to reassure myself. I look into her hair. She's had it fresh done to come to see us. Blow dried. She doesn't

95

bother with rinses or dyes any more. Her hair is a light blonde grey.

When I was a teenager my mother got alopecia. It was a nightmare. We'd walk down the street and my mother would say, 'Millicent, is my bald patch showing?' holding her hand anxiously up to the side of her head on a windy day. She'd carefully comb her hair to cover her pale bald patch, but the wind could threaten everything. Then it would suddenly appear, flat, white flesh, vulnerable, standing out in amongst all that thick brown hair. It made me love her intensely and despise her. Alopecia. It is a strange word; a dreaded word and a beautiful one. Like the name of a rare flower, alopecia. No signs of it now. It must have affected me deeply because I still have sly peeps despite the distance of all the years. The terrible intimacy of mothers and daughters. I notice dandruff on her shoulders and brush it off. The flakes of dandruff look quite unnaturally large.

Joss shows me a side to my mother I never knew existed. New people can do that. People outside your family can reveal another person, brightly lit, gleaming underneath all the tweed she's worn for years. I would never have dreamt that my mother would dance round my living room with my husband, that she would have a go on his trumpet, that she'd stay up late talking about how jealous a man my father was. My weak placid father. I actually found my mother interesting when listening to her conversations with Joss. I heard stories I'd never heard before; or I heard stories I'd heard many times, but now suddenly they were entertaining, fascinating. I couldn't understand it. Had I done her a disservice all these years? Or do all children do that to their parents?

On one of my mother's visits, Joss had a terrible flu and was quite feverish with it. My mother kept insisting on calling the doctor. She believed in illness like some people believe in God. She was fervent, righteous, informed. He'll need antibiotics. It could be one of those killer foreign flus. You've heard about them. The China flu. They come in on the winds from abroad. There was a programme about it on the television. Unless you see your doctor straight away, Millicent, it goes for you. It can take your life. Why in heaven's name won't you call a doctor in? I wanted her to go, just leave me to tend him. Joss would never see a doctor. One doctor's visit could ruin our lives. Even when he was dying Joss didn't want a doctor.

My mother wanted to go into our room, to turn it into one of the dark sweet rooms of childhood illness. Close the curtains. Change the sheets. Wipe his brow every little while with a cold flannel. Hold his hand. Listen to his fever talk. But I wouldn't let her in. I kept telling her Joss is a very private person. 'He doesn't seem that private to me,' she'd say, back to her old ways of contradicting everything I say.

My mother was always saying, 'You never know what goes on behind those four walls. Families have their own dark secrets. You just don't know.'

Or she'd say, 'Each to their own. Who am I to judge?' Or, 'It's their private business. Keep your nose out of it.' Would she say that now, if she were alive? Would she come to my defence and stand up for me? Would she push them aside and say, 'Leave her alone.' Or would she too have talked to the press, along with the old school friends, the boys in the bands, our neighbours, our neighbours' neighbours. The newsagent. The barber. The funeral director. Our own son. No, she wouldn't. My mother would have stood firm. Wouldn't she? She would. She would have stood firm.

When I look up I find I am in Colman's room. I don't remember coming in here. But I'm sitting on his low single bed with an old bottle in my hand. An old green glass bottle. Colman used to enjoy digging these up by the sea. There's a photograph of Colman and Pickles on his sideboard. Colman's fifteen or so, wearing an Afghan coat with his hair big and wild looking. I can't remember that girl's real name. She was just Pickles because she loved everything pickled. Gherkins, onions, beetroot, cabbage. I wonder where Pickles is now. I liked her. She was good for Colman. If Pickles were around now, Colman wouldn't be doing this book. I start packing all the stuff in his room away. I've been meaning to do it for years. The old comics, books, rocks, shells, bottles, boots, photos, records. Dark side of the moon. He played that every day for one whole summer up here. I pack it all away. It feels as if he has died as well.

When I'm done packing the small room is so bare it hurts. The bare bulb is a single tear. The bare bed needs someone from a fairytale to come and fall deeply asleep for years. I go outside and look back at the old cottage. It is crouched slightly to one side, defensive, waiting. I am going to the village to stock up. The air is crisp and has a bite at the back of its long throat. The sky is bloodless and pale. Drained of all pity. Drained of all passion. The sky cannot weep today. The sea is dark and wild. It is so loud I can hear it inside my own head. One thrashing after another like an interrogation. I go into Bruce Savage's butcher shop. I ask for four square sausage. Two slices of black pudding. Half a pound of mince. Two lamb chops. One beef steak. I will freeze some of the meat. The butcher has heard the news. He tells me he is sorry as his big hands place the square sausages in tracing paper and wraps them carefully. His fat sausage fingers are all soft.

He wants to know what Joss died of. Butchers do not shy away from grisly details. He wants the meat. He hopes it wasn't painful. This is a question not a statement. His voice goes up at the end and he is waiting. He sharpens his big butcher's knife. His eyes blink with sympathy; his face red as raw steak. 'Yes,' I tell him. 'It was so painful I am now afraid of death. I don't believe in painless deaths now,' I tell him. 'People lie about death, just like they lie about birth. They know it's the two things we've all got to go through, so they lie.

They say Fell Asleep. It's not like that.' I am about to go on, but I feel Bruce's eyes on me. I look deep into them and they are appalled. It seems as if his very soul is quaking. 'Could be any of us at any moment,' Bruce the son says. I ask after his father. He tells me his father is poorly and has become a vegetarian. 'What about you?' I say. 'Are you a vegetarian?' 'No, I like my meat,' Bruce the son tells me. 'I mean, come on,' he says with great bravado, 'I'm a meat man.' I like my meat too, I tell him, taking the bag from over the counter. But in moderation. You have to watch your heart. Bruce nods and laughs, he thumps his blood-stained apron with his fist, 'Oh, aye,' he says, 'you've got to watch the old heart. You've only got the one ticker.'

I leave the Savage shop with my meat in a plastic bag. I feel it, all soft and squidgy, against my leg. I walk up the main street with the sea behind me. The Lair bus stops and a man gets off who looks the double of Joss. I feel myself go weak. For a split second, I tell myself my nightmare is over. Joss is back. Joss is alive. I follow him round the corner. He turns for a moment and looks through me. He has the wrong nose. I feel sick with disappointment. I sit down at the bus stop seat and stare at the hills in the distance. If Joss hadn't died. If I had died first. The bus for Kepper arrives and I consider getting on it, then getting on another bus, and another till I am finally someplace I have never heard of. I summon up every bit of strength in me and make myself go and get my vegetables. I don't know how I am managing to do this. I don't know why I am still alive. If I had died first I wouldn't be going through all this. What does Joss care? The dead don't care, do they? I hate Joss.

Jean, in the fruit and vegetable shop, has one of those faces that understands everything. Nothing could shock her. She has never had an enemy. I could sit and tell my whole life to those great grey eyes of hers. I'm sure they would fill. When she smiles, wrinkles crease and dance around her grey eyes. She packs my messages carefully, as if she is tending to me. Heavy things at the bottom. Light at the top. The grapes are delicately placed on last. Even her hands look kind. She rearranges a few brown paper bags carefully. 'There you are, Mrs Moody.' That is the most she ever says. On days like these, I could die for that one sentence. There is something about the way she says it. Something intimate and fine. 'There you are, Mrs Moody.'

I walk back up the hill to Torr slowly, one bag in each hand to balance me. Everything is moving in the wind. The hedges, the trees, the roses. Everything is battling to stay steady, to keep balanced. The wind is in front of me pushing me back all the time. I could be walking through treacle for all the progress I am making. I stop by Rose Cottage and take a break. Not far to go now. When I get in I'll have a cup of tea and wait for the locksmith to come.

Mr Barton Todd arrives at 3.30. I have looked

at the strange face of the clock often today. He is punctual, as I knew he would be. You can tell punctual people by just looking at their punctual faces. They are usually sharper featured, punctual people. Joss was never punctual. He liked people waiting for him. When we were courting he kept me waiting outside Boots for thirty minutes. I thought he'd given me a dizzy. I was close to tears when he finally arrived claiming the bus driver had had an epileptic fit.

Mr Barton Todd is a tall lanky man, with stooping shoulders and a grey work coat. His hair is grey too and falls down over his face. He keeps pushing it backwards. His hands are locksmith's hands – solid brass knuckles. Nails short and well filed. Old. Right now he is cutting a hole in my wooden door, knocking one out with his tools. I feel safe for the first time in weeks. I feel like asking him to stay on and tend to me, my doors and my garden. Make me shutters. Fit a chain on the front lock. I tell myself I am better already. I have food for days. I have a new lock and key. I have window locks. I have always felt perfectly ordinary, but now asking Mr Barton Todd how much shutters would cost, I feel different. Window locks, shutters. Chains. This is Torr. Torr is still a relatively safe fishing village. Some people still leave their doors open. But Mr Barton Todd says, 'Better safe than sorry,' which seems a fitting maxim for a locksmith. 'There's more crime here now than there used to be,' he tells me. 'You never know the minute.'

Torr is not the same Torr any more. Since the letters came. It is a new place, with a new Chubb and Yale. It is familiar the way a memory is familiar, and changed each time like a memory too. Utterly changed. The size of the rooms are different today. Much smaller. The kitchen shelves are higher. The kettle's whistle is much shriller. The flush in the bathroom is so loud it makes me jump every time I flush it. The mirrors in the cottage make me look different too. I barely recognize myself. I am thinner. Most people either take off weight or put it on after a death. I am definitely a lot thinner. All that dieting and now here I am, suddenly gaunt on grief. The tall lamp in the living room looks fragile with its long fringes. Joss's armchair still imitates the shape of Joss's body, waiting for him to return, like Greyfriars Bobby. There's an empty vase on the table by the window. We'd usually fill it with scabious, cornflowers, campions. I should have brought some flowers.

This morning before I opened that second letter, I found an old note in Joss's handwriting. Lots of little jobs. Ring Harry. Chase accountant. Ring Big Red. Car. Each job done had one of Joss's daft little left-handed ticks by it. The little ticks moved me. One instruction puzzled me. Write EM. I can't think who EM is. All day, I've been trying to think who EM can be. It has an asterix beside it but no tick. I fold the little list away and put it in my purse. It could be a lock of hair. I would like to have a lock of Joss's black curly hair.

Joss had beautiful thick black hair. I wonder if it was always that thick, his hair.

I realize there is so much I don't know about Joss. She asks me to tell her all about his childhood. I don't know anything about his childhood. I know that his name was Josephine Moore. It took him a long time to tell me even that. It came out one day quite casually when we were watching a programme on Josephine Baker adopting a 'rainbow tribe' of children. 'That was my name,' Joss said quietly. What was? I said. I didn't have a clue what he was talking about. 'Josephine. My mother called me Josephine after her sister.' I was so surprised that time, I couldn't say much. I remember finding it slightly distasteful, the idea of Joss having another name. If I am honest, perhaps I found it frightening too. It unsettled me, the idea that Joss had not always been Joss, that Joss Moody had once been Josephine Moore. Sometimes, later on, I'd ask him what it was like. But whenever the name Josephine Moore came up, he'd say, 'Leave her alone,' as if she was somebody else. He always spoke about her in the third person. She was his third person. But I don't really know anything about Josephine Moore. I don't really know anything at all. I can't properly imagine even what she looked like. I can't imagine her hair, how she would have worn her hair. I don't want to.

It is getting dark now outside. Solemn and deep and secretive. When I come here the quality of the dark takes a bit of getting used to. The weight and the depth of the country dark. It is so absolute, so uncompromising. When I go outside to stare into the dark, it feels almost final. Even the stars don't change the deep dark of the hedges, the small lanes, the sudden corners. I close the curtains. The sea is out there getting up to no good. I light a fire, then put a newspaper over the front of it, holding on tightly to each side of the wall till I see the newspaper dip.

Death even for the dead is slow. I can feel Joss around this room with the fire going strong. He pulls and then lets go, pulls and lets go. Slack one minute, tight the next. I see his whole stomach suck in all the air then let it out again. When his stomach dips in like that, when he goes hollow, I rub the back of his hand until he lets his breath out again. I can see the dead Joss quite clearly now. He is quite different to the living one. He looked unlike himself when he was dying. Unlike the man I married. I don't know who he looked like. Maybe he looked more like her in the end. More like Josephine Moore.

What was she like, Josephine? Did she play hopscotch, marbles? Did she have friends? Was she close to her mother? Did she buy a 78 and rush home to play it? Did she climb trees? Did she play with dolls? Did she stand outside pubs playing jazz in the rain, tilting her head to listen? Did a stray dog pass by her and howl in the strange light of a paper moon? Was that the night she decided to change her whole life? I don't want to think about her. Why am I thinking about her?

If he comes with her I will say one thing and that will be all. I didn't think about it at all. Her letter says, with hindsight would you have done anything different? You don't live in hindsight though, do you? Hindsight is a different light. It makes everything change shape. When Colman goes through our house, pointing hindsight's big torch everywhere, he will find things in our garden that we never planted . . . One of the newspaper articles had the headline *Living a lie*. They found people who claimed to be Joss's friends who said things like, 'He fooled us completely.' But it didn't feel like that. I didn't feel like I was living a lie. I felt like I was living a life. Hindsight is a lie.

The cherry blossom tree we planted for Colman's first birthday waves behind the curtains. I noticed the roots of it today, clawing their way towards the house. The roots like long arthritic fingers, crooked and damaged. I might have to get it dug up before it topples the house. I check my brand new locks. Who would have ever thought that I'd be changing the locks to keep out my son?

When I go into our bedroom, the bed is just lying there. As if to say, it's only me again. I keep expecting that some miracle could happen, that I could just come up the stairs and find Joss in bed waiting for me. Each time I come into this room the emptiness of it punches me in the stomach. There is something so repetitive about grief. First the stupid hope, then the violence of remembering. The hope, then the carpet from under your feet. If Joss had lived and I had died. If Joss had seen a doctor. If I had made Joss see a doctor. The same things spinning every day and night. Each night I'm afraid to sleep. I know Joss will find me. I know I will wake up and forget and then remember.

Joss is wearing a pinstriped suit. His shirt has little buttons that hold his collar down. He wears the cuffs I bought him. He carries his trumpet. He motions for me to follow him, holding his long beautiful fingers to his lips. We are at Victoria coach station. Joss has got tickets which just say *Scotland* on them. He gives me a large plastic bag with *Selfridges* written on it. He shoves me into the Ladies and says, 'Quick! Get changed!' There's a pale green dress in the bag, a bit like the dress I wore on my wedding day. I put it on. I go out and Joss looks horrified. 'What do you think you're playing at?' he shouts at me, grabbing my wrist. I look down at myself and see that I am wearing a pinstriped suit. Not the dress at all. I look at Joss and giggle. He is wearing the green dress. But on his feet are men's shoes and on my feet are women's shoes. We both look ludicrous. I point at his feet, laughing hysterically. Now we are at the back of the bus frantically swopping shoes. I put my arm around Joss's shoulder to comfort her. She cries and dabs at her eyes. Then she starts to shrink. I am terrified. I want to tell somebody, but there is nobody to tell. Everybody on the bus is a dummy from a shop. There are no real people. She shrinks and shrinks till she becomes a little girl in a green dress. We are out on the street and I am holding her hand. A big yellow and orange bus comes towards us. I look at the driver and the driver is Joss. He is heading straight for us. I shout to him, 'Joss, you're killing yourself!' at the top of my voice.

I get up. I can't stay in bed any longer. The sun is not up yet. But I want to get dressed. I put on an old pair of camel-coloured trousers. An apple-green cashmere sweater. I stare at myself in the mirror as if I am somebody else, as if I am just saying to myself, 'Don't I know you? Didn't you go to Saint Catherine's School for Girls?'

I sit down opposite Joss's armchair. The last few days of his life keep replaying in front of my eyes, like a film. Like a special bit in a film that you watch over and over again. I can't stop it playing. Joss stares at me. He isn't trying to speak. He can't bear the weight of his own eyelids. He closes his eyes and opens them. I mop his brow. I plump his pillows with the expertise of a trained nurse. I tell him I am at his side. I am not going anywhere. I tell him I love him. He doesn't want the hospital. I know he doesn't want the hospital. I plump his pillows and make sure the bottom one fits into the small of his back. Then I make the pillows rise up in steps till they reach the back of his head. I have to do this regularly, every time they slide down. If the pillows are right, he is more comfortable. If the pillows are comfortable, he might manage a weak smile.

He struggles for three days. I don't sleep at all. I nod in and out of my own existence with him. Time is strange for us both. We have our own time now. The light glows and fades and glows again. Time is like a heron in the sky flying, gliding but not seeming to be moving anywhere, flying on the spot. Joss doesn't eat now. He takes slow sips of water. His eyes are closed now most of the time. He knows I am here with him. He can feel me and I can feel him. We don't use words any more. He can't speak and I can't either. We have gone beyond words. Out there – stranded, beyond time and language. He's propped up by his pillows and I am sitting by his side. I feel his brow constantly. I stroke his hair. It is sweaty and sticks to his scalp. I can feel his death inside me. We are as close as sex, as birth. I feel drained by his illness. I feel as if I am giving him my blood.

I walk right up to the border with him, supporting the weight of him on my shoulders. He is light now. I feel him crossing over. I know I have to turn back. I leave him there and at the same time I carry him back. I go to the bathroom. I can't stop myself. I try to move my heavy feet fast up the stairs. When I come back down, Joss is dead. His eyes are not flickering. His heart is not beating. I listen for ages to make sure.

I stare at myself in the mirror as if I am

somebody else. I don't know what feeling like myself is any more. Who is Millicent Moody? Joss Moody is dead. Joss Moody is not Joss Moody. Joss Moody was really somebody else. Am I somebody else too. But who else was Joss? Who was this somebody else? I don't understand it. Have I been a good mother, a good wife, or have I not been anything at all? Did I dream up my own life?

I open the bureau in the small dark hall and get out the shoe box. The old holiday photographs are in here. I look at snap after snap of Colman. Colman with his two front teeth missing. Colman holding up a pike by the bottom of its tail, grimacing. Colman in his oversized wellies. Colman and I smiling in our anoraks right into the future; the look on our faces, self-conscious, awkward, as if we knew this photograph would be still there years later, smiling the same smile of its time. Joss and I, lopsided, taken at an odd angle by Colman, holding hands. Joss adoring me. Me smiling at the camera, my small son. I can still see him the day he took that photograph, battling behind the camera, trying to keep steady. I can see him standing to the side as clearly as if I had taken that photograph. I wish I had. Sometimes you remember your life in photographs that were never taken. A moment after or before the camera's shutter. I wish we hadn't posed all the time, holding up a fish and a smile. It makes us look unreal, as if we were acting. Look at this one: Joss and Colman, playing at being chieftains. Colman has a tartan tammy on his head and a stick. Joss has our tartan blanket wrapped round his shoulders. I remember Joss joking that day, telling Colman that they were Black Jacobeans, that they could fight in any battle. This one is of all three of us. Colman is smiling up at Joss admiringly as if Joss has just invented something. Joss is squinting into the light. The sea is behind them. You can smell it.

Joss would never swim in the sea. He'd hardly take any of his clothes off on a baking hot day. He wouldn't take the risk. So I'd laze around in my variety of swimming costumes, ruffled ones, stripey ones, polka-dot ones, and Joss would be wrapped up in his layers. Colman jumped over the waves like hurdles and whooped like a cowboy. I tell myself I had a life, a family, family holidays. I tell myself to hold on to it. Not to let anybody make me let it go. Not even my son. I find myself staring at the photographs of Joss in search of something. I find myself looking at these pictures trying to see him differently. But I can't. Age made the biggest difference – some of these photographs are thirty years old. Joss has the look of the young in photographs, a kind of a permanence, a confidence, as if he didn't believe in old age, as if it was something that would never happen to him. That's all I can see. I can't stare at these pictures and force myself to see *'this person who is obviously a woman, once you know'* – according to some reports. I can't see her. I don't know if I'll ever see her.

The photographs of Joss on his album covers are the same to me. I can't change him. I can see his lips. His lips pursed when he played the trumpet. His lips open to talk. Him leaning over me, kissing me softly with his lips. All over my face. His dark full lips.

PEOPLE: *THE FUNERAL DIRECTOR*

Albert Holding handles the dead. He is used to making them look as nice as possible. Some people were born ugly, like him. Some people look more beautiful dead than alive. It is true what they say: there is nothing like a face at peace. Those who spent large parts of their lives moaning, blaming, cursing and regretting, look particularly beautiful dead. Sudden peace is an extraordinary sight. The rage, the remorse, smooth in a moment. The whole face opens out as if it has finally been understood.

Those that died before they were ready to go are often difficult corpses. Tetchy and irritable, stiffer than the rest, harder to move and handle. He puts powder on their faces and it slips off. Closes the mouth and it falls open. Has trouble with the eyelids. He is not one to find the dead unsettling. He does not get unnerved. But those who have been taken 'too soon' can be unpleasant. There is no doubt about it. Clenched fists. Clamped teeth. Frozen jaw. No matter what Albert Holding does, he can't loosen them up. Pity the families of those taken too soon; they always look appalled when they come to pay their respects. They never spend very long. In and out, quick as you like. A dart of a look then a rapid exit. The parlour door banging.

Of course there are always opposite personalities, even with the dead. There are those who have waited all their lives to be dead, who have spent their entire years on earth yearning to be on the other side. You can tell those 'Can't Waits' a mile off. In life they were pessimists, sure to make a mountain out of a molehill. Martyrs. When they die, their spirit is out of Holding and Son's so fast it leaves sparks on the parlour floor. The face left behind is empty, vacant, naive. Their corpses don't stiffen in the same way. They are soft, pliable. They practically float. Easy as pie to dress and move; when he is powdering them, Holding often catches the tail end of a smile. The families of those who couldn't wait to die will sit for ages as if they are just starting to get to know them properly, as if death suits them better than life. They relax into his parlour chairs like deckchairs on a beach. 'Stay as long as you like,' he tells them. He will offer a tall glass of cold water, ice clinking.

The friends Albert Holding used to have would never let him talk about his work. Too morbid, too depressing, they said. He thought his friends shallow, silly. Every one of you will die some day, he'd say, and you won't have a clue what's hit you. He has bodies come in here that didn't, by the looks of them, realize there was such a thing as death. There are people that deny death to such an extent that their corpse tries to feign life. Those are the corpses that sit up and burp and suddenly open their eyes to stare at you. People who say that's a reflex don't know what they are talking about. Albert knows what he knows. Knows the many differences of the dead. Can tell more about those distinguished, idosyncratic personalities than he can about the cause of death. It is the character of the dead that fascinates Albert. Astounding, how much he can tell instantly. The death of some people, the exact mannner that they have chosen to exit is often apt. Above Holding's door on the inside of Holding and Son is a sign that he had specially made:

> *Death hath ten thousand several doors*
> *For men to take their exits*

Written on a brass plate, it is the last thing anybody sees before they leave Holding and Son. If they were still in any need of confirmation, Holding thought the quote from *The Duchess of Malfi* would do the trick. He'd come across this quote when he was a student. It had always been his dream to put it up in his very own funeral parlour. There are as many different deaths as there are different people. Personality – people are born with one; people die with one. It might be the same one. Or it might change suddenly at the last minute in time for the next life. Most people die with the same personality that they were born with, only in extreme form – sometimes even a grotesque exaggeration of all their qualities. A naturally fussy person will become fussy beyond belief when they are ill, dying.

The undertaker had a girlfriend once who was a midwife. She told him she could tell the personalities of babies the minute they were born. He told her he could tell dead people's. He confessed to her one night, over a bottle of wine and a candle, that some people change personalities the moment they die. That's why, he told her, getting all excited and knocking back his wine, that's why you hear a lot of people say that the dead are unrecognizable. The reason the families can barely connect the dead person to the living person is because the dead person has changed! He clinked his glass down, triumphantly, and looked into his midwife girlfriend's eyes. What he saw made him reach for the bottle and pour some more. Her eyes were shining. It was only when he was walking her home that he realized the look was one of complete terror.

For twenty-five years, Albert has run Holding and Son even though he has no son and his father was not an undertaker. (The name So and So and Son is reassuring no matter whether it is a butcher's or a cobbler's.) He welcomes his newcomer to her temporary abode. He prepares those who need it for the long, long journey ahead. He takes their hands, and he says, gently, 'This is going to

116

be the longest journey you have ever been on. Did you have a tendency towards travel sickness when you were living?' If they nod, wink, or give him some other sign, he parts their lips and pours in a little Andrews Liver Salts. If he gets no reaction at all, he knows they are ready.

So many people seem to die nowadays. Holding is constantly up against it. They might be resting in peace, but he never gets a moment of it. If the terrible truth be known, most of the people are not at peace anyway. At least not when they first arrive. It takes quite a bit of talent and ingenuity on the undertaker's part to talk them into being dead. Some people are just not prepared to go through with it. Sometimes, he resents the time it takes up. He is not paid to be a counsellor! Like so many other people these days, his job involves more than what was on his job description. He has to be everything to everybody. It is not easy. The dead are rushing Albert Holding off his feet. The dead are so demanding. The dead are larger than life.

They might have been pronounced dead by a doctor but, as far as he is concerned, it's a slow business. It is a process. People don't suddenly die. Death is not an event. Not even when they have suffered a heart attack or been in an accident, do people suddenly die. There is life long after the heart has stopped beating. Of this he is certain. Years ago people knew this. They would sit around the corpse for nine days before burying it, just in case. Years ago, people feared being buried alive. Death is not the finite moment that we are told it is. Death is the infinite moment. People want to believe that death is quick because they are scared of dying to the rigid core of their being. But the truth is that death messes about, prevaricating, putting things off, being unreliable, carrying out several tiny displacement activities. Out with the dustpan and brush. The polish. The big yellow duster.

Several minutes after the heart has stopped beating a mini-electrocardiogram can be recorded. Three hours after the heart has stopped beating, the pupils can still contract. Twenty-four hours after the heart has stopped beating, it is possible to do a decent skin graft. Forty-eight hours after the heart has stopped beating, it is possible to do a bone graft. It is small wonder the atmosphere in Holding and Son's is crackling. It can take days for things to quieten down. A new arrival will have the others agitated and attention seeking, like a new baby on a baby ward. It used to be even worse in the days when burials were more popular. Death, like everything else in our society, has speeded up.

Holding is not one given to much gasping himself. He rarely gasps. Nothing ever shocks. When he is walking home in the early evening, a big man shouting at a small woman will shock him; or a boy battering another boy; or a glaring tabloid headline. But death, once you are used to the teasing, the prevaricating, the loitering, death is certainly not shocking. When his own mother died, he wasn't shocked. He tended to her personally. Gave her the full treatment. Didn't want her to go in the furnace. Buried her and wrote her stone. Still spends a small portion of every day at her grave. She is at peace, he knows. Lucky to have a son in the profession, to get a little special treatment, to land on her feet.

Holding is rarely shocked. Never gasps. But at one stage in his life, he seemed to have collected a bunch of gasping friends who were forever putting their hands over their mouths, or rushing for the toilet whenever he spoke about his work. It seemed a little unfair. Even his pathologist friend, Dr Norman Snell, found his conversation unseemly. Norman Snell is the one who says, 'I have a wonderful collection of livers,' as a chat-up line. The mystery is that it always works. The man has had a succession of good-looking men. One after the other. Holding has seen them, stroking his hair and laughing. Yet his conversation rarely veers from livers. He never goes anywhere without a jar of them to show people what a liver looks like that has suffered the devastating effects of alcohol abuse. It is Snell's crusade, like the dead are Holding's. He cuts livers up in front of appalled, hysterical friends. 'Look how the fat rises to the top, like fat on mince,' he says to uproarious laughter. 'The liver soaked in whisky is very, very fatty.' Then he brings from his jar of horrors his

119

second sample from an even worse alcoholic than the first. 'The tough liver is worse than the fatty one. To cut it you have to stab through the thick skin as if it were a haggis.' His friends' tears pour down their faces. 'The skin becomes tough like this when alcohol abuse has reached its heights.' The heavy drinkers knock back their bitters, looking, frankly, terrified. 'And then the smell is worse than a brewery.' There have been times after Dr Norman Snell's talks of livers when Holding has not been able to touch a drop for weeks.

Holding's friends do not laugh like the friends of Dr Norman Snell. Holding is always told to shut up or get out. Or worst of all, he is disbelieved. The old friends, who went to university with him, and once thought he was a good guy who had been driven barking mad by the company he kept, have mostly crossed him out of their address books. They used to joke that he couldn't stand up to the stiff pressure at work. Only when they are dying themselves will they believe him; and then it will be too late.

But today something did shock Albert Holding. Today, Albert Holding did gasp.

What happened has made him think new things and it's been some years since Holding has had a new thought in his head. He has been thinking about men and women. Ever since the young man got so distressed and pulled him back and forth, shaking him, he has been thinking about men and women. The differences between them. It never occured to him to think of those differences before, except of course those obvious ones that he is confronted with every working day of his life.

The body came in at nine-thirty this morning. One of Holding's men went to the house and collected it. There was nothing particularly unusual about the death. The man had had a fear of hospitals and had died at home, being cared for more than adequately by his devoted wife. Holding sat down for his morning cup of tea. He finished that, rinsed the cup in the sink, washed his hands with surgical wash and set about his new arrival, the famous trumpeter Joss Moody – though Holding had never heard of him until today. His funeral wouldn't be until Friday because it would take some organization. Anything over three days is a definite case for embalming. He had booked the embalmer and she would be coming in some time today.

He started to get the body ready for the embalmer. He took off his pyjamas, a rather expensive pair of pyjamas in a cream linen, very trendy for a man of his years. He took the bottoms off first. The first thing he noticed was that the man's legs were not hairy. Then Holding noticed that he had rather a lot of pubic hair. A bush. The absence of the penis did not strike him straight away. Perhaps because he was expecting it, he imagined it for a while. When he did notice after a few moments that there was no visible penis, he actually found himself rummaging in the pubic hair just to check

121

that there wasn't a very, very small one hiding somewhere. The whole absence made Albert Holding feel terribly anxious, as if he had done something wrong. As if he was not doing his job properly.

He began to take the pyjama shirt off. He noticed his hand was shaking slightly. (Under normal circumstances, he prided himself in having a steady hand with his dead.) The top button came away in his hand. It was an imitation bone button, quite lovely. Albert didn't know what to do with it. He stared at it in his hand. A few bits of cream thread were still attached to it. He pulled them out so that the two tiny eyes were clear. An image of himself as a young boy scrambling under the table to discover a much missed button of his mother's rushed towards him. His mother ruffling his hair, telling him she'd never been able to find another one like it. Albert put the bone button in his black trouser pocket to keep it safe, in case it was asked for. He took a deep breath and continued undoing the rest of the buttons. Underneath the pyjama shirt were several bandages wrapped firmly round the chest. He undid the large white safety pin. It was exactly the sort of pin you'd find on an old-fashioned nappy. And so he began to unravel the whole length of bandage. It was quite a difficult business, because of course Holding couldn't sit the body up. He had to keep turning the body on its side. Holding pulled a bit of bandage, turned it on the side, rolled the body over to the other side to pull some more. This went on for some time. Holding was sweating by the time he had finished. He could feel the heat of his own breath. He lay him on his back again. Even though Holding was expecting them, he still gave out a gasp when he saw them. There they were, staring up at him in all innocence – the breasts. In terribly good condition for someone of his years. Pert, alert. Small enough to have remained hidden beneath those bandages. The nipples were dark plum colour. Holding had a strange feeling staring at those breasts that was difficult for him to articulate to himself. It was as if they knew they had hardly been seen by anybody. As if they knew they were secrets. There was something in his surprise that made him feel the breasts were some sort of archaeological find, as if he himself had dug them up. Albert Holding looked at the pile of bandages on his parlour floor. They were like the bandages of an Egyptian mummy.

He didn't mean to but he happened to glance quickly at the face. It gave him quite a turn. The face had transformed. It looked more round, more womanly. It was without question a woman's face. How anybody could have ever thought that face male was beyond Albert Holding. How he himself could have thought it male! There she was, broad-boned face, black hair, with spatterings of grey, full lips, smooth skin. Quite an extraordinary looking woman. Her body was in good shape. Her stomach lean, muscles taut. Albert wouldn't have said she had a particularly womanly shape, but the fact that she was a woman was now beyond question.

It had never happened to him before. He had never had a man turn into a woman before his very eyes. He felt it to be one of those defining moments in his life that he would be compelled to return to again and again.

He wondered who knew about this woman lying on his table. Who knew what. The 'devoted wife' obviously knew. The doctor would surely have noticed. He would have to wait for the death certificate to come in to see what it said. Mrs Moody had mentioned nothing of this. Holding racked his brains to try to remember her exact words on the telephone. *My husband has died and I would like you to arrange the funeral. He already has a plot.* Yes, she had mentioned the plot. He remembered that because it was unusual these days. The graveyards were more over-crowded than inner cities. She had said her husband was rather well known; he remembered that too. Albert wanted to ring Mrs Moody and say something, but he was not sure what. Even although he had seen with his own eyes that the body lying in his parlour was that of a woman, he still found himself referring to it as 'Mrs Moody's husband'. He couldn't think what else to call it but 'Mrs Moody's husband'.

The thought of speaking to Mrs Moody filled

Albert Holding with terror. The son had phoned this morning saying that he would like to come round and visit his father and pay him his last respects. Holding had explained to the young Mr Moody that he'd be better waiting until after the embalmer had been. Less upsetting. Natural colour restored. But the young man said he wanted to see his father 'natural'. Jesus! The young man had sounded totally straightforward. He obviously didn't know. But then Mrs Moody had sounded straightforward too.

Holding looked at his parlour clock. The son would be round any minute! Holding rushed around her wondering how he could make her more presentable. Quickly, he dabbed some last minute powder on her face to take the slightly green tinge off. Not that the son would be looking at the face all that much. Holding's nerves were high. He was not good in a crisis. He could never think of the right words to say. He practised a few versions to himself, covering her up with a white sheet. Did you know that . . . Were you aware that . . . I presume you did not in fact realize . . . Nothing sounded that good to him. He would just need to come right out with it.

It seemed to Albert that he himself had a hand in the mistake. What if there was an inquiry? What if the doctor never properly examined the body? What if the medical certificate read 'male'. What if the wife turned up with the death certificate which said male too? Holding pulled open his special drawer to check that his red pen was still there. If there was anything untoward in the death certificate, he would be duty bound to correct it with this very red pen. He picked it up and rolled it between his thumb and forefinger. This pen would need to do the deed. He almost wished it would happen. If he could have the satisfaction of brutally and violently obliterating 'male' and inserting female in bold, unequivocal red, then at least he would have something to do. The idea of having nothing to do in such an unusual business, nothing official, was horrifying. Then, of course, there was the press to consider. If Mrs Moody's husband was as famous as Mrs Moody said then doubtless the press would be interested. The body might be refused a burial. If the registrar did not provide the suitable death certificate then the body could not be buried. What if he spent nights where she appeared to him as a woman and nights where he appeared to him as a man?

When the young man arrived at Holding and Son late Monday morning, Albert was struck by his good looks. He couldn't help but notice them. He was tall, dark, graceful, with shiny black hair cut into a very definite shape. He was dressed very casually in modern clothes. Mr Moody looked nervous, but no more nervous than most young men whose fathers have just died. Most people did not relish coming through Holding's parlour doors. More often than not, they entered hesitantly, almost stepping back rather than forward. There would come a small moment, as they were coming in through the door, which Holding always held open, when they would decide that it absolutely had to be done. At that pivotal moment most people would take quite a shocking large step into the parlour. Albert Holding would close the door behind them and say, 'Come this way.'

It was not like this with the son of Joss Moody. Holding couldn't possibly take him straight through. He had to delay. The words were a struggle. There was no language to make it easy for Holding. The young son had obviously steeled himself for the occasion and said, 'I've come to see my father, Joss Moody. I spoke to you earlier on the phone. I won't believe he's dead, you know, until I see him in the flesh.' Holding hid his face beneath his handkerchief and coughed awkwardly. 'Yes, that's understandable. A lot of people say that.' 'If you don't mind, I'd like to get it over with,' Joss Moody's son said. 'Yes, indeed,' Mr Holding replied. 'By all means,' Holding said, playing for time, 'I will take you through to see your father, but there is something I want to say to you first.' 'Can't it wait?' the young Mr Moody said. 'I've got to see him now or I'll lose my nerve.' 'Were you aware . . . I mean did you know that . . . I presume in fact that you must be conscious of the fact that . . .' 'What are you ranting on about? What's going on? Take me to see my father!' Colman almost shouted. 'What I mean to say,' Holding said, coughing into his fist, 'is that your father is not a man at all, but a woman. In other words he does not possess the male body parts, but instead the person lying through next door that I am given to understand is your father is actually a woman. She is in possession of the female body parts.' But somewhere in the middle of his second sentence, the good-looking young man grabbed his collar and shouted into his ear, 'What's your game? Tell me what's your fucking game? Is this some kind of a sick joke? Where's your boss? I want to see the real fucking undertaker.' He shook Holding back and forth, almost lifting him off his feet. Holding couldn't stop coughing. He felt like he deserved it. He deserved to be shaken like this. He deserved to be slapped across his face. He had never experienced violence before. His glasses skidded across the floor. 'I can quite understand—' he began.

'You don't understand nothing. You sick bastard. Get me the man in charge.'

Holding scrabbled on the floor, picked up his glasses. There was nothing for it. He said, 'Are you absolutely positive you want to see her?'

'What are you talking about? Let me see my father. What's wrong with you?'

Holding continued to speak quietly, forcing calmness into his voice. 'If you are quite sure you can handle the shock of it, come this way, please. You will need to see for yourself.' He took him through and pulled back the white sheet.

All afternoon, the son's face has repeated itself to Albert. That look of utter dismay and disbelief. That look of fury and sickness. It was quite an ordeal to witness. All his working life he has assumed that what made a man a man and a woman a woman was the differing sexual organs. Yet today, he had a woman who persuaded him, even dead, that he was a man, once he had his clothes on. That young man believed his father was a man; who was he to tell him any different? An entirely different scenario occured to Holding. What if he had said nothing at all? Who would have been the wiser? What if he had simply waited until the embalmer had come and done her job? Dressed her up in the man's suit and tie. After all, Holding was well used to the business of disguising dead bodies – making them look presentable even when they had suffered quite horrific injuries, making the face resemble the old face, using make-up unsparingly, dressing the body up in presentable clothes, even if it came to Holding in rags. Holding had made many a corpse look absolutely stunning in his coffins with his beautiful silk cloths and fine woods. Of course some people could only afford the standard box, but he always did his best for everybody. There was nothing he had not seen. Until today. This was a first all right. This was a first.

INTERVIEW EXCLUSIVE

The first time, right? Right, the first time I brought a girlfriend back home, my father was weird, come to think of it, very weird. Name was Melanie. Why I liked her was she told me her mum had had another baby before she was born that she called Melanie as well. The first Melanie died, cot death I think, something like that. My Melanie was originally called Ruth, but when her mum took her out in her pram all her pals forgot she was Ruth and called her Melanie. So Melanie stuck; her mum called her Melanie and so did everyone else even though it wasn't nowhere on her birth certificate. I liked her for that. I felt sorry for her. Didn't seem a good start in life being called after a dead sister. She said a strange thing to me once. She said she felt like she was both of them. That freaked me. But I liked being freaked. I was at that age – what fifteen? sixteen? – when being freaked was the next best thing to sliced bread. That's the only state we really liked to be in, completely freaked out, sucking in our breath. Strung out, rattling.

I told Melanie that I was originally called William

Dunsmore and we pissed ourselves laughing for ages.

When I first took Melanie home, my mum made a good fuss of her. My dad shook her hand and said, 'That's a real firm handshake you got there, Melanie,' as if he was an American or something. I took Melanie to my bedroom and kissed her and called her Ruth as an experiment and she called me William and that turned both of us on. I was playing Freddie Mercury and doing his high Queen voice. My dad couldn't stand Freddie Mercury so when I heard the knock at my door I thought that he was going to say, 'Turn that noise down.' I opened the door and my dad's standing there looking weird. 'Can I have a word, Colman?' he said. 'Can it wait?' I said, indicating that my girlfriend was there. 'No. I'm afraid it can't.'

So I go downstairs then and sit in the kitchen listening to my dad cough and splutter. 'What is it?' I says, irritable. He's looking worried but more than that, something fucking more than that. He's looking jealous. As if he'd like to be in my shoes, know what I mean. I thought at the time that he's just pissed off getting old. I says, 'I'm not doing anything that need worry you.' He says, 'One thing can lead to another, Colman. I want you to be careful.' Pronouncing every syllable. All I need to do to get rid of him is play ball with him. So I says, 'Fair enough,' and 'Thanks for the tip, old man.' He goes to the living room looking sad as shit. I go back and tell Melanie and we piss ourselves laughing again. 'Where is he living?' Then she calls me by my other name and pulls me towards her. But that's enough of that.

He was edgy around Melanie, that's for definite, always asking her too many questions. I'd have to interrupt and say, 'Hey, what is this, the Gestapo?' and he'd throw me a burning scowl. 'Just interested,' he'd say. 'Is there something the matter with being interested in somebody? Would you rather I just ignored your friends? Melanie, Colman doesn't want . . .'

'That's enough,' I'd shout and pull Melanie to my room. Melanie would say, 'What's the problem, Colman? I don't mind your dad asking me things. He's sweet.'

Melanie became the second of my friends to be favoured with a trumpet lesson. She picked up what my father told her right away – not to blow straight into it, but just over it. He said seriously she had real talent and could become one of Britain's best women trumpet players. He went on about this: trumpet players were mostly men, it was time a woman like herself gave the guys a fright, a nice wee fright. No kidding. She could do it if she was interested; that's all it takes, interest and intuition. Oh, and practice. My arse. He could help. That's what I felt it was about. He was trying to steal my girlfriend, give her these fake lessons, and completely screw me up. I wondered if all fathers did this to their sons to stay virile, or if it

133

was just mine. It was around that time that he started offering Mel and me a glass of wine with our meal – which we didn't refuse.

The day Mel said to me, 'Cole.' (We liked that, Mel and Cole, Cole and Mel. We liked writing it down on windows, notebooks, bus stops, toilets, bedsteads; we were a team. An item.) 'Cole, I think your father's really attractive. He's so gentle, so different from other men.' The day Mel said that to me I chucked her. Fuck that for a bowl of bananas. My parents asked where she was, if we'd rowed, what was the matter. They liked her. I wouldn't talk about it. I retreated into my sulky, no-speak world. That was it. Fuck the lot of them. I didn't come out of that world for a long, long time.

She turns the tape off. Leans forward. 'This is exactly what we want,' she says smoothly. 'Perfect. The details are wonderful. Wonderful. I think we'll leave it for today and continue tomorrow. Is that OK? It's a fascinating story. How do you feel about telling it?'

'I dunno,' he says, and ruffles his hair. 'It will take me ages to come to terms with it all. It's too much.'

'I think you're coping marvellously, if you don't mind me saying so. Just give yourself time. Give yourself permission.'

'Permission? Come again?'

'All I'm saying is don't feel bad about feeling bad.'

He stares at her long enough to make her feel nervous, stupid. 'Time is a great healer,' she says. 'Oh, yeah?' he says, raising his eyebrows. 'Who says so? I think that's crap actually. I know I'm not ever going to get over this. Simple as that. See, I'm screwed now. Do you get it?'

She shifts in her seat, pulls her skirt down at the sides in an attempt to make it cover her knees. He's a bit of an asshole really, she thinks. But cute. 'Look,' she says, 'let's get out of this room and go down to the lounge.

'What we really need is the early stuff. What did she do before she played the trumpet?'

'I haven't got a fucking clue,' he says. 'Always was a bit cagey about his past as I remember. With good fucking reason.'

She giggles. 'Yeah, right.' she says. 'Right.'

The lounge of the hotel is throbbing with people: people with money, having afternoon tea.

'I was thinking,' he ventures, 'of going back to Greenock where he came from. I thought it might help me to work things out.'

'Good idea!' She pours herself some more Earl Grey tea from the pot and takes a biscuit.

'More tea?' He shakes his head. He can't stand all those scented teas. It's like drinking fucking perfume. What he needs is a Jack Daniel's. Quite a few people are drinking bottled beers by the bar. He doesn't want to ask her though. She should offer.

'Yeah, I thought I could snoop around. See what

135

I can dig up. I want to get on his case. I can see myself as a kind of private dick investigating him, know what I mean?' He smiles the first broad smile of the day.

'Of course we'd pay expenses,' she says encouragingly.

'Funny,' he says, staring at a couple who are talking intently together. 'Funny, I always thought one day I might get round to tracing my other father. Ironic, isn't it? Pretty ironic.'

He likes that word, she can tell. 'Yes, it's very ironic,' she says back. 'You can say that again.'

'Eleven o'clock tomorrow OK again? I'll be in room 413 waiting.'

'It's worse than the dentist. How long have you got that room for?'

'For as long as we need it. It's good, isn't it? It gives us some privacy.

'Oh, and Colman? Remember you told me you had a letter from your father? Well, I think it will help the book. If you don't want to read it, I will. Bring it tomorrow.'

It's her that's calling the shots, Colman thinks. Really. It's her that's getting him to say things and not others. She seems to want only a certain kind of thing. He is not sure what that is. But he will need to find it. If he can find the way she wants him to tell the story, he will get the money. It shouldn't be that fucking difficult, should it. He noticed when he was shaving this morning, the first actual shave he's had since his father's death, he noticed himself looking different. His own eyes gave him a bit of a shock. The shaving mirror, the old-fashioned shaving mirror in his bathroom, the wooden brush, shaving soap and razor were a present from his father. He's had them since he was a teenager. Gets the blade changed regularly. Replaces the soap with the same kind of soap. Back then his father even bought him a small jar of Nivea cream in case he cut himself. He still buys that too. He wonders how come his father shaved. How the hair got there. Or was there never any hair. Did he just pretend? Did he take hormones to make himself hairy? Fucking Jesus. What did he do? He was into the shaving business. He got all elaborate about it. Loved the ritual of it all. He passed that on to Colman. Colman still enjoys a good shave, the extravagant lather, the clean swipes at himself, the tiny hairs mowed right back. Colman remembers the excitement of that first shaving set, the honour, the coming into manhood. It was something to do, a fine thing to do. Should he tell Sophie Stones about the shaving brush?

Colman hears himself say, 'Well, it's obvious, isn't it . . .' (He can't quite believe he is saying it, but he is.) 'Obvious. He got a kick buying me that shit because he wasn't a man. He had to do this big masculine number on me because he didn't have one. He wanted one and he didn't have one, did he. We know what he had. So, it was perfect that he had a son to play with. He had it made.

137

It's pure sick, man.' Sophie Stones fixes her eyes on his. This is more like it. This boy gets better every day. He's grasped the plot. 'Good,' she says and turns the tape off and writes down something in her notebook. Squiggles. Must be shorthand. She could be writing anything; it's all jibberish to him.

Maybe he's doing him a disservice. He bought him a shaving brush because he needed a shaving brush. Isn't that all there was to it? Does he need to go through his whole life working out his father's motives for every fucking thing? He'll be dead himself before he's finished. How can he do that? He thinks of saying something to Sophie. He can't think how he'd put it but something simple like, 'Do you think this is the truth?' But so what if it's not the truth exactly. He told a lie, didn't he? His whole life was a fucking lie. What does it matter if Colman himself changes things a bit? He's getting paid for it.

MONEY PAGES

I wake up every morning at exactly the same time. Sophie Stones has never needed an alarm. 7.10. I've got a small, slick flat in the city. I seem to lurch from one obsession to another. It's my sister that's done that to me. She's like me, only better. My current preoccupation feels different from the others. The others I had to force myself into a state of extreme interest by playing tricks on my mind, putting up pictures round my flat, repeating radical words. But this one. This one is just with me all the time, day and night, night and day, all I'm doing is thinking about this Joss Moody and what made her tick. I've thought up some brilliant titles for this book. But none of them have clicked yet. I don't know which one is the best. My sister would know. She knows things straight away. Sarah's what you call a decisive person. When we were young, she'd decide for us both – just like that. Then she'd turn and say to me that I was too fat to be decisive. I didn't even know what decisive meant then. I had to look it up when she wasn't looking. Bloody cheeky cow. Believe it or not, I was a heavy little girl. I was.

Being plump made me feel silly and inferior so I went on a diet and I got thin. But I can't be too careful: there is always the fat person, lurking around, waiting for a chance to take me over. If I looked away, she'd be in there quicker than I could snap my thin fingers.

The Trumpet Man/Woman. The Life and Times of the Transvestite Trumpet Player. Now You See Her, Now You Don't. Must discuss with Colman. It would be good to have a title. The publishers want one for the catalogue. Dreaming up book titles is good fun. Perhaps Transvestite and Trumpet should go the other way round. *The True Story of a Trumpet Transvestite. Blow Her Trumpet. Daddy, You Blew It. Blow That Thing. Joss Moody's Gamble.* A headline is only around for a day, but a title's permanent like a hair dye. I've got to get it right. They should have no problems selling this book. People are interested in weirdos, sex changes, all that stuff.

I'm interested myself. Always have been as far as I could remember. If I heard my mum or my dad hinting something about somebody, in those soft voices that went down then up, my ears would cock like a dog onto the scent. They were always whispering about the house. Talking in low serious tones, enjoying all the world's badness. My odd uncle. My malicious grandmother, my too tall aunt. I never quite caught what they were talking about; so I'd make things up. Next time I saw my uncle or my grandmother, I'd be absolutely terrified of them. There's nothing more fascinating than gossip. My sister Sarah says gossip doesn't utilize the intellect. I say, What intellect? All the bloody theories in the world can't get me hooked like a piece of strange news does. I'd just need to hear my mother say, 'There's something distinctly odd about her,' to be in seventh heaven. People: that's what interests me. People are weird.

Colman is coming along nicely now. Each time he divulges a little more. Soon I will crack him. I plan to trumpet the story everywhere. Spark up a blaze of publicity. Ignite the paparazzi. I could do a search on the Internet and find the cities that have had famous transvestites live in them. I have just read a piece about New Zealand being the first country to have a tranny mayor, Wellington. Stilettos in Wellington! The word transvestite has got more in it than the word cross-dresser. What is a cross-dresser anyway when he or she is at home? Someone who dresses in a fit of fury. *Transvestite* has a nice pervy ring to it. When we have finished The Book, Joss Moody's records will be selling better than they ever did. We're doing her a favour. We're making her immortal.

The last book I did wasn't the success I'd hoped for. The timing was wrong. I lost money on that book. That's the way it goes. In this business we are more like gamblers than anything else. This one is a cert. A synch. I wonder what I would have felt if I had been Mill Moody. Would I have fallen for Joss Moody too? When I look at her, she looks just like a handsome big fella. I could have been taken in. Maybe that's what happened with Mill Moody. Maybe she didn't actually know to begin with. Must find out when she found out. The question of Mill Moody's attraction to Joss Moody intrigues me. She married a woman who pretended she was a man. Why? A woman who stuffed wet cotton wool into a condom and tied on a couple of walnuts to fake the balls and penis. (Well, I don't know if Joss had a so-called 'three-piece suit' or not; but I've read about that somewhere.) Wild! It will do. She might have stuffed socks down her knickers, who knows? It's all as weird as fuck as far as I'm concerned. Weirder than anything my peculiar family could have dreamt up and that's saying something. A woman who slicked back her hair with oil, shaved daily to keep up the pretence, who always went to the sit-down part of the Gents. A woman who, even in the baking heat of a Greek summer, could not be persuaded to strip off and swim in the sea. A woman who wrapped bandages round her breasts and wore at least two T-shirts beneath her shirts. She must have had small tits. She couldn't have carried it off if she had Barbara Windsors, could she? Find out the exact cup size. *Chapter One – 'Even though it turned out that my dad had a 32C cup, he still wrapped bandages round his breasts in the curtained secrecy of his bedroom.'* I could just sit down and write this book in one gulp. Once I've got the details it won't take long. I won't even need to check it with Colman. He can look at the proofs when it's done. He won't be all that bothered. Anyone can see the guy's out for revenge. Don't blame him.

All for the sake of playing a trumpet. Wasn't that the issue that I read debated in the quality Sundays? Friends quoted as saying that Joss Moody lived and died for his music. Balls. I'm not buying it. I'm not keen on jazz anyway; can't imagine anybody going through all that just to blow a horn. The music angle is a red herring for definite. Let the rest of the wankers go down that road. My book will be the business. Snatched off the shelves, scandalous, piping hot.

What I want Colman Moody to find out is this: what made Joss Moody into a transvestite? What was the real reason for pretending she was a man? She is different, I'm quite sure, from other transvestites. Joss Moody only returned to being a woman in death. The rest of the time she dressed like a man, lived her life as a man, her own son believed her to be a man. No, this isn't a straight-forward tranny. Wasn't there an army officer that lived her life as a man? Good background. This isn't going to be your usual hack book. But there's not a lot of time. It needs to get out quick. Forget about the background, on second thoughts. Was she just a perv or what? Which came first? What's the story? How did she manage to pull it off? How come none of the smart journalists that have interviewed and reinterviewed her over the years never noticed? Nobody called her bluff. And yet now, in hindsight,

143

everyone is saying it was staring them in the face. Bollocks. I look at Sophie in the mirror. I pull my hair up and put some pins in. I look clever with my hair up. I knew I had it in me. Clever Sophie.

I drift into my small kitchen and put the kettle on. I take some fresh coffee out of the fridge and put three generous spoonfuls into the cafetière. I get my favourite cup and saucer, black and white spots, from the wooden shelf and arrange it on the table. Colman probably doesn't like fresh coffee. How did he end up like he is with those parents? He's rough at the edges. He doesn't like jazz. He's pretty conservative really. He's a rubric, that one. A rubric. It occurs to me that Sophie here is starting to find Colman more puzzling than Joss Moody. I pour my coffee adding a spot of milk. I've never been to Scotland before. I've heard the people are friendlier there. I wonder if that means they'll *talk* more. It should be quite a trip. I'll come back from Scotland a changed Sophie. My parents will have to stop saying, 'Sarah this and Sarah that,' to everything. This time is going to be *it*. I can feel it in my bones. Something lucky is about to happen. (Will they love me? Is success lovable?) It will completely change my life, place me in another league. I can see myself suddenly very rich in Italian clothes, my hair thick as my sister's and swept to one side. When the moment comes, I will look back and say, 'It all happened the moment I met Colman Moody. I knew from the second I saw him.'

I get out my personal money file. Currently I have £3,300 saved in an Abbey National Investor Account and £2,500 in Premium Bonds. I have £1,000 in an instant access Halifax building society account and £700 in my current account and that is it. Too much of my money goes on designer clothes. If I pull this off, it will be a case of Armani, Givenchy. I can visualize the money columns in these blue books changing rapidly like a wild cash register. 'We're talking big money,' I say to my bank book. 'Big Money.' Disgusting, I know. But Sophie deserves it more than anybody. I kiss my blue bank babies and put them back in my drawer. What I need to start thinking about is how to invest the money. I don't want to piss it up against the wall. I lock my white door. I notice an extra flourish to my wrist the way I turn the Chubb. The moment is coming, Sophie baby, it's coming.

MUSIC

When he gets down, and he doesn't always get down deep enough, he loses his sex, his race, his memory. He strips himself bare, takes everything off, till he's barely human. Then he brings himself back, out of this world. Back, from way. Getting there is painful. He has to get to the centre of a whirlwind, screwballing in musical circles till he is very nearly out of his mind. The journey is so wacky, so wild that he sometimes fears he'll never return sane. He licks his chops. He slaps and flips and flies. He goes down, swirling and whirling till he's right down at the very pinpoint of himself. A small black mark. The further he goes, the smaller he gets. That's the thing. It's so fast, he's speeding, crashing, his fingers going like the hammers, frenzied, blowing up a storm. His leather lips. His satchelmouth.

And he is bending in the wind, scooping pitch, growling. Mugging heavy or light. Never lying. Telling it like it is. Like it is. O-bop-she-bam. Running changes. Changes running faster, quicker, dangerous. A galloping piano behind him. Sweating like a horse. Break it down. Go on, break it down.

It is all in the blood. Cooking. Back, from way. When he was something else. Somebody else. Her. That girl. The trumpet screams. He's hot. She's hot. He's hot. The whole room is hot. He plays his false fingers. Chokes his trumpet. He is naked. This is naked jazz. O-bop-she-bam. Never lying. Telling it like it is.

The place down there: it forces him to witness his own death. He watches open-mouthed the card he's going to be dealt. He watches himself in flashback. He's a small girl skipping along an old disused railway line in a red dress, carrying a bunch of railway flowers for her mother. He goes further back till he's neck in neck with his own birth. There's the midwife, Kathleen. (His mother always said he was either going to be Kathleen or Josephine.) Kathleen, with her big thick midwife's hands. The hands of a butcher. Fleshy and too soft. Kathleen pulling the slippery powdery, slimy baby out and up in the air. The cord wound right round. Right round the baby's neck. Kathleen has to unhook the wee girl first before she can cut the cord. 'A lucky, lucky girl,' she says to the mother. He gulps on the trumpet. The music has no breath, no air. Small ghost notes sob from his trumpet. Down there at the bottom he can see himself when he was a tiny baby, blue in the face. The trumpet takes him back to the blue birth. In the music at the bottom the cord starts to swing. It swings round and round and up and down until he slices it, cuts the cord and watches the cord slither into

147

a bucket. Looks just like a perm of snakes. The drums start to hiss. His trumpet plays gutbucket. Kathleen scrubs the baby hard and hands the wee black girl to her mother. He turns away, still playing, pulling out the past or the future, looking at the faces. What the fuck are those faces doing in the music? The mother licks her baby. He licks his trumpet.

The face of his own undertaker scares him the most. Albert Holding. He is wearing a brass sign round his neck. Death hath ten thousand several doors for men to take their exit. He leans out of the music and calls out, 'See you later.' When he is in the groove he can see Holding's long fingers unbuttoning a shirt, his shirt. Unwrapping him. Holding's hands are cool. His breath hot. His fingers are tough at the edges. He can see him bent over the table he will lie on. Cold, soft, bare. He can see the pine drape. The pad of stiffs. The other unlucky bastards that have quit it at exactly the same time as him. It's strange to share a birthday, but it's even stranger to share a deathday. There they all are, his stiff comrades inside their coffins. He can see right through the pine. Snuffed it. All at exactly the same time. This is their meet. One last jam. Dead meat.

The picture changes with the light. He can taste himself transforming. Running changes. The body changes shape. From girl to young woman to young man to old man to old woman. The old woman sits up on the cold table and looks straight into his eyes. She says, 'Who are you kidding?' He watches the flame eat the body up. He is an ear man. He can play it all by ear. He is bending the ears of everyone in the bar.

When he starts to come back from the small black point, he finds himself running along the old railway line that his mother never trusted although there were never any trains. Running along he realizes his mother was right never to trust that track. The trains hurtle alongside him, whistling and steaming. People who fall off the train are met or unmet, loved or not loved. The train charges through the flame. Alongside the track, the yellow railway flowers are in full bloom. He finds himself standing on a stage clapping, standing on the one spot, clapping the blur. He spots Millie and the whole club sharpens. A nose. A laughing face. A clapping hand. A bright red silk scarf.

There is music in his blood.

Stomping, stamping, hooting, whistling, cheering. They want more of him. 'Talk to me!' they shout. 'Talk to me!' 'Gone yourself!' They want more blood. He dives back down again. He has barely come out. When he plays his trumpet, his left leg is uncontrollable. It bends and cracks like a tree in the wind. His foot going out and coming in. His eyes shut tight to keep out the light. He is the music. The blood dreaming. The long slow ache. All the light is in the music – soaring, flying. The trumpet gets him off, takes him up or down.

He could float. He could fly. He swings with his cats in the dim light. There is no level ground. He feels himself going down; he feels one of his cats going down too. He can go all the way to the bottomless ground. There's the sensation of falling without ever stopping. Each time like dying. His number up. Each time he returns to the faces, intent, peering down at his grave, throwing mud on his face, showering him with blooms.

The trip shakes him up. It is painful. But there is nothing like that pain. That pain is the sweetest, most beautiful pain in the world. Better than sex. Soar or shuffle along, wing or glide, trudge or gallop, kicking out, mugging heavy, light, licking, breaking, screw-balling. Out of this world. He could be the fourth horseman, the messenger, the sender. He could be the ferryman. The migrant. The dispossessed. He can't stop himself changing. Running changes. Changes running. He is changing all the time. It all falls off – bandages, braces, cufflinks, watches, hair grease, suits, buttons, ties. He is himself again, years ago, skipping along the railway line with a long cord his mother had made into a rope. In a red dress. It is liberating. To be a girl. To be a man.

The music is his blood. His cells. But the odd bit is that down at the bottom, the blood doesn't matter after all. None of the particulars count for much. True, they are instrumental in getting him down there in the first place, but after that they become incidental. All his self collapses – his idiosyncracies, his personality, his ego, his sexuality, even, finally, his memory. All of it falls away like layers of skin unwrapping. He unwraps himself with his trumpet. Down at the bottom, face to face with the fact that he is nobody. The more he can be nobody the more he can play that horn. Playing the horn is not about being somebody coming from something. It is about being nobody coming from nothing. The horn ruthlessly strips him bare till he ends up with no body, no past, nothing.

If it wasn't for his horn he would be dead and gone. Years ago. Dead in his spirit and still living. It doesn't matter a damn he is somebody he is not. None of it matters. The suit is just the suit the body holds. The body needs the suit to wear the horn. Only the music knows everything. Only the dark sweet heart of the music. Only he who knew who he was, who he had been, could let it all go. The sender would shout a word and he would go. The word could be 'baby' or 'cooking' or 'take it'.

So when he takes off he is the whole century galloping to its close. The wide moors. The big mouth. Scotland. Africa. Slavery. Freedom. He is a girl. A man. Everything, nothing. He is sickness, health. The sun. The moon. Black, white. Nothing weighs him down. Not the past or the future. He hangs on to the high C and then he lets go. Screams. Lets it go. Bends his notes and bends his body. His whole body is bent over double. His

151

trumpet pointing down at the floor then up at the sky. He plays another high C. He holds on. He just keeps blowing. He is blowing his story. His story is blowing in the wind. He lets it rip. He tears himself apart. He explodes. Then he brings himself back. Slowly, slowly, piecing himself together.

SEX

Since his father died, Colman has not seen any of his friends. He has cut himself off from them, cast himself adrift. Brady, Michael, Lucas, Sammy. Sammy is the most persistent. Leaves loads of messages on his machine; has been to his flat and pounded on the door. Colman can't face him. He's known Sammy the longest and Sammy knew his father well. Sammy will be gobsmacked.

For a year before his father died, Colman had been working as a courier on a motorbike. He liked it, wearing his big helmet. People made way for helmeted guys like himself. He could see them, but they couldn't see him. It was like having a disguise. He could hide his laugh behind his visor. He liked the big leather gloves, the tall black boots, and the rest of the gear. It wasn't the kind of gear he was used to wearing. It made him bigger. His presence loomed in the mirror in his hall. Nobody messed with him. People found him frightening. He found himself frightening. He could jump queues and nobody would challenge him. He could dart in and out of the traffic doing the fingers

153

up to any of the stupid fuckers out there who didn't realize they had a wing mirror. He'd whizz past them swearing and pointing first to their mirror and second to his helmet to let them know how stupid he thought they were.

When he was a courier, he felt liberated. Like he could suddenly act the part of the biker and nobody would know any better. Everybody hates bikers. He could just put the gear on and join the clan and nod at other bikers on the road. When he stopped to get a bacon roll, people would instinctively let him go in front of them. It was quite a discovery. Actually the rest of the couriers were just mild men like himself, but nobody let on. When he stopped to deliver a package and get a signature on his board, the signature was always written in a hurry and the door closed before he revved up and screamed away. He was always in a fucking hurry. You had to move fast to make any money. The money was crap actually. The bosses didn't seem to realize they were working in a totally constipated city. People used to get around faster in London in the days of the fucking horse and carriage. You couldn't even fart in Piccadilly.

The day after Colman saw his father in the funeral parlour, he went into work. He thought it would keep him sane. He told the boss that his father had died and he said, 'Sorry to hear that,' and continued with what he was doing. So Colman just walked out. It made him angry. He felt angry at every fucker. He didn't like any of the other couriers anyway. They could all go to fuck.

A new name and a new job, that's what he'd like. A new start in life. The thought of carrying the name Moody around with him for the rest of his life is no joke. Maybe he should change back to his original name. What would William Dunsmore do for a living? Insurance? Insurance against shit happening. A doctor? A doctor who would specialize in – what? Plastic surgery? Sex changes? Hormones? Christ. Where is this coming from. Is it coming from him? Is he spinning out or what? His brain is mince. William Dunsmore. William Dunsmore. He would do something plain and ordinary with no element of risk in it. What job has no risk at all? He can't think. He just can't think. Fucking forget William Dunsmore. He won't fucking come to life.

Colman Moody is convinced he has started to grow backwards. He is watching *Star Trek*, the new one, even though some bald bastard has taken over the *Enterprise*. He is eating cornflakes, at least ten bowls a day. He is reading the *Beano*. He's got out his old copies of *Oor Wullie* and *The Broons*. *The Broons* upset him so he stops reading them. They remind him of his father. How his father liked them all to have Scottish things, daft naff Scottish things to keep them in touch. Every time they went to Torr they returned with packets of tattie scones, slices of square sausage, bottles of Barrs irn bru. Shortbread. Black bun.

He gets up and pours himself a very large Jack Daniel's. It's a night for the box, he can't handle anything else. It's knackering talking to that Sophie Stones about his father's life. Half the time he imagines his mother sitting in the corner of that hotel room just staring at him, just fucking staring at him. It gives him the creeps. Today, for a minute, his father even put in an appearance. The worst of it all was he was smiling, smiling at Colman as if he didn't have a care in the world. It made him waiver a bit. But then he thought of the money.

He gulps down his whisky. Jack Daniel's. You are a traitor, he tells himself, drinking JD instead of a good Scottish malt. There is a crap murder on the box. Just the business. He settles himself down, knocking back his drink and pouring another one. He imagines lifting Sophie Stones onto the desk in the office he has not seen. He pulls down the zip of his jeans. He gets it out. He runs his finger up the crack of her arse. This is what she'll like. All tabloid hacks must like it. Fucks full of cruelty and sleaze. He mutters filth into her ear. Moves it slowly back and forth. His cock seems bigger since his father died. Bigger and harder. He has a slow smile on his face. He's shoving it right up her, swearing at her. He pulls at his balls, grasping them and then pulls his cock faster till he lets it out, swearing to himself, ah fuck, fuck, fuck, till it is everywhere, too much of it, too much. How many kids could he make with that? A fucking population. He could make a whole generation with that. There's more come too since his father died. That's weird, but it's definitely true. He's losing it. He gets up and gets some toilet paper, wipes himself down, doesn't do up his zip, and sits watching the rest of the murder with his Jack Daniel's in his hand.

He's meeting her this morning. She wants the letter. He puts it in the front pouch of his bag and pulls the zip. His father's handwriting startles him each time he gets the letter out to look at it. He gets dressed: loose baggy top and baggy trousers made in America. Pulls on his white sports socks and his big trainers. He is particular about the way he does his laces. He does not tie a knot, but tucks them in at the side of the tongue, so that they look done and undone. He pulls at the fat tongue till it sticks out properly. He looks in the mirror. Shaves thoughtfully and dabs some of his aftershave on. He finds his place very silent at the moment, unsettling. Why is it so quiet? No music, that's it. Since his father died, he's stopped playing music. He didn't even realize it until now. He can't wait to get out. Get the fuck out, he says to himself, patting his hair into shape. Get out, you asshole. He smiles at himself. Women tell him he is handsome. But he was not a handsome boy. His glasses spoiled it. He was the last one to get a girlfriend in his class. He still can't see himself as handsome, but everyone tells him. Sophie Stones will be after him. He will have to be careful. It's been a long time since he got his rocks off.

* * *

157

Sophie Stones is armed with tape recorder and notepad and fancy fountain pen. 'Let's write down our objectives vis-à-vis going to Glasgow,' she says, scribbling as she speaks. Colman looks at her blankly. She has a great weakness for the word *objectives*. As soon as she says it she can start writing, but not before. 'Right,' she says, happily. 'Objectives. What are our objectives? Well, for starters' (she writes number one) 'to find out about Joss Moody/Josephine Moore's childhood. What else, what else? Let's see.'

(She writes number two.) 'To collect any information from any source – old friends, relatives, school.'

'OK. OK.'

(She's on a roll now.) 'Number three!' (She practically shouts.) 'To do detailed interviews with the people who knew him/her well.'

Colman interrupts. 'Don't bother with this him/her bullshit. That's bollocks, man. Just say him.'

'But it's important that we remember that "he" was a "she" first.'

'Tell me about it! I'm not fucking forgetting, am I?'

'Four.' (A bit deflated.) 'Describe the house he grew up in.

'Five. Get the birth certificate.

'Six. Get all old photos, records, letters, etc.

'Seven. Trace all living relatives. Get their reaction.'

'There are no living relatives. What are you talking about?'

Sophie Stones smiles a very small smile into her sleeve.

Colman hadn't reckoned on any of this. He thought he'd follow his own nose, let one thing lead to another, naturally. But this is more like fucking Operation Transvestite. He hears Sophie saying somewhere in the background, 'So, I am going to accompany you.' Shit. 'Separate rooms of course,' Sophie says, and pats his leg. He gets a hard-on and feels suddenly embarrassed. Feels himself scrambling around, knowing things aren't quite right, wishing he had another brain. A sharp brain that could lay out a different plan. Just like that. All he says is, 'Did I invite *you?*' to see if that bothers her, but it doesn't. 'No,' she smiles, 'but I'm coming. You can't do without me. Nobody can. You need a journalist's special powers. People don't talk any more without this.' She rubs her thumb obscenely against her fingers. 'And besides,' she says, 'I've discovered that Joss Moody's mother is still alive.'

PEOPLE: *THE DRUMMER*

Some guys said Moody had a baby face, but the drummer didn't think so. Big Red McCall beat up anybody who came out with those things. One time he caught a guy saying, 'There's something strange about that Moody,' in the Wee Jazz Club not long after they split with the Witnessers and made out on their own as the Boogie Woogie Moody Men. McCall never let anyone get away with anything. McCall was six foot two and weighed twenty-two stone. He cornered the guy, poked him hard with his fat fingers. Who, jab, are, jab, you, jab, calling, jab, strange? The guy stood his ground – 'Moody's voice is high like a woman's,' McCall knocked him down. He had one of those tempers where he literally saw Red. The minute after he knocked someone down, he'd help him up, spit on his hands and dust down his jacket. 'Sorry, but I had to do that. It was fucking crucial.' Then he gave his famous short snorting laugh, which sounded like a pig fucking, went to the bar and growled, 'Two Scotch on the rocks, please.' Moody took his whisky grinning like a man. Big Red winked and said, 'Canny staund assholes. I've no patience for them. Did you see the face on it when I walloped him?'

Big Red's temper earned him his nickname. He was proud of it. Ever since he was a boy he's been graffitied with nicknames. 'Big Man' at three, his nervous granny set that one rolling. 'Brassneck' at around six, after he asked Sandra MacGregor to kiss him and she said loud enough for the whole street to hear, 'You've got a brass neck, Malcolm McCall.' 'Poacher' at twelve when he was poaching with his great-uncle Tummock. 'Bunk' for a long time because he was always bunking off school. 'Malki' until he was nineteen till when he took up the drums. Malcolm McCall was his proper name, but he'd never answered to it all his life. Who was it who first called him Big Red? He can't remember. But Big Red spread quicker than wildfire, quicker than blood on a bar-room floor.

Big Red was his favourite because he believed in communism and had a red hot temper. Nicknames were magic; they let people know what they were in for. Big Red was all for them. When he was wee, only the unpopular swots were not granted the gift of a nickname. The wee pains in the ass. Some of those clever bastards would skulk into smokers' corner and make a nickname up for themselves! Then they'd find some sly way of forcing the nickname to catch alight. But it never did. It always spluttered out like the damp match that it was. The boys who were called David, Peter,

Walter and John tried to metamorphosize into Mince, Spider, Peanuts and Crow only to find themselves chucked back onto the slagheap of their dull names. Nothing they could do about it. You had to be in the running to be crowned with a nickname. You had to have a bit of what it takes. Yes. You had to have a bit of this. Panache. You couldn't try it on if you were just a wee nyaff. Or you had to be so slick your own name sounded too cool for anybody to ever want to change it. Imagine being born with a name like Miles Davis. You've already got it made. If you had a name like Miles Davis maybe, you already sounded like you were driving a Mercedes. No need to tamper wey a name like that. Miles Davis. Charlie Mingus. Joss Moody.

Big Red first met Moody when the drummer of the Witnessers took food poisoning. One of his pals asked him to stand in and he did. He went up to Moody and asked him straight, 'What kind of rhythm shall I play for you?' From that day on Moody and him were tight as fists. McCall could drum the same rhythm every night. He had total recall for what he'd done before. Moody was private with his trumpet and McCall was extrovert with his drums. They were a great team. McCall's showmanship was hilarious. He made more verbal asides than a character in a Shakespeare play. He always played with this huge powderpuff for his armpits. He dressed in loud green chalk-striped suits and bright ties. He could roll those drums like thunder. When they started to make records together Joss joked that he would knock the needle off the wax. McCall felt he had a calling for the drums. They were his babies. The big bang and the wee tom-toms. He got them all to practise drumnastics until he got so out of hand Moody told him to cool down or split. He was in danger of nabbing the limelight.

McCall loved nothing better than a wee jam with Moody. A wee practice. Just the two of them. Blowing room. They'd doodle and noodle and smear. They'd make the odd clinker. It seemed, to Big Red, that they understood each other perfectly like bad twins. There have been more times than Moody was aware of, when Big Red McCall rushed to his defence. Big Red McCall was not the least bit interested in private life. He was no gate-mouth. He had never clyped in his life. Some blokes liked to blether and gossip but McCall wasn't one of them. He acccpted Moody had a bit of a squeaky voice. Big deal. Lots of people squeak. As for baby face, millions of jazz men have baby faces. Look at Baby Dodds, Baby Mack, Baby Riley. The jazz world is full of big pudding faces, cheeks like cheese puffs. A man with a baby face could send you to town. A man with a baby face could have you away ta ta on a big raft sailing for an island you've never heard of. Big reefs. Rocks the size of drums. Trees playing trombones. Big Red McCall and Joss Moody together had people reeling and begging for more.

163

The claps they got! They weren't normal appreciation. They were fucking desperate. Jazz was their fix. Jazz was in the veins.

Most of Big Red's mornings are hangover mornings and all of his friends, acquaintances and fellow bums know better than to ring him before three o'clock. So when the phone goes, when the phone rings and fucking rings and rings, Big Red already knows it is something not nice. And sure enough, right on the end of his line, dangling, is a woman by the name of Sophie Stones. Big Red's hangover is throbbing enough to make him want to dress to twelve Bessie Smith numbers. He isn't feeling well. He isn't feeling well at all. Non communicado. She says to him, 'You were Joss Moody's drummer, weren't you?' Big Red said, 'Aye, what's it to you? Who is asking?' The sleek voice comes down the line. 'My name is Sophie Stones, I work on the *Daily Sky*.' Big Red is almost ready to hang up. He loathes the capitalist press. What a bunch of weak-willed unintelligent bastards they all were. But he hangs on, out of curiosity.

'I'm writing a book about the amazing fact that Joss Moody turned out to be a woman,' she says. 'Were you aware—?'

He interrupts her, 'Nope. And you should concern yourself with the music. The guy's a genius.'

'Don't you mean the girl's a genius?' Sophie says.

'Whatever. Christ, do you think I'm bothered? Do you think anybody's bothered? It's the fucking

164

music that matters.' He hears her drawing her breath.

'But did you know before the funeral?'

'Nope.'

'So you must have got quite a shock? Come on. This is somebody you toured with for ten years. How come you didn't suspect?'

'A lot of people said Moody had a baby face,' Big Red says, 'but I didn't think so. I beat up anybody who said that.'

'Can you tell me what Moody did when the rest of you were in urinals?'

'Women think that men spend all their time gawking at the size of each other's pricks in the bogs. I've more to do than watch men pish.'

'But that's just it,' Sophie says triumphantly, 'Moody never "pished" in front of you, did he? Did you never notice, touring together like you did?'

'We were in jazz clubs. We were musicians. We werenie interested in wur wee-wees.'

'But, come on,' Sophie says again.

'Naw, you come on. Away and write yir stupit book. It won't tell us anything aboot Moody. If you want my advice, you'll drop it. It ull only upset his family. Anyway, I'm having nothing to do with it. It's not on.'

Sophie says, 'We will of course be paying a handsome fee.'

Big Red pulls himself up to his full height in his hall. 'Are you trying to bribe me? Away and raffle yourself.' Big Red slams his phone down and goes back to bed. His head is still sizzling and his temples are singing songs. 'Christ almighty,' he says to himself, 'I'm strung oot. Rattling.' He pulls the covers over his head and mutters to himself, 'Stupit fucking cow,' before giving himself up to sleep.

In his dream Moody is there with his shining trumpet. He walks towards him and he says, 'You've heard I'm dead, Big Red.' In his dream, he hears himself tell Moody, 'Yes, I've heard the news. Every fucker is talking about you. The jazz world is going fucking mental. You won't believe how much you're missed.' Moody says, 'Is that so?' Big Red can't help but notice that dead Moody is the same as live Moody. Big Red reaches out for Moody's arm. He is about to say, 'You bastard, I still can't believe you did it,' but Moody starts walking backwards through the club's doors. They are in a big bright yellow field. Big Red is running after Moody. Moody is fit and Big Red is not. He sweats and runs. Must lose some weight, he thinks. Finally he shouts ahead to Moody, 'I still can't believe you did it.' Moody shouts back, 'Did what?' Big Red shouts, 'Died on me, you fucking bastard!' In his dream, Moody's face lights up. 'Oh that,' he says. 'That. You had that coming. You needed to be the bandleader.' Moody starts to run. In his dream he is the same age that he was when they first met. 'Was it me?' Big Red shouts after the running figure in the yellow field. 'Did I do something?' Moody turns and shouts, 'Don't be soft, McCall. You knew all along!'

McCall wakes, clacking his tongue to the roof of his mouth, wondering what the fuck Moody died of. He can't remember. With all the hullabaloo, he's just plain forgotten. Was it kidney problems? Fuck me, Big Red thinks to himself. I don't fucking know what claimed him. Big Red lies awake in bed, trying to remember deadly illnesses. AIDs, naw, cancer, don't think so, diabetes, naw, emphysema, no. Glandular fever. Hepatitis. Irritable bowel syndrome. (Can you die of that?) Jaundice. Kidney failure. Liver failure. Meningitis. Narcotics. Osteoporosis. Parkinson's disease. (Hadn't Moody been shaking strangely the last time he saw him?) Quadriplegia. Rheumatic fever. Salmonella. Tuberculosis. An ulcer, one of them exploding ones. A deadly virus. White cells. Yellow fever. (Where was the last place they'd been?) Z? Z? What the fuck begins with Z? Big Red has exhausted himself. Maybe he just died in his sleep; maybe that was it – zzzzzzz.

It's bugging him. He can't come up with it. He can hardly ring Millie and ask her. Maybe it'll come back to him. The last time he saw Moody he was looking a bit jaded, but no' bad. Just tired. He didn't look like he was dying. If Big Red had realized he would have said different things. He would have handled it differently. It's awful when you get deprived of a last word. There was Moody going to his grave with most people none the wiser.

167

If he'd known, if he'd been able to tell him, 'Look, Moody, don't worry about me because I don't give a fuck.' Moody was just the same in Big Red's head, except Moody was dead. That was the fucking awful thing. Moody was dead. No more Moody Trumpet. No more scooping pitch. No screaming. No hubba hubba. He seemed like he would just go on playing the trumpet till he dropped. Dropsy? Give in. Big Red punches his fist into the pillow saying to himself over and over, 'I can't get fucking comfortable.' He dents and winds and batters the fuck out of his useless pillow until he tastes salt on his lips. It's been years since he had a cry. At first he can't believe those are tears sliding down his face. Then the sound comes out of his mouth and he knows. Once it starts it goes on for ages. After a bit McCall gets into it. Just fucking cry, he thinks to himself. 'Go on, you stupit bastard, you big fat wean, cry your eyeballs out their sockets.' He doesn't get a hanky. He lets the snot run down his face till he has to wipe it with the back of his big hand.

HOUSE AND HOME

Her hand on the envelope. Third letter. Being blackmailed must feel like this. The sight of Stone's white envelope makes me sink, as if the floor of my house has turned to marshland for a moment. Her handwriting now has a terrible familiarity; I don't want to recognize it instantly, but I do – the big childish letters, the pretentious 'e's and 'a's. She uses a fountain pen evidently. *Mrs Millicent Moody, 10 Sandy Road, Torr, Kepper*. I hold it in my hand gingerly as if it smells. I open it slowly as if it might explode. This time she says I should reply to Glasgow. She says Colman and her are going to Scotland together to write the book. She says they are working together. Will I cooperate? I notice my hand holding the letter. It is an old woman's hand. I shall keep this one. I can't keep burning them. I want the evidence now. I want people to know some day that this is what has been done to me. It is like torture. I don't know who I could trust. I don't know whose advice to ask. There must have been somebody in that life of ours who would know how to handle this. I can't think of anybody. I've forgotten them all, suddenly.

I can barely believe that Colman would get himself involved in something like this. He is not a bad boy. He can be difficult; he's always been immensely capable of being difficult. But not malicious. I would never have associated him with sleaze. Did I give him no sense of morality at all? How is it possible for him to sell and tell the story of our life? Can he not see that lives are not for sale? I could shake him. Every time his face flashes before mine I feel so furious, so violent. It reminds me of how I used to feel when he was a boy, when he would disappear into these moods, these long domineering sulks for days. Those moods affected the atmosphere of the entire house. I remember I wanted to slap him. I itched to draw my hand across his sulky face and shout, 'Snap out of it!' Occasionally I actually did hit him. Once I had my hands round his neck and was shaking him uncontrollably. It wasn't me, the woman who suddenly leapt out of me at those moments. I had never ever hit anyone in my life. I don't know where it came from. One moment the hatred, the next the love. When the love came it was molten, hot, rushing forth out of all the guilt. I didn't know I was capable of feeling violence at all before I had Colman; I didn't know I had it in me.

It is a real plot. I have to keep reading her vile sentences over and over to convince myself it is true. When Joss was alive, life was never like this.

It was real. We just got on and lived it. Everything has stopped since he died. Reality has stopped. 'Will you cooperate?' This is such a strange notion to me: the idea that I could cooperate with a book about my life, that I could graft myself into this life that they think I had. I am going to have to contact my lawyer and get some advice. Perhaps I can stop the book. Perhaps I can get an injunction. I can't just sit here until they turn up. His story is not going to be my story. A story with a price tag is never going to be true. His story will not be true, even to himself. He has always been naive, Colman. I can just see how it will all go. He has never been that articulate. This Sophie Stones will be putting words into his mouth. I could never write my version of our life. I don't know what I'd say.

I used to find the amount of publicity that Joss created terrifying. I hated the constant interviews, the articles about his life and music in the newspapers and magazines. The description of our house always incensed me. It was their myth of our house. Every word I read about Joss was a myth. It wasn't him. When they quoted him in articles, he never sounded like himself. I used to ask him, 'Did you say that?' and he'd say, 'Yes.' I'd persist, 'Were these your exact words?' They never were. Perhaps Colman doesn't know that Sophie Stones is sending me these letters. What do they know about his life? What do I know about his life really? What do I know about my own life?

My life is a fiction now, an open book. I am

trapped inside the pages of it. Anything is possible. My life is up for grabs. No doubt they will call me a lesbian. They will find words to put on to me. Words that don't fit me. Words that don't fit Joss. They will call him names. Terrible vertigo names. I can see myself holding the book out at arm's length, to see what words they have used, sinking with them. Down to the bottom, below the green film, to where the thick black mud lies.

I won't read it. I won't go near it. It won't come to that. I will stop it before it happens. No comment. No comment. When he died, I kept repeating that sentence whenever they fired questions at me. I kept saying I don't have anything to say. I couldn't understand why they wouldn't stop. They kept on bombarding me, more new faces every time I went out. In the end, they all looked like the same face. The same white sharp face.

I am here because I became convinced that they were stopping Joss from resting in peace. I had to get away from them so that Joss could get some peace. He didn't get a proper night's sleep for days before he died: he was in and out of sleep, fretful, snapping awake and dropping off, like a baby. If I could hide from them for long enough, Joss would be able to find his peace. When you die, you don't leave straightaway. I know this. I feel it. After they took away his body, I felt Joss desperate for peace. He still hasn't been given his proper death. The one everyone expects – a good send-off. His funeral won't have helped; he wouldn't have been satisfied with that funeral. No, he is still hanging around in limbo. They say that when there is trouble, the dead hang around. I believe it completely. Joss is here in me. I find myself thinking thoughts these days that I know are his thoughts.

I find myself standing over the kitchen sink with the tap running at its full capacity. The dark brown basin in the sink is overflowing. My hands are plunged into the cold water. I have no idea how long I have been standing like this. I know my hands are cold, freezing cold. I know my mouth is wet. I know that I have been looking for ages in the water to try to see if I reflect. I don't. The letter keeps chiming through my head. It is like a bell rung in an old town to tell people that somebody is about to be tarred and feathered or publicly whipped or hung. If Joss was here we would at least be in it together. Joss has forsaken me.

I dry my hands and pour the water down the sink. I must remember things. I look out of the kitchen window. It has been raining. Tiny beads of rain have been painted on the window pane when I wasn't looking. It is a fine Impressionists' rain. Next door's rowan tree is quite still, not at all flamboyant; it is not the season for flamboyance. I can see Elsa at her kitchen window peeling potatoes. The intimacy startles me. Seeing me staring, she waves at me. I wave back, suddenly glad of the human contact. If I pin myself down and remember the ordinary things, I will be able to manage. To get up each day and get washed and eat and sleep. To live a life without my companion. To live this life where I am exhausted with my own company, terrible thoughts spinning morning to night inside my head. Maybe this is what people mean when they say they are lonely. Maybe they mean they are exhausted even with their own company. If I could just say I am lonely how lovely and ordinary that sounds.

What a wonderful common sad ring it has to it. Lonely. It is light and graceful the way old women are, old women who hurry into their small houses at twilight and pull the curtains fiercely. I am just a lonely old woman. I will admit to being old now. I will admit that my body does not behave the way it used to; that my walk is not as fast; that my bones are not as strong; that my breath is shorter; that my energy is sputtering and sparking. I will admit now that I am my age, I am not the girl or the woman that I once was. Old. I have shunned the word and rushed away from it. I have laughed and said smugly to people, 'You are as old as you feel.' But today I feel old. It is a comfort to me. Old people should be left alone. They should not be troubled with nasty letters. It is outrageous when you think of it: fancy sending a nasty letter to an old woman! The minute I put it like that you can see how ridiculous it is. How wrong. Fancy hounding an old woman, chasing her with a pack of dogs that have all been given something of hers to sniff. Chasing her right up to the door of her house and howling and barking to get in and have a piece of her. Old women should be left in peace in the gloaming to sit and contemplate and ruminate and go over the bright, sharp details of their memories with their kind old hands, picking and peering and muttering to themselves.

I make myself a list so that they won't surprise me. A list of potential betrayers. People who will talk for cash. Kiss and tell. There are certain people I know for certain would never divulge a single detail. Maggie wouldn't ever talk or Ragnail or Big Red or Harry or . . . But there might be people Joss knew that I don't. These swines are capable of digging anybody up. Is it possible that Sophie Stones could discover somebody Joss went to school with? Anything is possible. There is no line I can draw which says: 'Stop here.' It will all be over the top, crossing the boundary. All hell let loose. Money talks.

LETTERS

There were people who said he had a baby face. There were people who said he had a high voice. I'd fight anyone who said those things. I never suspected a thing.

Big Red McCall, Joss Moody Trio

I was surprised, but I don't see what all the fuss is about.

When it all blows over, we'll be left with his music. That's what matters.

Soloman Davis, Joss Moody fan

I am writing the authorized biography of the trumpet player, Joss Moody. Please refer all correspondence to me. My book will look into the fascinating details of every aspect of her life. I would like anyone who knew her, who played in a band with her, or who corresponded with her to get in touch with me urgently.

Yours, Sophie Stones

We question this notion that somebody who lives their life as a man and is discovered to be female at the time of death was really a woman all along. What is 'really' in this context? What is the force of that reality?

Transvestites Anonymous Group (TAG)

We are planning to bring out four CDs to mark Moody's phenomenal impact on jazz music. They will be called *The Best of Moody: The Man and the Woman*, to acknowledge the strange circumstances surrounding the trumpet player's death. These will be available later this year.

John Anderson, Columbia Records

What I can't understand is how he managed to go on the road with us. I never noticed anything exceptional. That takes some doing. I mean we shared rooms and shit. I don't remember him going to the john. I'm trying to remember him going to the john but I can't. The point is he seemed just like the rest of us. I suppose if I'm looking for something I'd say his features had something about them – I don't know what, something about the soft face, the lips. Once you know, it's staring you in the face. And the laugh was

177

way over the top and sounded a bit . . .
girlish. But we loved that laugh. It was
crazy sounding.

Sean Lafferty, UK Trumpet Society

Can we please let the dead rest in peace?
Has this country forgotten how to do that?

Ann Gray, address provided

INTERVIEW EXCLUSIVE

If I stop talking you won't have a book. If I shut my fucking trap, you're grounded. You can't just write shit about people if you don't know the facts. To tell you the truth, right, I'm starting to get a sore throat. It's like there's fucking gravel in my throat or something. My father used to make brilliant hot toddies for things like this. Cloves and shit.

But you know I can't stop, don't you? I just can't shut the fuck up. You ask me things and I tell you things. Simple. It's not the money any more. I don't know what it is. You're bad news. I should stay away from you. What the fuck am I doing here with you? I can't stop telling you things. Fuck me, maybe it's doing me some good. Maybe it will do someone else good. You know and I know that I don't believe that. You believe that. Well, you say you do.

I used to enjoy winding my father up. I could see a chance coming and I'd take it and the end result was always the same. He'd go mental. I knew how to do it to him. I could get right inside his head. The best time was when I was a teenager.

That was crucial. I was bad then. Really bad. I didn't want to do any school work. I just liked hanging out with my mates and having a spliff. I didn't stand a chance really. There was all this pressure on you not to do anything. Not to do well. Not to work hard. I mean practically every black guy my age that I saw on TV had just been arrested for something. Or was accused of mugging. It's like we only had the one face to them. The same face. The one that was wanted for something. I can tell when I go out and about, fuckers staring at you as if you've done something. I've been picked up by the police countless times, man, for doing fuck all. Just for being black and being in the wrong place at the wrong time. But my old man, he didn't take my side about all this. He thought I had it coming to me. He thought I was a waster. He'd try to get me to stay in and concentrate. Concentrate on anything. He got exasperated the way I couldn't 'apply' myself. He was always saying that to me. Why don't you apply yourself? I remember telling him he was a hypocrite, that all his doped out jazz mates would be shocked at him, treating his son like this. They were all cool. Most of them had kids that were embarrassed about *them*; they were out of it half the time, turning up to collect them at school with strange coats on. Some of those kids have grown up to be business managers. They were the first fucking yuppies on the street. But me and my dad were conventional. He wanted me to get the head down and concentrate. Once he lost his temper and called me a talentless bastard. I was gutted. So I picked up this new album of his that had lots of regigged old tunes on it and I said, 'New release, old man?' Then I said, 'What do you want me to be? Wynston fucking Marsalis?'

He goes into this long thing about jazz being improvized and being different versions of the same thing. I says, 'Bollocks, when did you last have a truly original idea?' Then he looks sad, he says something about people being only talented for one moment in time. Something like that. Some gifted people have a short time of pure talent. Some people longer. The ones that have a short time can't believe it when their talent runs out, so they scramble to get it back, impersonate themselves. Mimic. Parody. Act themselves. He says jazz can get away with that better than most stuff. He looks sad then. Like he's a conman or something. I feel bad in the pit of my stomach.

My father couldn't cope with me becoming a man. Couldn't handle it. Probably jealous of my cock now I think about it. I'd see him standing around some days, staring at me with this sick look on his face. When I was a wee boy he was a great dad to have, cool, funny, easy. But when I became a teenager, he flipped out. Started all this business of checking up on me. Finding out if I'd done my homework. Clocking the time I came in. It was like living with a fucking dictator. It was at the same time as his career took a bad dip. Maybe he felt his life was over and it was down to me to come up with something. I don't know. Whatever it was it was pure hell for me.

Once, he comes out with, 'I can make people listen to me from London to Japan, but I can't get my own son to hear a single word I'm saying.' Not when you talk pish like that, I said. I mean, man. That's heavy stuff. Doesn't do to take yourself too seriously, Joss Moody, I said to him. He didn't like it when I said his name like that. Joss Moody will know, I'd laugh. Joss Moody always knows. Then I said, in my gimmicky jazz voice, 'Let's call the whole thing off.' I slammed the door for special effect and went out. I wasn't exactly a pleasant boy. But I mean everyone goes through it, don't they? Everyone needs space at that age. I was raging all the time. Don't ask me about what. I was just furious from winter to spring. Generally obnoxious. I can see that now. Doors in our house were always being pulled off their fucking hinges. They got Bob, the big handy man, to fix the doors frequently. Bob would look at me and say, 'What are you doing – swinging on them?' I'd just stare coldly back and say, 'Yeah, that's right. I think I'm Tarzan.' Bob laughed one of those knowing adult laughs and exchanged a look with my mother. She looked away then, disgusted and sometimes she'd raise her hands as if to say, 'I can't do anything with him.' I'm not proud of all that now.

I used to use half a bottle of shampoo every time

I washed my hair. I ate a packet of cornflakes a day. I had a slab of meat every evening. Steak and chips. I had long sessions in the bath and always left the ring around it for my mother. I left all my dirty clothes all over the house. My room was a dustbin. I smoked out the window in the bathroom. I didn't want them knowing I smoked. I didn't talk to them about anything. Once I was held up at the police station till four in the morning. I hadn't done anything. I didn't call them. I don't think they know half what I went through. I made a lot of noise eating. Especially cornflakes. I went about, according to my mother, with a huge chip on my shoulder. Not just a chip, my father would say, a whole fish supper. I was surly, sullen, selfish, shameless. It's true. I was a total animal.

Another time I remember was when I wanted to go to this party and my father wouldn't let me. Said I had too much school work to do. I said, 'Since when have you bothered about my school work. It's fucked anyway. That's down to you, dotting about the world playing your horn, man.' He grabbed hold of me. Fuming. Smoke coming out of his nostrils. He shouted, 'Show some respect.' And I pulled his hands off me and said, 'Get real.' It's funny that, when I think about it. Me telling him to get real.

When I left home, I got on better with the old man. Just before he died, I'd say we had a pretty good relationship. We liked each other. He was

183

always disappointed and guilty that I hadn't done more with my life. But who could do something with a father like that? I mean I was never going to be as good as him; so forget it. You only need one in a family, that's what I reckoned. It was difficult having a famous father like that. He never understood that. But plenty people in the world have been screwed up by their famous parents. I'd have needed to have more talent than him to do anything with myself. And he was talented. I've got to say that for him. All this doesn't change the way he played that trumpet. I mean I've got to hand it to him, he was a talented bastard. Even when I wasn't into jazz all that much, I still liked the way he played the trumpet. The minute I'd hear him start I could see myself as a wee boy again. It was like getting back something I'd lost. Have you ever listened to any jazz at all?

When I was a little boy I liked being Joss Moody's son. I even liked the hat he wore, the cream fedora. The way he wore it on his head, slightly tilted to the one side. I liked going to gigs with him and overhearing people say, 'That's his son.' I liked the looks they gave me, those fans of my father's. It was quite something being his son. Everybody knew about it. In school I'd always have to talk about it, my father the jazz musician. It came under, 'Parents who do something unusual.' I wrote a story about it. My mother kept that story.

But he wanted *me* to be talented. He'd have liked me to play something. Not the trumpet; something else. The piano. He always said I had nice hands for the piano. The galloping piano. Flexible fingers. Then he'd say he didn't mind whether it was music, sport, science, whatever. As long as I had an occupation, an obsession with something, it would be good for me. He wanted me to be cleverer than him. But I reckon each generation is now turning backwards. People are more stupid now than they used to be. That's why you keep hearing people say things like, 'They don't make them like they used to.' About all sorts, good shoes, clothes, you name it. What's happened to the cobbler? Mass production has done away with talent, that's what I reckon. All the talent is sliding away back towards the sea. This is the anti-fucking-evolution age. There's not as many clever bastards out there as there used to be. Even the jazz musicians nowadays have got nothing on my father's generation of jazzmen. Where are all the dukes and the counts now? Where's the big guys?

I was born the same year that Captain Scarlet first appeared on the box. One thing we had in common, my father and me, was that we both liked *Star Trek* and all that kind of stuff. My father liked Captain Kirk and I liked Spock. I sympathized with Spock and his big mental ears and what happened to his mother. Sometimes all the guys in the current Moody band would come round to our place and we'd watch it together, munching on a big bag of potato sticks. Then they'd have their jam at the end of it. To boldly

185

go. And the jazz would shake the whole house like a train.

Later on my father was obsessed with the sixties. Every person has their favourite decade. He said it was the decade for everything that mattered. An enthusiastic decade was what he called it. Jazz, politics, sex, science fiction, peace. He'd sit up late at nights ranting to anyone who would listen, about how a bad decade always follows a good one. (He got that right. Didn't he? He got that right.) I'd say something reactionary to please him and get him to spout off more. Bring back capital punishment. Never failed.

I decided to do the son thing one day and ask my dad about sex. I thought it would please him. I started by saying something like: there's a few things I need to know, Dad, seeing as we're living in a permissive society. He had a drink in him. It was late and he'd just come back from somewhere. My mother was asleep.

He sits down on his chair, lights a fag and doesn't offer me one. I sit watching him, dying for a fag. Then he says, 'Fire away.' He's got a drunk smile on his face that is also a bit sexual. I say, off the top of my head, have you ever had an affair? He says, No. He says, No, with complete sincerity, no effort involved at all. Do you want to know why, he says. Because I am not interested in anyone besides your mother. Only she can turn me on. I'm shocked at this, this expression. He sees that and repeats it drunkenly, relishing it. Only she can

186

turn me on. Then he smiles, a slow smile, pleased with himself and exhales a ball of smoke. I breathe in, trying to get a hit from it.

So, I say, is sex good with Mum? And he says, Aren't you getting out of your depth here, son? I pour him another glass of whisky. Oh no, he says. You don't get me that way. Yes, it's good. It's really good. Of course. Of course it's good. How often do you do it? I say, appalled. Oh come on, he says, still enjoying the conversation, lighting a new cigarette. Fathers should tell their sons stuff like this, I say, it's educational. Three times a week, he says. You're exaggerating, I say. You asked. I don't care whether you believe me or not, he says. And I believe him because he says that and because of the look on his face. Do you always do it in bed? I ask, knowing that at any minute I will be stopped and cursed. He laughs, throwing back his head. Come off it, he says. Your mother and I like variety. The spice of life. Any old place will do. A dressing room . . . A dressing room, I shriek. Why not? What else are dressing rooms for?

My father never got a leg over. Had a hard-on. My father was never tossed off. He never stuck it up, or rammed it in, never spilt his seed, never had a blow job. What did he have down his pants? A cunt – is that it? Or did he wear a dildo? Shit. If he did, he would have rammed it in, I promise you.

He leans forward drunkenly towards me. 'Your eyes,' he says, 'your eyes are the same colour as my Jack Daniel's.' He is holding the glass up to my face, ridiculously close. He looks pleased with himself, as if he's discovered something really crucial about me. This is more like it. I make a mental note always to give Colman a good few drinks when I'm interviewing him. Since we talked about going to Scotland, Colman has started dishing the dirt. This is exactly the kind of stuff that will sell the book. The nineties are obsessed with sex, infidelity, scandal, sleaze, perverts. The nineties love the private life. The private life that turns suddenly and horrifically public. The sly life that hides pure filth and sin. The life of respectability that shakes with hypocrisy. The government minister who wanks himself to death with a rope around his neck to achieve the ultimate orgasm. Love it. The priest who has been screwing half of his worshippers. Love it. The upper-class English movie star who has been caught having his cock sucked by a Hollywood prostitute. Love it. The respectable 'family values' MP who sucked on the toe of a bimbo. Love it. All of it. The dirtier the better. The more famous, the better. The brother of the princess who cheated on his wife twelve times. The higher they are the lower they fall. Lesbian stories are in. Everyone loves a good story about a famous dyke tennis star or actress or singer. And this one is the pick of the bunch. The best yet. Lesbians who adopted a son; one playing mummy, one playing daddy. The big butch frauds. Couldn't be better.

I can't *wait* to get this book out. It is my book really. Joss Moody will have been dead for at least a year by the time the book comes out. Colman Moody and his ghost writer, Sophie Stones, will be so close we'll be interesting. Even my sister Sarah will be riveted. I am Colman Moody's ghost writer. His psyche. I like the idea of finding his voice. His subconscious. If I use my nut, my loaf, I'll be rolling in it before the millennium. I need to get right under Colman Moody's skin. It will not be the first time. Why should I have scruples when men have been using me for years? As long as it takes to make good copy. He's playing the same game, isn't he?

I feel like his shrink when I say, 'How do you feel now all that is said?' I know he is lying when he says, 'Cool.'

PEOPLE: *THE CLEANER*

The first time Maggie arrived at Mr and Mrs Moody's house, Mrs Moody took her aside, and in a strange voice, one that was a mixture of whispers and pride, said to her, 'Do you know who my husband is?' Maggie didn't. Mrs Moody said, 'My husband is Joss Moody.' She said the name 'Joss Moody' as if she expected the whole world to know who Joss Moody was. Maggie reckoned he must be famous, so she said, 'Oh, really, how amazing!' quickly trying to rack her brains to see if the name rang a bell. Wasn't that the name of that new Games man on the TV? Mrs Moody went on to say, 'If my husband is at home, he practises from eleven in the morning till around about two. So it's important that you always do the hoovering first.' Maggie knew better than to ask what it was that Mr Moody practised.

A beautiful family house. Nice smells. Always smelt of fresh coffee. They were good to her. If she had any problems with her young son, with her mother, with her bills, they listened to her and they helped her. Mrs Moody always gave her a cup of tea the minute she arrived at ten o'clock.

(Most people liked to see you sweat before they offered you a cup.) Cup of tea two hours later. Mr Moody was a bit of a special man. The first time Maggie met him, she knew straightaway. She could tell things about people. Mr Moody was at the top of the stairs that day. Maggie watched him coming down. The man had style. He wore unusual shirts that had five cufflinks, specially ordered. Beautifully stitched. He never looked like he'd just got out of bed. His trousers always creased. She never saw him wear anything casual, although plenty of his music friends turned up at the door in jeans and T-shirts. A few of them looked in need of a bath.

The other thing Maggie noticed about Mr Moody was how gentle he was. Once, Maggie had arrived at the Moody house upset. She couldn't help herself; she cried. Mr Moody made her a pot of tea. She'd never seen him make the tea before. Then he sat down with her at the kitchen table and listened. He never spoke all that much, but he was polite. After a good half an hour Maggie got to her feet and apologized profusely. 'I shouldn't be taking up your time like this.' 'It's no bother,' he said and went off to his room. Mrs Moody was good-looking as well. She had a good head of hair. You could tell them two loved each other. They were always giving each other looks about the house. You know the kind, little special looks.

It was on the third visit to the house that Maggie heard it. At first she wondered what on earth it was. She was in the kitchen, bleaching the sink and emptying the dishwasher. It was the first dishwasher she had ever seen. Not many people had them then. She heard this unbelievable sound coming from Mr Moody's room. It was low at first, almost a growl. Then it started to become quite frantic. It agitated Maggie. It put her on edge. If only they let her listen to Radio One like the rest of her houses.

Mrs Moody was a bit fussy as to where everything should go. But then everybody was a bit fussy. Some people were a headache. Telling you to put this there and that here when you were already in the middle of something. There was nothing you could do about it. You had to do what they wanted and you had to do it 'now'. Well, she wasn't all that bad. The thing she was fussy about was all her ornaments. Ornaments from all around the world in that house. Huge Russian dolls, those ones that hide inside each other. Mrs Moody showed her one one day. It took up ten minutes to get to the baby hiding in there. The smaller they got the less details on their faces. Mrs Moody said to her, 'We're all like that, aren't we? We've all got lots of little people inside us.' Maggie said, 'When you think about it. It's true, you know.'

Mr Moody gave her some of his records. She still has them. Two CDs, two tapes. It's not her kind of music, but it's not every day you know somebody who does something. Sometimes, she sat down with a cup of coffee and a cigarette and played Mr Moody's music. 'I know him,' she said to herself. 'I've worked for him.' After four years cleaning the Moodys' house, Maggie had felt something for them that was akin to love.

When she stopped working for them two years ago, they bought her a holiday. Told her to take her son and go. It was the first time she'd been abroad. She'd popped round to see them from time to time. But you know how life is. You mean to do something and the time just goes.

It is difficult for her to remember what happened when. The first she knew of it was a phone call from a neighbour who knew she had worked for the Moodys. The neighbour said, 'Maggie! Have you seen the papers?' She hadn't seen the paper. 'Why?' The neighbour's voice sounded oily. 'You know those people you worked for, the Moodys?' the neighbour said. 'Oh God, don't tell me something awful has happened to them,' Maggie shouted, picturing them murdered in their own home, tied to chairs or hidden in wardrobes with all those pieces from around the world missing. She felt she had to sit down. She pressed the phone to her ear. 'No. No. Nothing like that. The one you thought was a man, is dead, and they've discovered he wasn't a man after all.' 'Well, what was he?' Maggie asked stunned. 'A woman of course. It's in the paper. Will I bring it round?'

The next thing was a woman from the *Daily Sky* newspaper asking if she could come to interview her. Maggie said there was no way she was going to talk about her employers. They were kind to her. But the woman said it wasn't going to be nasty, it was just to try to understand. Given Maggie was so close to the family, she thought she could help. Also the son, Colman, was helping. Also, there would be a sum of money.

The very next day at eleven in the morning Sophie Stones is sitting in Maggie's front room, sipping a cup of tea – pretty cup with a saucer. The coffee table has been well polished up before she arrived. The carpet hoovered several times; you can't get a carpet to look brand new unless you go over and over it. The cushions on the couch turned and plumped. The curtains taken down and fresh ones hung up. The sheets on her double bed changed. (Not that she will be showing Sophie Stones her bedroom, but she always changes her sheets when she has a guest in the house. It's just habit.) Her sink scoured. Her toilet bowls bleached and shining. Air freshener sprayed. Inside windows cleaned. The front step brushed and washed. Every door in the house wiped down on the inside. All her kitchen units washed. Kitchen floor swept and mopped.

Maggie can see the girl look at the cleanliness of her home out of the corner of her eye. Too late now to tell her to go home and stop wasting her time. Anyway, it's not every day she has a journalist in her front room. And Maggie has never seen her name in print.

The girl pulls out the tiniest little tape recorder Maggie has ever seen. She gets out a tiny tape too. Maggie doesn't trust all these tiny things you can buy these days. 'Just talk for a minute,' Sophie says, 'till I check it's working? Tell me what you had for breakfast.' 'Well, I don't eat breakfast,' Maggie says, suddenly shy, like the tape is some kind of camera snapping her. Her voice has become self-conscious. She can't stop it. The lilt flying up towards the sky like her voice is a helium balloon and she is running on the ground trying to get it back down. She can't. Everything goes up at the end. As if everything is a question.

'Say a bit more,' Sophie says. 'Count to twenty.' Maggie feels silly sitting on her armchair counting to twenty into this tiny tape recorder in front of this Sophie Stones. How did she get herself into this? She must have spotted her nerves. She says, 'Don't worry, this is just a mini-interview.' Tiny tapes and mini-interviews; what is the world coming to?

'Great,' Sophie says. 'I'll just ask you questions and you can answer them in your own time. Don't rush. Don't worry about the tape. Pretend it's not there,' she says, pushing it a bit closer to Maggie. The tiny thing looks quite sinister on her gleaming coffee table. 'All right then,' Maggie says. 'Let's

195

get it over with.' Her voice sounds all breathy now, she can hear herself breathing in and out with the rush of words. 'What exactly was your job for the Moodys and for how long? (Tell me the years.)' 'I worked for the Moody family for four years.' (She can hear her own breath back to herself. She never realized her breathing was so loud. How to shut it up? How to simply talk?) 'I stopped two years ago because of family problems.' 'What did it involve?'

'Well, I cleaned the whole house from top to bottom. It was a big house. Four bedrooms. Two bathrooms. Nice house. I liked it there. I liked seeing the place looking nice.' (She can hear it herself. The falseness of her own 'speaking' voice.) 'Of course, it didn't stay that nice for long because by the time I came back the next week, the place was in a state again. They weren't tidy people.' The minute she's said this, she regrets it. She doesn't know what made her say it.

'Were you ever at all suspicious about Joss Moody? Did he seem like a regular guy to you?'

'If you are asking was he ordinary, no, he wasn't ordinary,' Maggie says. 'The man was a musical genius. He could play that thing!'

'I'm not interested in the music. I mean did you know he was a she?'

'No. Could have knocked me down with a feather.'

'Really?'

'I still don't believe it. You don't think they made some kind of mistake?'

'Oh no! This is for real.'

'You hear about undertakers making mistakes. Look at that woman they pronounced dead and nearly buried her when they discovered she was alive.'

'Look, it's all fact. Her name was Josephine Moore.'

'And that family who had to have the funeral twice because they had forgotten to put the body in the coffin! Are you sure there weren't two bodies in the same parlour, one woman, one man, who looked alike and they just mixed them up? If they can mix up babies in the hospital, can't they mix up the dead?'

'So, you didn't have a single inkling?'

'No. Not one.'

'What about his clothes? Did you do his laundry?'

'They had a laundry service come and pick up his shirts and bring them back like brand new, all folded with tiny pins and covered in cellophane.'

'So, nothing strange at all, as far as you could tell.'

'There was one strange thing,' Maggie begins.

Sophie leans forward tense as a cat. 'Yes?'

'One time, I'm cleaning his work room which was an amazing room, let me tell you. Full of photographs of musicians like himself, playing instruments. I don't know all their names.'

'Yes, yes. Go on,' says Sophie Stones impatiently.

'He had a big desk in that room. I always put back the papers exactly where I found them. But I'd lift them to polish underneath. He had strange writing, very small and curly. There were always lots of his own notes to himself about music everywhere. My eye caught a letter. I didn't usually read his letters. It was the way the letter began that interested me. It began, "Dear Mum," which was odd since Mr Moody told me his mother had died a long time ago.'

Sophie is right forward on her chair. 'Really!' she says. 'Really!' like she's just won on the lottery. 'What else did it say? Can you remember?'

'Yes,' Maggie says. '"Dear Mum, I am enclosing some money for you. I miss you. I am very busy." And so on. But the strangest thing was how the letter was signed. It was signed *Josephine*.'

'My God!' said Sophie. 'So surely that made you wonder?'

'No. What was I going to wonder? I thought to myself, Mr Moody must have written the letter on behalf of somebody else, maybe. But I remembered it.'

Sophie Stones smiles a huge mile of a smile.

'I don't suppose you still have keys to the house?' Sophie Stones asks her.

'No. I gave them back ages ago.'

'Pity,' says Sophie.

Maggie opens the door and Sophie Stones leaves her spotless house. Sophie takes Maggie's hand and shakes it warmly. 'You've been wonderful.'

Maggie says nothing. She watches her go down the three steps and get into the waiting taxi. She doesn't even wave. As she turns to go back into her house, she sees the neighbour, who phoned that day to tell her the headline, standing at her window.

The money is sitting on her table. Five hundred pounds in cash. Maggie can't stop herself. She has never in her life been handed five hundred pounds in the one gulp. She has to count it. And count it again. When she has finished counting it for the third time, she feels tired, exhausted. Maybe this is what it feels like to be rich, she thinks. Maybe the rich just get knackered all the time counting and thinking about money. She wonders what to do with it. Quickly, as if she's just robbed a bank, she puts the money into a canvas bag, runs up her stairs and hides it in her wardrobe, behind the shoes at the bottom. That won't do. She takes the bag from the wardrobe and puts it in her top drawer among her pants. She sighs. She pulls the money out of her underwear and puts it under her mattress. It comes to her again for the umpteenth time. Why did she do it? What could she have been thinking of? She leaves the money under her mattress for the time being. It is not a satisfactory place; she will have to do better than that. She will sleep on it. She goes back down the stairs and puts the kettle on. She sees the keys to the Moodys' house still hanging out of habit on the hook by her kitchen door.

TRAVEL: *LONDON*

Colman Moody lives in a ground-floor flat in Tottenham, north-east London. His father paid half of the sixty grand mortgage when he first bought it. Even so, he can't manage the relatively small mortgage and is in debt at the moment, behind with his payments, receiving repossession threats. His damp flat, with its regular mice, ants and other livestock, is now worth twenty thou less than what he paid for it in the time when people like himself were encouraged by the government to buy. He is trapped there: the livestock, the wonky electrics that gobble up light bulbs, the smell of rotting mice under the floor-boards, damp peeling paint on the dripping radiators, the kitchen units with their drawers falling through, the linoleum with its holes, its strange inexplicable bumps, trapped there unless he can get the money to split. His father told him he'd have to learn to manage his money and not do crazy things with it. But Colman has never learned to manage money. His father stopped giving him handouts. Told him it clearly wasn't helping him. He'd need to stand on his own two feet.

He gets up this morning and staggers into the shower. The fucking shower doesn't work properly and incenses him every time he uses it. It is either freezing his balls off or burning his back. He soaps himself, dashing in and out of the too hot or too cold water, swearing, fidgeting with the taps to try to get the blend right. Thinking, thinking all the time now about doing this book. He has been offered a sixty grand advance which would allow him to dump this heap of a flat and get the fuck out of the country. The need to escape, to go to a place where no one has ever heard of Joss Moody, where no one knows him, grows daily. He can't imagine any more money, though he has had calls from all sort of creeps offering him dosh to tell his story. Better the devil he knows. Sophie Stones is all right underneath that slick act she puts on; it doesn't fool him. She's vulnerable just like he is.

Scotland, his father's country, the country where Colman himself was born. He is going to Scotland today on the train. Sophie Stones is taking the shuttle in the early evening. Colman never flies unless he has to. Since he read that the majority of air disasters take place either in the three minutes of the plane taking off or landing, he has found take-offs unbearable. The sick moment when you are at the wrong angle completely to the earth.

Out of the shower. Dry the body. He stops to look in the mirror at himself. He can never decide if he is good-looking or ugly as shit. There are two Colman Moodys in the mirror: the boy with the glasses from the past; and the man now. The man now has got a good body, no question about that. A good sized cock, long arms, good shoulders, flat stomach, long legs. It's the face he can't decide on. It is as if he can't actually see himself properly; as if the sight of himself always gives him a bit of a nasty shock. He looks straight into his dark eyes. Shadows underneath, evidence of his insomnia and the amount of alcohol he's been packing away. Never could take whisky. His eyes seem to have got smaller, closing in on him. They used to be bigger, huge. People were always going on about his big beautiful brown eyes. His long, long lashes for a man. But now the lashes aren't curled back on themselves and the actual eye socket is smaller, the eyelid thicker. Definitely. Shit. His one big asset is closing in on him. He stares again at himself in the mirror, at the green towel hanging over his shoulders, at his wet hair. Just get dressed, man, get out the house, he says to himself and then rubs his hair affectionately in front of the mirror, trying to be his own friend.

Think of the money. Money is uplifting. To shut these repossession wankers up, buy himself a new sound system, go on holiday, pay the gas, the electricity, the phone, buy some new black jeans. Soon, he won't be here. He'll be travelling on a boat, a train, foot down in the hire car. Away ta-ta. As his father would say. Away ta-ta.

Colman Moody walks down West Green Road towards the tube, light-footed. Loose stride, taking long, bouncy steps. He looks like he's not exerting himself, like he's walking slow and casual, but he's actually covering a lot of ground with those long, long strides. Stepping.

West Green Road has two kinds of shops in it: barber's shops and fish shops. That's all the dudes in Tottenham do, get fancy shapes cut into their hair and eat fish. Colman passes quite a few guys he knows, they call out to him from the barber's shop. They are all sitting in a row waiting to have half their head shaved off, the hair taken away behind their ears, the straggling hairs on their neck sorted. The buzzing razor going over and over the same ground. What is this thing with hair? Colman thinks. White guys aren't as interested in their hair as far as he can see. Black guys keep reinventing themselves through hairstyles. Shapes – in one minute, naff the next.

His father liked going to a barber that was good at cutting black hair and whose customers were almost exclusively black. He liked sitting silent, waiting, watching himself in the mirror whilst the barber took his hair off in slices, slices of hair falling on to the floor. Colman always went with his father when he was a boy. They'd get done together. An initiation ceremony. His father must have had some nerve to sit in a barber's shop full of black men getting a man's haircut all the time knowing he was a woman. Must take quite a lot of balls to pull that off. Maybe he enjoyed it. Maybe he liked the danger of it. Maybe it didn't feel dangerous at all. If he was to have a chance to pull his father back up out of the wet muddy grave, have a chance to wrench open the wooden coffin and sit him up for ten minutes, that would be the first question he would ask him: did he like going to the barber's?

He stares at the fish in the window as he passes. Ghoulish looking. Dead mouths hanging open. Jelly eyes. Scaly slippery skin. Red mullets. Parrot fish. Grey mullets. Huge strange fish, exotic looking, as if someone from a children's story had caught them under the sea in the old world, and brought them back for people to see in the new world. Eyes staring blankly at him as if they remembered nothing. As if they'd forgotten they ever were fish. Some of the guys in the barber's shop stare like that, empty-eyed, as if they've forgotten who they are and have just landed some place without a past. The eyes of fish and the eyes of guys. Colman looks straight ahead down the road. A train passes over the railway bridge. The sky is a burden to itself, grey and heavy and passionate about rain. This is the strangest summer he can remember. Every day is a different weather. Not even the fucking weather can make up its mind.

Three steps at a time, down into the filthy hole of the tube. Down into the underworld of rubbish and stink and piss and poor people with their kids begging and guys holding up bits of brown cardboard that read 'Homeless'. Gets his ticket from the ticket machines that freak tourists. Remembers to get a single. He's not coming back. Not for a while. Pats his holdall. He's packed one pair of black jeans, two long shirts, one pair of brand new trainers – that he's bought with his card – four pairs of clean boxer shorts, one of them silk, just in case. A couple of sweatshirts and T-shirts, all American. One smart suit.

He passes someone at the bottom of the steps huddled between the entrance to both platforms who says, 'Any change?' Change in what? Change in the weather, change in government. Change – what do you mean, any change? Do you mean you want money? Well, why don't you ask for money? If you'd asked for money I'd have given you some, asshole. Learn to ask for what you want. Doesn't say any of this. Thinks it. But the guy shuffles back as he passes him as if he could read his thoughts. The sight of the broken man, with his dirty fingernails, filthy long matted hair, dirty beard, dopey eyes, hangdog look on his chops, and his millions of bits of rags that pass for clothes wrapped round him, his stupid mongrel dog that looks as defeated as him – but protective – infuriates him. It grates, seeing people broken like this. He is repulsed; doesn't feel any pity or mercy. Just raging fucking irritation. Doesn't want it in his face. The sight of it, in his face. His mother and his father were always sympathetic to poor people, to people with no money or power but, even as a boy, he wasn't. He still finds himself thinking these sour thoughts about people like this guy, thoughts that spring right into his head, barking. Barking. He thinks these kind of thoughts every day. Go and get a job, you useless pile of shit. The exact opposite way of thinking to his upbringing. Sponger. Waster. Parasite. Get up and get a job for fuck's sake.

He panics for a moment. Has he got the tickets that Sophie sent him? The Glasgow tickets? Did he leave them by the phone? He can see them by the phone. Stupid fucker. He calls himself names. This is another thing he has taken to doing recently, calling himself names. He pulls out his wallet and checks through. His head is buzzing, making a high noise inside his ears. There they are. Thank fuck for that. He says that out loud to himself. Thank fuck for that. His father used to say that all the time and he's always liked the ring of it. He looks into the eyes of the guy who asked for change. The guy's actually been thinking he was getting out his wallet to give him some money. He gets a fiver out of his wallet and drops it into the guy's empty box and says, 'Now stop staring in my face.'

Colman gets on the tube and turns to look at the homeless guy who is turning the fiver round in his hand, staring at it, pulling himself up, gathering his plastic bags and his sad dog together. He'll be off to the butcher's to buy that mutt a bone. Colman pictures the look on the sad dog's face when the bone is put down in the street for him to pull and tug and crunch and suck in a long, long dance of the bone in a homeless London night.

The black woman opposite him has a son that looks her double. He's cute. He's staring at Colman. He winks at the little man. The boy keeps staring, pleased. So Colman winks again. And again and again. The boy is two or something. He's still staring at him. Shit, I can't spend my whole time winking all the way to fucking Euston, Colman thinks, and turns his head away. He's relieved to see them getting up to get off at King's Cross. He gives the boy a nod and the boy gives Colman a smile to die for. Doesn't cost much, Colman thinks, doesn't cost much to nod at a little geezer and make his fucking day.

Colman never reads a book or a paper on the tube. He likes to keep his wits about him in case somebody tries to do him over. This is a mean city. You've got to watch out. London is not the London it used to be. It's all broken up. It's defeated. It stinks. He's relieved to be cutting loose. Going somewhere on a train. Actually escaping. He is getting the fuck out of it. He feels something in him lift and float, something light and fluffy. Time is a dandelion clock now. He can blow each hour off and make the time up.

The big departure board at Euston blinks down at him with its frightening list of the wrong cities and times. He stares at it panicking. It's a while since he did this, get on a train on his own. He stares at the wrong cities, sweating. Where is Glasgow? Why isn't Glasgow up? He realizes he's looking at arrivals and not departures. Asshole. There it is. Glasgow 11.15. But no platform. Why isn't the platform number up? Who can he ask? He'll just need to stand watching the big black board till the number appears. Fuck. The number will appear at the last fucking minute and every anxious fucker will be rushing down the platform, banging their trolleys into the backs of others' legs and struggling with that tight gang of trolleys to get their quid back. Carlisle. The train is stopping at Carlisle. That's on the border. 'The minute I hit Carlisle, I know I'm in my own country. My heart starts beating the minute I cross the border,' his father would say. Well, why don't you go back and live there then? Colman would ask him. He'd just shake his head. Not enough work.

Not enough work, my ass. His mother. That's why he didn't live there. His mother was alive.

His mother is alive. Does Josephine Moore's mother know that her daughter is dead? Will he have to tell her? Shit. He rushes and buys a tuna sandwich and a Diet Coke. Still no platform number. He scoots into Menzies, gets one of those puzzle books where you find words, diagonally, horizontally, vertically. They make him feel clever; he can't do crosswords. He hates crossword people: conceited bastards, always humming to themselves, thinking, thinking with all their thoughts showing on their face, sitting with their sharp pencils or their fancy pens, sly, working out their cryptic clues. Saying 'Ah' ostentatiously and triumphantly filling in another anagram. His mother can do crosswords. His mother has tried to teach him the secret of crosswords on and off through the years. His mother would have loved that kind of son; the kind of son who would have listened, got it and in no time been filling in his own puzzles in the *Guardian*.

Colman moves about in the queue from foot to foot. Impatient to get going. What is it about travelling that makes him so anxious? He sees other people looking harassed and wound up, shouting at each other. Over the top. Everybody's over the top, except for a few business wankers with suits who will probably sit in the first class, cool as fucking cucumbers. Well, he's cool really. He's got his ticket, his sandwich, his reservation. Everything's cool. No problem. No problem.

He strides down the platform, longer steps than usual, easily overtaking all the old people and the women with children. He is looking for H. He can never understand the order of this carriage business. It doesn't seem to be straightforwardly alphabetical. He has to walk practically the length of the train before he sees the hopeful H. He hopes someone else is not going to be sitting in his seat. He's had that before and he's always lost the battle of the train seat. Even though his ticket has said the same thing. He's always lost. Got himself into a fight with the railman, the other customer, the other fuckers on the train staring. It is not easy to travel in this country. Black guys like him. People always think they are going to be wrong or they've done something wrong or they're lying, or about to lie, or stealing or about to steal. It's no fucking joke just trying to get about the place with people thinking bad things about you all the time. He knows they think these things. They don't fool him with their surprise and pretence. It's written all over their faces. They are wary of him, scared of him, uptight. How many times has he had to say, Hands up, it's OK. I don't bite. He doesn't want the hassle of it, someone else sitting on his seat and treating him as if he had no fucking right to a seat anyway. Out of the window another train pulls out slowly giving the impression that his own train is already moving. The sensation scares him. He panics, wondering if he is on the right train, or if he should be sitting across the line in that other train with those people that are pulling out. When he hears the word 'Glasgow' he relaxes. Should he eat his sandwich now? His stomach is empty and weird. He keeps forgetting to eat. Since his father died, his eating is all over the place. His stomach has started to make weird noises every time he does remember to eat, noises that remind him of science experiments he did at school, bubbling and garbling. He keeps having to fart or burp to get any relief. Just as well nobody is sitting next to him. He decides to open the sandwich at Milton Keynes.

How many years is it since he lived in Scotland? Twenty-five years? His father was always telling him: you are Scottish, you were born in Scotland and that makes you Scottish. But he doesn't feel Scottish. He doesn't speak with a Scottish accent. He can do a good one, like all children of Scottish parents, but it's not him. What is him? This is what he's been asking himself. It's all the train's fault: something about the way the land moves out of the window; about crossing a border; about seeing a cow's tail spin round and round its arse to get the flies away. Why is he even on this train in the first place? He is going to find out about his father. That's right, isn't it? He's going to meet the woman who is supposed to be dead. Find out about his father's real life.

He looked real enough playing that horn in those smoky clubs; he looked real and unreal like a fantasy of himself. All jazz men are fantasies of themselves, reinventing the Counts and Dukes and Armstrongs, imitating them. Music was the one way of keeping the past alive, his father said. There's more future in the past than there is in the future, he said. Black people and music. Black people and music; what would the world be without black people and music. Slave songs, work songs, gospel, blues, ragtime, jazz. ('Rap?' Colman would say. 'What about rap?' 'No, that's just a lot of rubbish,' his father would say quite seriously. 'A lot of shite. Rap isn't music. Rap is crap. Where's the story?') The stories in the blues. All blues are stories. Our stories, his father said, our history. You can't understand the history of slavery without knowing about the slave songs. Colman doesn't feel as if he has a history. Doesn't feel comfortable with mates of his that go on and on about Africa. It feels false to him, mates that get dressed up in African gear, wank on about being African with a fucking cockney accent, man. Back to Africa is just unreal as far as Colman is concerned. He's never been to Africa, so how can he go back?

Where is he supposed to begin? Who is he meant to start talking to? Sophie Stones says she is going to find old school friends, neighbours. People come crawling out of the woodwork if you offer them a bit of dosh, she says. The thought of talking to anyone who knew his father when he was a girl makes Colman feel dizzy. Staring out the window, swallowing hard, his throat still sick and soar, seeing a black horse gallop along with the train and then disappear into the distance, Colman tries to imagine himself back in that place of his childhood, in Glasgow, walking down Accident Street, turning the corner. That sweet shop, the one where the weird sweet-shop man liked children too much, what was its name? He always gave you extra pokes. The thought of arriving at Glasgow Central fills him with excitement. He hadn't reckoned on feeling this way. He hadn't reckoned on feeling anything at all.

He can't go through with it. He can't go and

talk to all these people who used to know his father. It's not possible. It's crazy. He's crazy but he's not that crazy. He'll have to tell her. Just tell her. What can she do to him? She can't make him do it. He'll visit his father's mother. He's got to do that. He's got to see her. See what she's like. See if she actually looks anything like his father.

His father never talked much about having a white mother. Didn't like the subject. Know who you are and it doesn't matter where your mother or father was from, he said. Did he? Did he really say that? How could he when he didn't fucking know if he was a man or a woman? Black men need to be more gentle, his father would say. They could learn a lot from women. What a laugh. What a laugh he must have had to himself in bed at night. Chortling and choking. What a fucking scream. Colman likes talking about white people. He likes talking about black people and white people and how they do or do not get on. His father liked talking about the past. Colman said to him once, why are you always on about the past, old man? What's Martin Luther King doing for you now? Is he going to help sell your new album? It incensed his father, talk like that. How can I have such a stupid son? What did I do to deserve you? All the black guys his father loved to talk about were American, black Americans. Black Yanks, Colman would say. You spend your whole time worshipping black Yanks: Martin Luther King, Louis Armstrong, Fats Waller, Count Basie,

Duke Ellington, Miles Davis. Black Yanks all of them. You are not American, are you? Colman grins to himself munching his tuna sandwich, remembering. I never said I was an American. What is the matter with you? No, that's right, you're Scottish, aren't you? Proud to be Scottish. Why don't you get a kilt and play your horn in a kilt? The jazz world would love that. And you know you are not allowed to wear anything under a kilt, don't you. The Boogie Woogie Moody Men would have a brilliant time, peeking up your kilt.

He drifts off to the strange sleep of trains. Half of him is sleeping and dreaming about Scotland and the other half is shouting, *Shut the fuck up!* to some screaming kid who keeps saying over and over, 'But I want that one there.' And the mother's voice saying again and again, 'Ewan, I'm not going to tell you again.' A man's voice behind him says, 'I'm telling you. If it wisnae fir me the place wid have been ransacked. They didnae know I wis there.' And a woman somewhere down the train talks into a mobile phone, or rather shouts into a mobile phone. Mobile phone voice, 'Hello, hello, I'm all on my ownio. Hello? Hello hello hello.' Shut the fuck up, Colman says to himself, trying to get his dream to drown it all out. He is there at the very back of himself, bare knees, long shorts, running across some field, a big hay field on a farm.

The dream has slipped away completely. He checks for his father's letter in his holdall, in the side pocket.

He still hasn't given it to Sophie Stones. He keeps pretending to have forgotten it. He looks at it again. 'To be opened after my death.' He wonders if he should open it now. If now is the moment. But he can't. He puts it back in the zipped side pocket. At least two or three times a day, he checks to see that the letter is still there.

The black man is carrying two cups of tea and is swaying from side to side. Graceful. He doesn't bang into anyone or trip over any foot. Colman watches him come along the corridor when suddenly he sees that it is his father. He starts to sweat. The coat is the same dark coat. The shirt. The shirt's the same. He's coming towards him. He's smiling. Christ almighty, he's smiling. Staring straight at Colman, swaying with the cups of tea from one side to another, coming towards him. Walking down the train with such dignity, such fine balance, his back straight, his eyes staring straight ahead, with neither kindness nor cruelty in them. Walking down the train as if that is all he does with his day, walk up and down the infinite train in this way, as if that is all he has been doing his whole life. Colman stares at the man in disbelief. The man passes him. Colman turns round to see where he is going. The man keeps walking.

Colman gets up to find the guy. He walks down the aisle, stumbling. He trips over some asshole's foot and nearly goes flying. He can't find the guy. Where's he gone? He can't see him. Maybe he's in the john. It says occupied. Maybe he's gone to hose off. Colman waits outside. But the one further down says occupied as well. Maybe he's in that one. Just as Colman is about to go back to his seat, the man comes out the john. It is not his father. Of course it is not his fucking father. Now he's up close, he doesn't even look similar. Colman goes back to his seat. Walks right past it, turns, walks back again and finds it. Losing it, he says to himself. Spinning out. This is out of order. He gets out the puzzle book and finds DOUBLE-TAKE right away. Circles it. That's better.

This morning Colman phoned Sammy. He wanted someone to keep an eye on his flat, but more than that he wanted to tell somebody he was going away. He always liked to tell somebody when he was going away. Sammy was surprised to hear his voice. 'Cole, where are you at?' Sammy said. Colman was not sure if it was his imagination or not, but Sammy sounded embarrassed, awkward. He told Sammy he was going to Scotland to do a book.

'What kind of book?'

'You'll see. I'll give you a signed copy when it's done.'

'Don't do anything you won't like in five years,' Sammy said.

He gets his holdall down from the top quickly. Zips up his black anorak and gets off the train. Tells the taxi the name of the hotel and sits back staring at Glasgow to see if he remembers anything.

But he doesn't see anything he recognizes. Nothing. The buildings look the wrong colour. Sammy's sentence rings in his ears: 'Don't do anything you won't like in five years.'

HOUSE AND HOME

Ialways liked Sundays with Joss. Sundays with Joss at home, not travelling with the band. Sundays at home with me. We wake and fall back into sleep together several times before we get up. Each time we wake we smile kindly at each other, full of sleepy love. Our faces have the lines of dreams on them. Joss's pillow is damp from dribbling in his sleep and this tiny pool of dampness makes me feel tender towards him. Sometimes I wake alone for a bit and lie watching him sleep. I love watching him sleep. His face often looks quite moody when he's sleeping and it makes me laugh. He lies on his side facing me, one arm thrown back over his head the other hand, possessive on my hip. In his sleep he strokes my hip, the dip of it is his favourite place, the dip where my hip meets my waist. In his sleep he loves me terribly; he remembers me, whether he is conscious or not. He knows every part of my body. If I was sad, he would wake and ask me what the matter is. I drift off with him, back to sleep, another ten minutes, just another ten minutes.

I wake to Joss kissing me, lightly on my cheeks.

His lips just brush my cheeks, patiently over and over again. His hands move up my body and across my chest. I stare at him. He has that look on his face. His eyes are very serious, intense, dark. He wants me. I know he wants me. He wants me so badly he will sulk if he doesn't have me. I pretend I am not interested. It is late. We've slept for so long. We need to get up. Get up and get on with our day. We want to go for a long walk. Remember. A long walk. His breathing has changed. His breathing is fast. His breathing excites me. Come on, he's saying. Come on. He's pulling open my legs and moving down me. His fingers move first slowly then faster and harder deep, deep to the back of me. I feel myself being taken away. Transported to another time. Another place entirely. I am barely conscious any more of what is happening to me. I can hear my own noises through the blur. I don't know if they are loud or soft noises. I can feel my mouth open to make them. I feel myself being turned around. He straddles me. Pushes himself into me. He pulls me back round again and kisses me, kisses me everywhere, muttering things to himself. He touches me firmly, getting faster and faster till I'm shaking with desire with the need to let go, to climb really high, right to the very very top and let go. I feel myself falling down, exhausted, tearful, exhilarated. I curl myself into him and he holds me, rocking me back and forth, telling me he loves me again and again. He is smiling. Full of himself. I am weak. I am totally and utterly loved.

I like Sundays. First the lovemaking, then the newspapers. Sometimes there's an interview with Joss in one of the supplements; or a review of one of his gigs or new releases; or some gossip about the trio. I usually laugh heartily at whatever is written. Joss often gets bad-tempered about it, or too sensitive, or too conceited. But I go easy on him about this sort of thing on a Sunday, especially if he has just taken me to our other world. Our secret world that is just his and mine. Nobody else's, just his and mine.

We get up and Joss makes the breakfast. He is good at breakfasts, talented. We have perfectly scrambled eggs, not too hard and not too soft, creamy and yellow, toast, bacon, grilled tomatoes, black pudding (What's a breakfast without some sheep's blood? Joss says to make Colman squirm). Freshly ground coffee. Joss loves coffee. Loves the smell of coffee shops and choosing his own beans. Moroccan, Kenyan, medium roast, dark. Loves the description of the beans in the shop. Like personalities, he says and laughs. Comes home and grinds them in his newly bought grinder, that is his current favourite toy. Fresh coffee, hot milk, which he heats in the pan and then whisks till it is good and frothy. Freshly squeezed orange juice. More newspapers.

We never miss Sunday brunch if we are at home. 'Sunday brunch!' Joss always announces it, as if we were in a restaurant and he was shouting out the menu for his customers. 'Joss Moody's Sunday

Brunch.' Colman is rarely impressed. Joss sings to us as he puts each plate down on the table with a flourish. Da da da dah da da da dee da didi bum bum bum brup brup brup baaaaade dup dup. Scatting. Making it all up. If Colman is irritable he will shout, Stop it, Daddy, or latterly, Shut up, and Joss will start singing louder and louder, stamping his feet and moving the plates in time to his rhythm dancing across the kitchen floor. Just give me my breakfast, Colman will say. And I'll look at Colman reprovingly. Why do you have to spoil everything? I'll ask him. Your dad's just having fun. What is the problem? Be nice.

I am being nice, Colman will say. I just want my breakfast. So we will sit down to eat. Joss completely unbothered by Colman's bad humour, and me trying to rise above it and be pleasant but all the time feeling this terrible rage inside me, that these days springs from nowhere. I have never felt angry towards anyone in my whole life like the anger I can feel towards my son. It scares me. Right, let's have a nice breakfast, I say in my bully's pleasant voice. In other words, I'll want to punish him in some timely way if he doesn't manage to bring out the best of himself.

You know I don't like scrambled eggs, Colman will say. He is, what? Nine, ten? Anyway, whatever he is, he has been eating scrambled eggs happily for years. I get up and yank him from the table, pulling him along to his room. I throw him into the room and say stay there until you do like

222

scrambled eggs. I know as I am doing it that this is not quite fair; but neither is he fair and I am sick of him trying to ruin my weekends. Sick to the back teeth of his sulky ways. I hear him throw something in his room. I resist the temptation to open the door and have a piece of him. The table is still perfectly laid. The bright yellow tablecloth and the bowl of fruit and the coffee pot are all unchanged. The sun is coming through the window and making light of the apples.

Joss looks up from his paper. 'There's no need for that. You make him worse when you do that,' he says. 'Come back when you *do* like scrambled eggs?!! Are you out of your mind?' I laugh and stand behind him. I kiss the back of his neck. 'You've hurt me,' I whisper in his ear and he smiles, shamefaced. I bend over him and kiss him on his soft lips. 'You go and get him,' I say and sit down to my Sunday brunch.

When Colman is back with us at the table, eating his eggs and trying really hard, I feel all guilty again. My lovely boy. He looks beautiful. He is a good eater, really, I say to myself. Why was I so hard on him? He's only a boy. (Show me the boy and I'll show you the man.) Why do I let him annoy me so much? I'll need to try to be better. Try to be a better mummy. That's a nice boy, I say to him and smile. His eyes look all loving and hurt. Like a tiny pityful Oedipus.

We get in the car and drive to the Heath. We like a long walk on a Sunday on the Heath. It is the only place in London that makes us feel that we are not in London. The trees are shyly blooming and the May sun shines through the leaves towards our faces. Joss and Colman walk and run hand in hand. We play games as we walk. Make up stories. I spy. Catch you out if you say No. Make up a song with a car in it. Make up a song with the word San Francisco in it. Make up a song with the word bitter in it. We can never catch Joss out. No matter how unusual the word. I even tried Shakespeare on him and he got a song. Brush up your Shakespeare, he started singing, pretending he was sweeping the Heath with a big broom.

Sundays. Perfect, ordinary Sundays. Today is Sunday. I have missed five Sundays now without Joss. Five. He died on a Sunday. I wish he had died on a different day. The last few Sundays before he died were not like our Sundays at all. He was so ill and we both knew he was dying. We didn't know when it would be.

I remember things each day about the Sunday Joss died. Things I don't want to remember. It was a while before I called anyone. I just sat with him, waiting for his soul to travel. I have never believed in such things until the moment that Joss died. But I do now. Because in our room as Joss was dying, I could feel two of him there. One was the ill person, lying on his bed, constantly making clacking sounds with his dry mouth, opening and closing it, trying to make it moist. The other did not have a body, but was more like a spirit in the

224

room. A spirit that had miraculously managed to get out of his body early and comfort me, tell me to let go, tell me everything was going to be all right, only I needed to let go so that he could too. For some moments I wrestled with the voice of this spirit. I didn't want to let go. Right up until the last minute, I believed in miracles; I believed he might pull through, get better. You hear of people all the time that are at death's door and turn back to life. I was waiting, wanting more than I've wanted anything in the world for Joss to turn back to life, just get better. I prayed. I clasped my hands together like a child; I went down on my knees and prayed. I am not religious, but I prayed. I prayed. So help me God. I didn't want to let Joss go. I held on to the sick person's hand. I felt sick myself. Weak from lack of sleep and pure terror. A kind of terror I have never ever felt. A kind of terror that is so pure, so powerful, it goes into your body and claims it. Your temples sing the terror. Your sweat smells of it. Your mouth tastes of it, metallic, poisonous. Your hands shake with it. Your voice, even though you try to sound soothing, comforting, reassuring, your voice shakes and is not your own voice any more. It is the voice of pure terror and you know it; you know it when you try to speak with your old voice and this new voice comes out. This new voice that is saying please to itself, please please please. Not now. Don't go.

Until I realized that this was agony for him. That

the first Joss and the second Joss both wanted to go. That the spirit was kind but it was also at the end of its tether. The vehicle was ready and waiting, it couldn't wait any longer if it was going to take Joss to where Joss needed to go. So I kissed his hand and took some initiative. I said, it's all right now, darling. You can go now. You can go now. It is all right. You can go now. I kept stroking his hand, stroking it smoothly in the one direction. Feeling the ghost of a pulse still beating. I left the room. I went to the toilet. When I came back his pulse had gone. His hand had fallen out of the sheets and was hanging over the bed. I tucked it in. He was lying half-covered in a white sheet. He had on a pair of cream linen pyjamas. His hair was still damp, his skin was still clammy. His hands were still his hands. I couldn't take my eyes off him. He looked different. I've heard of people who pull a sheet over the dead person to cover the face. But I couldn't do that to Joss.

Joss told me a few days before he died more about being a girl than he had ever done in a lifetime of marriage. Two days before he died he had an unusual request: a tin of Ambrosia Creamed Rice. His favourite pudding when he was a girl. He had said those words, for the first time in his life with me: 'When I was a girl my favourite pudding was Ambrosia Creamed Rice.' I spoonfed him a little bit of the rice and that was his last meal. He told me to remember the bandages, to remember and put the bandages back on. So I unbuttoned the pyjama jacket, managed to pull it off. It was hard work. I wrapped the bandages around his chest for the last time. The bandages that were part of our life together. I wrapped them round and round tightly till his small breasts flattened underneath the cream-coloured bandages. I did not cry when I was doing this. I had no way to express this feeling I felt. It was worse than anything I have ever felt. I still have that feeling. That same sickening feeling. I had it this morning when I woke up and thought for a moment that Joss was alive. I put his pyjama top on and did the buttons. All this must have taken a very long time. I put a fresh sheet over him and another blanket. I would call the doctor, the undertaker, get him moved soon; but first I had to tell Colman.

I wanted to wash my hands now. Wash my hands and my face with cold water. I could still feel the other Joss in the room, hovering. The spirit Joss. The kind understanding one. I stood up on my own two feet. I went into the hall and stared at the black phone. I stared at it for ages trying to remember Colman's number. It came to me some time later. I know it must have been quite a while because the dark shades deepened. I had looked at my watch when Joss died. It was 1.12 a.m. when I came back into the room and found him dead. I had heard that in hospitals they are strict about the time of death as well as the time of birth. I wanted to get the time right. That night before he died, I had left the room for a couple of seconds to phone

227

1 2 3, so that I could be sure that my time was the same time as the rest of the country. The disembodied voice told me it was nine-thirty and twenty seconds. It is half-past two. Colman's number enters my head, fully formed – 802 0464.

I cradle the phone. I say to the spirit that I know is still there: I'm going to phone our son. I'm going to phone our son. I push the numbers. My fingers feel barely strong enough to push the numbers. I get Colman's answerphone. I have always hated them. How can he have it on at a time like this when he knows his father is dying? I hold on waiting for the bleep that everyone tells you to wait for. When it comes it frightens me, it is so loud and thoughtless. I say, Colman? Colman, are you there? And the real Colman is on the line in a flash. Your father died an hour or so ago, Colman, I say. Can you please come round?

I don't know what I would have done without him. He came round, quite soon I think. But he didn't want to see his father. He said he'd rather remember him alive. If only he hadn't changed his mind. If only he'd never gone to the funeral parlour. It wouldn't have made any difference, I suppose. Somebody was bound to tell.

When Colman came he started behaving in a way I had never witnessed: he became super-efficient, organized, understanding. He made hundreds of phone calls. He made me many cups of tea. I wanted to ring the undertaker myself. I had to think now of the person lying in that room as Joss's body. I remember noticing daft things. A neighbour of ours that had never been all that friendly weeping in the street when the body was carried out, early on Monday morning. I watched at the doorway. I had to watch him being taken away. I had to make myself. A little boy, two houses down – his name has gone – came running up to me. Did your husband die? Did your husband die? he asked till his mother came rushing out and shooshed him. I stared at him for a moment then I said, 'Yes. My husband died.'

My husband died. I am now a widow. That is what I will tell them if they come and ask me. My husband died. I am now a widow. My husband died, I am now a widow.

Why can they not understand how ordinary that is? Many women have become widows. Many women have gone through what I've gone through. Many women know the shape, the smell, the colour of loss. Many women have aged with loss. Grief has changed the face of many women. I am not alone. I have to tell myself this. I am not alone.

I am lying to myself. I am always lying to myself and I really must stop it. I am alone. My friends don't know how to talk to me or write to me any more. They are embarrassed, confused, shocked. Perhaps angry. I don't know. Perhaps they are angry like Colman is angry. I don't know. Perhaps they want to know how I 'managed' it.

I managed to love my husband from the moment I clapped eyes on him till the moment he died. I managed to desire him all of our married life. I managed to respect and love his music. I managed to always like the way he ate his food. I managed to be faithful, to never be interested in another man. I managed to be loyal, to keep our private life private where it belonged. To not tell a single soul including my own son about our private life. I managed all that. I know I am capable of loving to the full capacity, of not being frightened of loving too much, of giving myself up and over. I know that I loved being the wife of Joss Moody.

I managed to live with a genius. Not easy, I can tell you.

Maybe all widows feel misunderstood. The widow who takes to her bed and pulls her curtains down, does not do the done thing – pull herself together, put on a brave face – perhaps she feels like I do. I am putting on a brave face. I have pulled myself together.

Today is Sunday. The fifth Sunday without Joss. I have made myself a brunch. My scrambled eggs are not as good as his. My coffee is always too weak. My bacon is overdone. I sit down at the wooden table at Torr and eat. Joss would approve of my making a Sunday brunch in his honour, in his absence. Later, I will go out and get a newspaper. I haven't read a whole newspaper for quite a while. Those disgusting articles scared me off. But today I quite fancy a couple of the Sundays.

If they come I will be ready for them. I will tell them all about being Joss Moody's widow. I will not be shy. Now that I come to think about them, I realize that I actually want them to come. I know that if I actually see Colman and he looks straight into my eyes, he will not be able to do this book. Not possible. When they come for me in the morning, or the morning after that, or the afternoon after that, or the following week, I will be ready.

OBITUARIES

JOSS MOODY

1958 *Millie's Song* (Centre)
1960 *Night Hiding* (ACR)
1963 *Prodigal Son* (ACR)
1966 *Fantasy Africa* (Heygana)
1967 *Moody Moanin'* (Power Label)
1968 *Wee Blue Bird* (Sugar)
1972 *Torr* (Sugar)
1975 *Rainstorms in Italy* (Columbia)
1979 *Blues in a Wild C* (Columbia)
1982 *Rubric* (Columbia)
1985 *Slow 'n' Moody* (Columbia)
1987 *Sunday Brunch* (Columbia)
1991 *Joss Moody* (Columbia)
1994 *The Best of Joss Moody* (Columbia)

Joss Moody, trumpet player, born 1927;
died 27 July 1997

GOOD HOTELS

He must have been away with his father at least seven or eight times in the past five years. Little trips, a couple of days with the band. If there is a Toblerone in the minibar, the hotel scores top marks. If there's a white bath-robe in plastic in the wardrobe, it scores top marks too. The only time Colman ever wore a dressing gown was on the road with his father. It was fun. His father always insisted Colman have his own room. If the room service menu includes a hamburger in a seeded roll or a steak sandwich, it's doing not bad. If it has Sky TV and a movie channel, it's in with a shout. If it has none of these little luxuries, it stinks. This one, in Glasgow, has the lot, the whole package. Colman checks for everything, sees it's all there, then feels depressed. He doesn't know why. Feels himself sinking. There is no old man to meet in the bar for a drink.

'What do you like?' she asks him, pulling her white napkin over her black silk dress. 'Would you like a gin and tonic to start?' 'You order everything for me,' Colman says and watches Sophie's eyes. Her eyes are large. Her lashes long. Her hair is blonde; she wears it up. A few long fallen strands of hair line the edge of her cheek. Her cheeks are high and sharp. She tilts her head to one side, looking at the menu. Her lips are slightly open as she thinks. She's wearing a bright lipstick, a startling red. Her lips are not full, and not thin. The bottom lip looks as if it could belong to a different mouth from the top lip. 'Are you sure you want me to order for you?' Sophie asks, looking up from the menu. 'Sure, positive,' he says. The waiter comes and she orders two Dover soles and a bottle of Chablis. 'That's us then,' Sophie says.

Colman can't think what to say. When the fish arrives, he is relieved to have something to do. He lifts the bone out carefully. It is pleasurable to airlift the bone to safety. He puts it at the side of his plate. The fish is excellent. Sophie Stones talks incessantly about the book. She calls it, 'Our book.' It's starting to grate on him. 'Our book.'

Alone in my hotel room, I go over and over Colman in my mind. Strip him bare. Picture his back completely bare, his arse, his thighs, the inside of his thighs, his balls, his cock. All of him. It is not a game any more. It is not even a story. Tonight for the first time, I felt sorry for him. I felt sorry for myself. Feeling sorry for him only made me want him more. Damn, Colman loves his father. He loves his father. It agitated me to discover that instead of hate or fury or spite or repulsion, the emotion, that I saw clearly written across the wide high bones on Colman Moody's cheeks, was love. Love! It was like the first time in my life I'd really seen it.

I take off my black silk dress and hang it up. I put on the white towelling bathrobe and run a bath, pouring the bubble bath in. I slide underneath the foamy bubbles, close my eyes. Something is wrong. Must ask him what is the matter. Tonight, at dinner, he was on about how he couldn't meet these people, how it would do his head in, I had to do it. Wanted to meet Mrs Moore on his own. (Had to give in to that.) I mentioned this Torr place to him and he just about blew up. Not going to visit his mother. Not taking me up the road to Torr. Couldn't do it. He said, 'I'm not taking *you*!' as if I was tainted or something. It hurt my feelings. As if I was the gutter press. I might write for the *Daily Sky*, but I'm freelance. It annoys me when people assume we're all the same. Colman didn't even pause on my hurt look. He loved that place, Torr, he said, with its windy roads, the wind on the top of the cliffs, the wild walk down to the harbour, the boats. The men fishing, endlessly, patiently fishing. The smell of fish and rain. The little café that'd been there since he was a kid. Torr was sacred. Couldn't be touched. Neither could his mother. She needed to be left in peace. No matter what she'd done. She must be grieving, he said, as if it had just that moment occurred to him that his mother would be grieving. 'Grieving badly, man,' he said. I didn't know how to react. I wanted to say to him, 'Look, you've got me all wrong.' I didn't want to risk it, to risk antagonizing him. I had to play it cool. People often get cold feet just before they spill the beans. Quite common. Not the first time a great story has pulled out on me. A scoop scuttling backwards. Never thought I'd have any problems with Colman Moody though. 'Look,' I said, 'it'll be good this book. It is just trying to explain the phenomenon of your father. It'll help other people.'

'That's bullshit and you know it,' Colman said. 'Phenomenon of your father!'

So I tried to soothe him and calm him down, but when he gets worked up he gets worked up. Bloody hell, I thought to myself, he must have been a handful. I felt a moment's fleeting sympathy for Joss and Mill Moody. Let's both get a good night's sleep and talk about it in the morning, I said. Chill out.

When I first wrote to Millicent Moody, I had Colman's word that we would visit Torr together. At the time of the second letter, Colman seemed less sure of the visit. He told me his mother would never cooperate with such a book in a month of Sundays. Then he wondered for a moment what a month of Sundays would actually be like. That's the kind of thing he does – goes off at a tangent.

Colman is awake in room 310. He is smoking and drinking whisky from the mini-bar. Glenfiddich.

236

Now that his father is dead, he will always drink malts. After years of hating the bark and the flame of a peppery malt, Colman now finds himself relishing it. Strange that – how your mouth can suddenly switch allegiances. From now on it will be one 'wee nip' after another. Colman knows all their names. His father was a malt fanatic. Glenfiddich (if there's nothing better), Glenmorangie, Laphroaig, Jura, Lagavulin, Port Ellen, Talisker, Cardhu, Braes of Glenlivet, Ardberg, Caol Ila. High peat, low sweet. No more Jack Daniel's or Bell's or Teacher's or any other common stuff. Colman sips away, smiling to himself. High peat, low sweet.

Sophie Stones has found out Edith Moore's address. Colman looks drunkenly for the bit of paper Sophie had given him. Here it is; Number 12 The Larches. A sheltered housing scheme, one of those places where old people don't lie dead for days unnoticed, where they can ring a red bell and see somebody before they drop dead. How would he feel if he was an old woman living in a house with an emergency bell and some stranger turned up out of the blue with a blonde journalist asking questions about her estranged daughter, Josephine Moore. Maybe he should let it be, let sleeping dogs lie. Maybe he shouldn't visit her at all. What a shock he was going to be. Fuck. She might have a heart attack or something.

The idea suddenly occurs to him that he needn't mention anything to Mrs Moore about his father.

He could simply say he was a friend or something. Wouldn't that be kinder than the truth? But it would be tricking her, lying to her. How can lies be better than the truth? Good lies. What they call 'white' lies. Lies that are harmless, innocent, told from the mouths of innocent harmless white people. He isn't that, is he. Can a black guy like himself tell a white lie? If he says Josephine Moore was his mother it would stop the old girl having to hear about all the transvestite stuff. The tranny stuff has just about knocked him out so what would it do to an old woman? What would he say to Edith Moore? My father was a black man when I was a little boy. He was a famous black man who had a beautiful face and a high laugh. My father played the trumpet. He was so good at it that the whole world loved the sound of his trumpet. He played his trumpet so brilliantly that people listening would suddenly remember things they thought they had forgotten. His trumpet told stories, he used to say. Old, old stories. That was all, he would never say what the stories were exactly. You tell me, was what he said. As a treat sometimes, he would ask for ingredients to his story. Everyone present had to give one. Whatever you could think up. A butterfly. A chest. A little girl looking through a keyhole. Hair. A baby ape. An old woman in a house by the sea. And then he would make up a song on his trumpet, a song that would tell the story of all these things together, and sometimes it was possible for each person to recognize the music of the butterfly, of the wooden house, of the little girl. My father was a trumpet player. Internationally known. At the time of his death, he had made fourteen albums. He had won several awards and had played with other famous musicians of his day. My father was brought up in a small Scottish town called Greenock. His mother was white and his father was black and in his day this was very unusual. Does any of this ring a bell? My father was your daughter. Colman Moody tips the last of his third Glenfiddich into his glass. Drink always makes him rant in his head. He quite likes it. He's one of those guys that is actually more articulate, at least to himself, when drunk.

That's totally unrealistic, he thinks to himself. I can't say any of that crap to the old woman. Maybe it won't matter. There's a good chance that Edith Moore won't be all there. She could have senile dementia or Alzheimer's or something like that. Yep, good chance that she won't be the full shilling. But, she's bound to have a couple of photographs. Just one would do. One picture of Josephine Moore.

TODAY'S TELEVISION

Every morning in life Edith Moore wakes at 6 a.m. If she has been lucky she will have slept between 2 a.m. and six. Most of the night she sleeps fitfully, the sleep of an insomniac who can never, even whilst asleep, quite trust the fact that she is actually sleeping. The older she becomes the more difficult it is to find a good night's sleep. She has to picture herself walking through the woods of her childhood, past her old house with the big men's booming voices, past a steel tub where she scrubs the backs of her uncles, past a long line of shoes and boots that stretch the length of the hall in her childhood house. These days, awake or asleep, she returns to that house. The past is so vivid; the present is so dull.

At six in the morning, the daylight arrives at last. Edith has watched it coming for some time. She gets up thankfully. Another day of life for the old body giving out. There is life outside her small house; she listens to it: the paper boy, the milk lorry. The warden will come in a few hours, to do her rounds, check that they are all still living! She moves her legs round to the floor, before trusting her feet to carry her weight, pulls on her needle-cord dressing gown. She walks into her bathroom and washes her face with freezing cold water. She never had hot water as a girl and still regards it as a luxury to wash her face with hot water. Edith Moore hates waste. She was so accustomed to hardship, she cannot allow life to go easy on her. She lives off her pension and never dips into her savings. She does not want for anything, but she worries about her bills, her gas and electric. She worries about the system for heating water that operates in this house. She never has found the switch that turns the hot water on, and yet when she does her dishes or has her bath, there it is, piping. When she goes to hand-wash her pants or her blouse or her bra or her nightie, it is still piping hot. She has asked her warden about the water and her warden has said hot water is always available because of the system. But where is the tank and the switch? Edith asked. 'Never you worry your pretty head about that!' the big warden replied, annoying Edith so much that she'd have loved to take a good swipe at her. The cheek of it. That beefy warden is so bone idle she can't take the trouble to find out the things Edith needs to know. She's too busy getting back to those big plates of noodles that Edith has spied her eating.

Edith likes the plain fare: boiled ham, cold chicken, a slice of tongue, greens, a bowl of

All-Bran, a nice banana. There's plenty foods she avoids altogether now that she is eighty-seven. She is not a great fish eater. The taste and the smell of it stay with her for too long. Once she suffered a bit of fish to be polite to somebody. She has forgotten them, but the fish is still memorable. The stench. Never again. She hates foods that repeat themselves, just like she hates people who repeat themselves, or she used to. She has the strange feeling that she might be repeating herself, but she is never quite sure if she has said something before or not. Whenever she gets an opportunity to talk, even if it is to the warden, Edith finds she just can't stop and has no idea afterwards what on earth she has said. But the sad feeling of her own words linger with her and she can feel them if she moves her tongue to the roof of her mouth. Pickled onions, pickled beetroot, gherkins, onions, sybies, blue cheese, anything curried, anything spicy. All to be avoided. All foods which repeat themselves.

The last time Edith saw her daughter Josephine, she brought her a carry-out curry. Edith had never tasted one before. She has in her possession many letters from her, safe in an old suitcase under her bed. The living, curly sight of her own daughter's handwriting. She has not had one for over four months now and fears the worst. There's one thing she'll say for Josephine: she kept sending her cheques, every week. Every week for the past thirty years. She has strapped the letters in with the elastic bit of the suitcase that is usually used to keep clothes flat for their journey. Safe.

It was a chicken curry. Josephine assured her that it was 'mild'. Which gave Edith the wrong idea; how could a curry be mild? Curries were wild, hot foods for hotshots and show-offs, for daredevils. The chicken was covered in a yellow spicy sauce that did not agree with her stomach. Edith remembers the unnaturally bright yellow colour of the sauce. And the peculiar fat bloated bread that came with it, the exaggerated bread that was named after a grandmother – what was its name? You were expected to tear wee bits off this giant bread and dip it into the yellow swimming sauce. Josephine sat there on that chair, quite the thing, dipping and licking her fingers, showing off. Which house was that? 20 Aberdower Street? 26 Graham Road? 35 Lochore Road? 18 Duncan Drive? Cracking a bit of a giant's crisp named after a grandfather. Thingimibob. Edith can't remember names any more. Pop. Pop goes the weasel.

The more she tugs, the more unravels. The night that Josephine brought the carry-out chicken curry she was wearing a man's suit. Edith still asks herself about this. Why bring her a curry in a man's suit? Why bring her a curry when she doesn't like foreign food?

Old words she cannot reclaim, old phrases she cannot bring back to land, old memories that float further away from her as one day ebbs into the other. She imagines herself right over on the other side of the coast waving to the wee girl she once was who is walking with her skirt up gingerly into the sea.

Some memories have become more vivid as time has gone on. Some have shocked her by just shoring themselves up, like unexpected booty, treasure brought in by the tide. When those memories arrive home, and they tend to arrive at three in the afternoon when she is having her afternoon cup of tea with her gingernut biscuit dooked into her tea to soften it against her gums, when they arrive in through the back door she is shocked and still. But delighted. Old memories are like old relatives. She grabs the stick of liquorice, shoves it eagerly into her own mouth. Attacks the sherbet fountain.

Edith Moore passes a lot of her time remembering her husband, John Moore. Sometimes, he will spring up into her mind, fully formed. Other times, she will be trying to capture him. John Moore was different from any man Edith had ever met. His skin was very dark, his eyes the deepest darkest eyes she had ever seen. She saw John Moore's eyes in the eyes of her little daughter. John Moore has been dead such a long time now. A whole lifetime away. So far back that she could have made him up. Except there he is, on the mantelpiece, smiling in his grey suit. The new homehelp – a nice girl, Cathy, but asks too many questions – picked up the photograph and said, 'Oh my! He's handsome. Who's he?' When Edith replied, 'That was my husband,' Cathy was shocked. Aye. She might have tried to hide it, but Edith saw it just the same. Shocked at her this auld, auld woman, going out with, no, *married to*, a black man. It was written all over her face. Edith watched her hoovering, thinking things. She watched her dusting Edith's china, thinking things. She was sleekit, but she wasn't sleekit enough for Edith. Sharp as a tack is Edith. She may not be 'all there' but she is still sharp as a tack with certain things. Not much gets past her. For a long while, John Moore's picture was away in the cupboard. But she missed him. Missed having him in the room in his grey suit.

But it wasn't just the suit. (She can still see that suit. It was dark, big broad lapels, linen. Very fine. No doubt about it. It had cost a penny or two.) It was the tie that did it. A hand-painted silk tie. It looked almost tropical. Pinks and blues, exotic. Now why had she gone and dressed herself like that and what was it she had been saying to her? Edith can't remember a single word. The memory has no sound. It is a silent movie. There is Josephine, eating her curry with the sleeves of her shirt rolled up and her tie flicked back over her shoulder to stop it getting stained with the bright yellow sauce.

In her memory, her daughter is moving in the

245

jerky, uncoordinated way that people move in the silent movies of the past. Her arms look big for her body and her elbows are awkward and her eyes move too fast. The suit jacket is over the back of the wooden chair.

You never know the minute, Edith says to herself. When you are a mother you never know the minute that your child will go and do something downright peculiar and then go missing. Josephine was all she had. Josephine hasn't written for ages now, nor sent the regular weekly money she is usually so good at sending. The money that Edith cannot bring herself to spend, but puts away in her savings for a rainy day. Perhaps she went away abroad for a while. Perhaps she's been awful busy. Why won't she come and visit like she used to? Nobody knows her like Josephine knew her. And if nobody knows you how can you be yourself? Edith could be somebody different every day and most probably nobody would notice.

Even her doctor wouldn't notice. He sees that many crabbit old women, he probably gets them all mixed up. Edith had to have Doctor Ferguson out the other morning with her angina pains. The doctor said to her, 'Well, Mrs Moore, you're no getting any younger.' And Edith said, 'That I'm not, doctor.'

Edith opens her paper to see what's on the telly today. The telly keeps her better company than anybody now. It's a good day today because the snooker is on and Edith loves watching the snooker. And at eighty-thirty on BBC 2, there's a big romance with costumes. Edith enjoys seeing them, all dressed up in their fineries from the past.

INTERIORS

It is 9.27 on Colman Moody's digital watch. He gets up and staggers into the shower. The shower thunders down on him, pounding and shaming him awake. If only his shower could work like this hotel's shower, he'd be laughing. Today he needs to be conscious, fully awake, in charge of himself. He whistles in the shower.

It is 10.47 and he is ready for the off. He's nervous now. He couldn't eat much of the big buffet breakfast downstairs or take in anything more than a headline. He has on clean trousers and a denim shirt. 12 The Larches, Colman says the address out loud, 12 The Larches.

It is 11.18. A row of bungalows in a round with a clump of larch trees in the middle. A few curtains go back in the round of houses and an old suspicious face peers from each one. There is no face behind the lace curtains of Number 12. Maybe she is not in. Damn. He meant to get here earlier. Mini-bars are bastards. He'd have been all right if that ominous dwarf fridge had not been waiting for him when he got back, had not opened its wee door and offered itself up to him.

He chaps the door cautiously, then louder. He hasn't used the word 'chap' in his puff. He is becoming his father. Jesus, he is turning into his father. His father would often say, 'Who's that chapping at the door?' Where did that come from? Was it because only men used to knock on people's doors? He chaps again and peers through the letterbox. She might be dead on the floor. Nobody answers. He knocks harder. She might be deaf. The old biddy is what? Eighty-seven? Eighty-eight? Something like that if she's a day. The blue door of Number 12 remains closed. Colman tries to imagine the door opening and a woman emerging from behind it, looking him up and down as if he was going to rob her, mug her, murder her, lock her in her wardrobe for days, tie her to her armchair, make off with her tin box of savings, under her bed. Pull her mattress back and yank out her savings. Men that look exactly like Colman are always in the news. Some top arsehole in the police said recently that black guys were more likely to be muggers than white guys. It is quite possible that Edith Moore is somewhere in that small house spying on him, terrified that he has come to mug her. So he shouts something just in case, through the letterbox. 'Mrs Moore? Mrs Moore. I knew your daughter. Mrs Moore. Mrs Moore. Are you at home?' Colman is close to tears. Perhaps it's the hangover, but he shouts, his voice nearly breaking, 'I won't do you no harm.'

The curtains at the nearby Larch houses are

pulled back now. Mrs Tweedy is out in her bit of front garden. Mr Harrison is on his path. Mrs Scott is at her window. Mrs Saviour and Miss Innes are all standing staring. The other folk are ailing and cannot get to their windows so easily, but they are listening. Mrs Mason, the warden, is on her way to find out who the young man is who is banging at Edith Moore's door.

It is rare for somebody to turn up at the Larches that nobody has ever seen before. People know that Mr Harrison's daughter comes twice a week. That Mrs Sinclair's daughters take it in turns. That Mrs Tweedy has no one. That Miss Innes has a couple of mobile friends. That Mrs Saviour has the minister and the doctor out regularly. But nobody has ever seen this young man before.

'Can I help you?' Mrs Mason asks Colman.

'I'm looking for Mrs Moore. This is her house, isn't it?'

'Yes, a Mrs Moore lives there right enough. She's probably out. She goes out more than anybody here. For her messages. Likes to get them fresh every few days.'

Colman is wondering how he can prove who he is. His head is full of the news. Perhaps they think he's a criminal. Why else are they all staring at him? 'She's the only one around here that still goes out for her own groceries,' Mrs Mason is saying. The name Colman Moody won't mean a thing. 'Don't worry,' he says, 'I'll try again.' 'Dear,

dear, from your accent, you've come a long way, have you not?' 'London,' Colman says. It is on the tip of the warden's tongue to offer Colman a cup of tea at her place whilst he waits because Edith is never out long. 'Why don't you go down to the shops and have a look for her. If you turn right just there at the top of . . .'

'I don't know what she looks like,' Colman says, before he manages to stop himself.

'What did he say?' asks Mrs Saviour.

'He doesn't know what she looks like. He doesn't know what she looks like,' says Mr Harrison, whose hearing is absolutely perfect.

The older Edith Moore gets, the more she suspects that other people want to pry into the business that is her own life. The older she gets the more certain she is that all the other Larch folk want to do with their time is drink Edith's tea, eat Edith's light sponge and pry into Edith's past. The old people at the Larches can take over your life. None of them invites her back to their place. All they want is to come to her place and take up afternoons and afternoons of her time. She is fighting fit compared to most of the old buggers – apart from her angina pains. A hospital doctor recently told her that her heart and her lungs are the youngest looking organs he had ever seen for someone of her years. Perfect, he said, perfect organs. Edith felt quite proud. She can still walk. A bit shaky on the old pins, but she can make it there and back to the row of shops on the main street.

This morning she is out shopping. A pint of semi-skimmed milk. Four ounces of Edam. Three slices of tongue. A small turnip. A *Daily Record*. A small granary from the bakers. Edith hates supermarkets. For a while, she consented to going on the 'Big Shop' where they hired a minibus once a fortnight and took the whole pack of them to Safeways. It was hell on wheels. Edith couldn't concentrate on what she was going to buy without Jessie Innes telling her what to try and what was a good bargain, pulling at her trolley and once even plopping items in that Edith didn't even need. And then, the lot of them eyeing up each other's shop at the till. Mr Harrison has a very poor diet. No fresh vegetables or fruit. No wonder Mrs Tweedy is fat. The amount of cakes and biscuits and scones and pancakes for a fortnight was beyond belief. And it wasn't as if Mrs Tweedy had many visitors. When the funding was stopped and the minibus couldn't go to Safeways any more, it was a relief to Edith. The rest of the old buggers were devastated.

Edith Moore enjoys buying just enough, not too much. Edith is slim and has always been slim. Fighting fit and feckle. She regards overweight people with distaste. She'll often say to them, 'Putting on the beef, eh?' There's no need for it. The first person Edith sees when she turns the corner into the Larches is the massive body of

Mrs Tweedy. What on earth is everybody doing out when it is obviously going to rain any minute?

Then Edith spots him, the tall dark young man who looks oddly familiar. Mrs Mason approaches. 'Mrs Moore, just the person we've been looking for. You have a visitor here.' This is not how Colman had imagined it happening. This public meeting. He had imagined her behind the door, calling out first, then cautiously opening it, inch by suspicious inch. Colman half thinks of just running off at top speed. Let the old folks watch him run. Let them admire the sheer velocity of him, his large legs flying past their tiny houses, like somebody passing on their way to the Olympics. Let them stand and watch him go and say they've never seen the like. Let them say he looks like Linford Christie or Sebastian Coe or some runner from the past, some fine athlete who made history the way that Colman imagines he could make history this very minute. But he is rooted to the spot, looking for anything in the dignified, proud, but slightly wary face of Edith Moore that might remind him of his father.

The rain turns up too. The big splats of rain fall on the circle of the Larches, on the neat kerb, on the small well-kept gardens, on Miss Innes' own bush and Mr Harrison's own roses, big round drops of rain, like a giant's tears. Each of the Larch people are scared of catching the cold; at this age a cold can kill you. That's all it takes, just one bad sniffle and you're done for. They start to shuffle reluctantly inside. 'Come this way, son,' Edith says to Colman.

Edith Moore is well aware that the old buggers are peeking at her from their windows now. It is years since anything happened in Edith Moore's life that made people stare. It is rather enjoyable. This is a shocking discovery to her. The burning gossipy eyes of Mrs Saviour; the high-class nosiness of Mr Harrison, pretending to water his plant; the jealous fury of the beefy warden – who is still standing out in the rain, just to be sure. None of it escapes Edith Moore. Oh, they are always watching for something, the old buggers, and now they really have something to watch. They will sit at their windows until they see him leave. At last the ones who have been showing off during the winter, who have had their good sons and daughters come to shovel the snow off their path, who have looked down snootily on Edith's thick snowy path with disdain, at last Edith has got a chance for revenge. The shame of it during the winter. Every other biddy's path cleared except hers. And her next door's cleared even though she's not set a foot out since her man died last summer. Two daughters arriving. Always at it. Clearing something. You'd think the daughter could have taken the shovel to Edith's path when she knew she didn't have a single soul in the world.

'Who are you?' Edith Moore shouts into Colman's face, now she is right outside her own house. 'Who are you?'

'I knew your daughter,' Colman says.

'Who?' shouts Edith. 'You'll need to speak up, son.'

'I knew Josephine Moore!' Colman shouts, shifting on his feet uncomfortably.

'You're a friend of Josephine's?'

'You could say that,' Colman says embarrassed.

'What?' says Edith. 'Are you a friend of Josephine's?'

'Yes,' says Colman. 'Yes, I'm a friend of Josephine's.'

'Right then,' says Edith, rustling in her handbag for her keys – even though she's tied a big bit of string to them, they still manage to find places to hide in her big black handbag. 'Right then. Any friend of Josephine's is a friend of mine,' shouts Edith into Colman's ear. 'Ah, here they are.' She concentrates on unlocking her door. First the big Chubb, then the Yale. 'That Yale can stick sometimes,' she says to the lad. 'It can be awful tricky. You'll need to wait a moment till I concentrate.' Edith pushes her door open. 'There,' she says triumphantly. 'Come away in.'

'Come away in! Come away in!' Edith says everything at least three times. Colman has this strange fluttery feeling, beating away inside his heart, making his ribs rise and fall, his mouth and lips go dry, his hands shake and his eyes twitch and even his fucking eyebrow is starting to play up.

'I haven't seen our Josephine for years, you know, years. Is she well?'

Colman doesn't know what to say. 'It's a bit of a long story.'

Edith cuts him off. She doesn't want to hear it, not yet. Not yet. Oh, please, God, not yet. 'You can tell me all about yourself over a nice hot cup of tea. I'm not one to let my visitors go thirsty. There's plenty of them over there,' and she pointed to the Larches, 'who'll let their visitors go thirsty, but not me.'

She is in the kitchen right now. Turning on the tap and filling the kettle. Every noise makes him jump. Christ, how he wishes he wasn't hungover. What is going on? What's he got himself into? Is she mad or what? He can hear lots of banging and opening and closing doors and tins going on. She is taking for ever.

It is so exciting to have an unexpected guest that Edith Moore wants to make the most of it. She glances at the kitchen clock. It is lunchtime. Why not make the young man one of her lovely ham sandwiches. Just as well she went to the shops. Why not give him a piece of her light sponge to go with it. And a grape or two. And a bit of cheese on a cracker. She must hurry though or he might just go. Young men do that these days. They can't sit for a minute. They just get up and go. The young plumber the other day didn't wait for his tea. Nor the nice young man who came to do the rewiring. No patience. Edith has noticed, whenever she's had someone round to do something for her, fix something or hang something, or read the gas meter, they are all in an awful hurry. Nobody has time for a cuppa. She hopes the young man that knew Josephine is admiring her wallie dugs, her Chinese vases, her mahogany dresser. She's got a few nice pieces. Nothing's happened to Josephine. No, Josephine was aye a healthy girl. Even although Josephine will have just turned seventy, she is still Edith's wee lassie. Edith Moore has never given up on her all these years. One day, completely out of the blue, Edith will open her door and Josephine will be standing on her doorstep.

Colman looks at his watch. It is 12.00. He is not hungry. He is in no fit state to eat at a time like this. He tries to think about what he is going to say. Why didn't he learn it off by heart? He knows whatever it is he is about to say, he is going to make a cock-up of it. It's only natural. What is she doing? He hopes she's not starting to bake. Christ almighty, he hopes she's not going to bake some massive elaborate cake. She looks like the kind of old woman who would like to fatten a guy like him up. What is he going to say? 'I'm just emptying my messages, son. I'll be with you in a minute,' Edith shouts from the kitchen.

257

STYLE

Shopping is one of my favourite activities. I call it 'Savagery'. I can be spotted in the changing rooms of classy boutiques with feathers around my mouth and blood on my face. Shopping is a blood sport. 'Tally ho!' I cry to myself when Sophie sets out on a spree. 'Tally ho!' Every woman out for herself. Tracking down the minimalist look. Hunting John Rocha, Nicole Farhi, Clements Ribeiro when I want to be bold, when I want to parade wild patterns and stripes in lime green, tangerine and turquoise. The fash pack. DKNY. Always on the look-out for what's new, what's really totally stunning and different. Fishnet stockings. Sophie Stones doesn't just hunt down one look. If I fancy some glitzy glitter, I will get some glitzy glitter. If I want a Power Suit, I'll get a Power Suit. I will stalk a sparkly sequin number, then seize it viciously off the rack. 'Oh Gucci, Gucci!' I say when I've found what I'm after.

I will eye myself critically in the malicious mirrors of communal changing rooms. Glad at least that I'm size ten – still not as slim as Sarah – but not obese like the woman next to me, squeezing herself into a size 16 when she is probably a size 22, her Marks and Sparks bloomers riding the crack of her arse. Poor fat cow.

This morning it's Sauchiehall Street, then Buchanan Street, eyeing up the dummies in the window displays searching for something chic, glamorous, sexy. Something that would make other people say that Sophie Stones has a good sartorial sense. I like that word sartorial. Sartorial. Satirical. The need to shop cannot be suppressed or appeased. I buy up the shop. I don't shop for pleasure – sometimes it feels like I shop to save my life. A wardrobe thick and dense, black skirts with slits, gold mesh halterneck tops, and trousers and jackets and black lace tops, is a wardrobe of the woman I'd like to be. I know I'm not her yet; but the clothes can lie. Was that it with Joss Moody? That the clothes could lie?

A wardrobe crammed with famous names. You have to be somebody to wear somebody. I have a prized Sara Sturgeon black silk dress. An Armani waistcoat. A Calvin Klein shirt for men that looks devastatingly good. A rich boyfriend even once bought me a Versace dress. Donna Karan trousers. And shoes! Shoes. Oh God, shoes. Rows and rows of stilettos, of spike-heeled mules. I could murder for chic shoes.

Who shopped for Joss Moody? Did Millie buy all the shirts? Did Joss ever get measured? A tailor would surely know what was missing, no? What about the shoes? How big was her shoe size? She would have had to buy her own shoes.

What do I love more than shopping? My job. I love the tips-offs. The head hunts. The warnings. The sales. The competition. Competitive gossip. The goods. The inside information. I track down the lowdown, the nod, the wink, the kick under the table. I keep my ears pressed to the grapevine. I like to be in the know. Up to the minute. The confessions of a Colman Moody are the goods, the blood, the entrails. I can't help myself.

It fascinates me how clothes in shops look anonymous until they are owned; yet the minute it becomes part of my wardrobe, it looks so Sophie it could be tailor-made. As if whoever designed it was imagining me all the time.

It is not just 'The Shop' that has got me all worked up. Colman is at this very minute in the *Mother's House*. Hopefully, he will be getting her story right now. If he doesn't lose his fucking nerve. The Mother of Joss Moody. I have a newspaper picture of her in my head. It took me a while to find her, but I found her. It is just as exciting for Sophie as tracking down the mother of Peter Sutcliffe or Ian Brady or Fred West would be. The mother of the famous transvestite. Well, well, well. Colman has gone to the address. Number 12, The Larches. Pity the address sounds so innocent! It doesn't quite have the ring of 10 Rillington Place or 25 Cromwell Street. It is not an address that makes the hairs on the back of my neck stand on end. But Edith Moore would not have lived all of her life in that sheltered housing scheme! Of course! Find out all the other addresses, the childhood homes of Joss Moody, the teenage ones. One of them is bound to be gripping.

The minute I even sniff a whiff of depression coming on, or a slight wind of paranoia, I am out to the shops, sometimes before they have even opened their doors. Shopping staves depression. Definitely. If I buy the right outfit, Colman might like the look of me. I better not ever introduce him to my sister. He would go for Sarah. Men do. Men have always gone for Sarah. She nabbed my first boyfriend, Paul Ross. I never forgave her for that. The *first*. I'll never forget that feeling I had when I watched him holding Sarah's hand walking down our street. He gave her a look he never gave me. It was an admiring look. The worst of it was he didn't look like he was admiring her body, he looked like he admired her as a person. It just about knocked me out. I've still never seen a look like that on a man's face for me.

Colman likes casual stuff. Perhaps I should buy myself a pair of black jeans. A pair of black jeans and a red silk shirt. What about that then? Soon he'll be back from the Mother's House ready to tell all.

It is raining, soft at first, then full and heavy. I shelter outside a shop and punch the number of the hotel into my mobile phone. Room 310, please. I hug the phone to my ear with my shoulder, shoving the bags of new clothes between my legs, holding them together with my knees. Glaswegians are running in and out of shops. Sitting in the café opposite me, drinking cappuccino. A few passersby scowl at my mobile phone as if it was a fucking pit bull or something. Colman is not in. His number is just ringing and ringing. I leave a message on the hotel voicebox machine. 'Hey, Cole. How did it go? I'll check with you in another half an hour. How about dinner? I've found this great Thai restaurant. Hope you like Thai. Bye for now.' Did that sound stupid – 'Hope you like Thai?' I mimic the sound of my own voice. I click the little murder weapon into its soft leather pouch and toss it into the snarled open mouth of my handbag. I snap that shut. Where the fuck is he? I hope he hasn't mentioned our book. I told him to leave all that to Sophie. I hope he doesn't go soft and sell out. I don't trust him.

I must get back with my spoils.

Back in room 308, I try them all on again. Round 2. They look different here in the mirrors of the hotel room. I stand on the bed and unbutton my red silk blouse slowly and start to touch myself looking in the mirror all the time. I try his number after I come. No reply. It is 7.30. What is he playing at? I run a bath. Pour two of the chubby little bubble baths in, get a decent lather going. Call room service for a G&T.

Wait impatiently for the black suit and white shirt to arrive with it on a tiny tray. I get into the bath, G&T in one hand, *Hello!* in the other. Bliss. He'll be back soon. What is this? Is it The Book Sophie's bothering about or is it Colman himself? The Mother is not likely to stay up late, is she? Don't all old people go to bed ridiculously early? They must be catching up, I think, soaping myself, catching up with the past.

I try to act the part of actresses I've seen in foamy baths in the movies, but I can't manage it. The water is irritating. I can't relax. The bubbles are smothering. I jump out and rub myself viciously. The phone in the room isn't flashing. I check my mobile to make sure it is turned on and the batteries haven't run out. I gave him both numbers. Sophie can't suffer not being rung. I need a flashing machine, a spewing fax, a blinking e-mail to make me feel loved. Why hasn't he phoned me? What the fuck is he playing at? Is he playing hard to get? If he is playing games, I can play too. Let him ring and I'll tell him I'm having an early night.

It is 8.15. I've got my TV on. My hair is done. The gel is on. Blusher done. I sit back on the double bed in my room and flick through the channels on the remote control. Remote controls are wonderful. How did people watch TV before they had them? I like the quick pic, seeing something in a flash and moving on. This hotel has Sky and cable. I stop at the chat show long enough to hear a mother tell how she stole her daughter's boyfriend; on to *World in Action;* finally, I settle on the last bit of *EastEnders.* I feel like getting into bed, wrapping myself up in the duvet. But I don't. I lie on top of the covers, fully clothed.

HOUSE AND HOME

I wrapped two cream bandages around his breasts every morning, early. I wrapped them round and round, tight. I didn't think about anything except doing it well. Doing it well meant wrapping tight. The tighter I wrapped, the flatter his breasts. That was all he was concerned about. He didn't care if it was uncomfortable. It probably was a little. I don't remember us saying anything whilst I did this. I don't remember thinking much. I had to help him to get dressed so that he could enjoy his day and be comfortable.

I did it without thinking about it. He put a white T-shirt over the top. Over that another T-shirt. Over that, a buttoned shirt. He put on his boxer shorts and I turned away whilst he stuffed them with a pair of socks. He pulled on his trousers, constantly adjusting his shirts and the stuffing. He was always more comfortable once he was dressed. More secure somehow. My handsome tall man. He'd smile at me shyly. He'd say, 'How do I look?' And I'd say, 'Perfect. You look perfect.'

I have some of his bandages here at Torr. I don't know what to do with them. I can't throw them away. I can't give away these bandages. I can't burn them or bury them or throw them into the dustbin. They are in the top drawer of my chest of drawers here along with my white cotton underwear. They lie in there curled and sleeping like a small harmless animal. They smell of him still. They smell of his music; the peat smell of jazz. I have the bandages and I have his golden trumpet, his mouth pieces, his battered old box, his last flyer announcing his glorious return for a week at Ronnie Scott's. These are the most personal things I have.

Once I slept with two bandages under my pillow. That was light years away, in the bizarre couple of days after his death. I don't remember which days now. All days are the same day. I live the same day again and again and again and again.

When I open up the trumpet in its box, it stares out at me, using its dumb keys for eyes. It looks sad. Unplayed. It looks like it is saying to me, where has all the jazz gone? Where is my master? I put my lips to its tight gold mouth. But I can't make a sound. I put it back, laying it down in its furry case. It is lifeless. I shove it under my bed, the battered case.

His breasts weren't very big. They flattened easily. Nobody except me ever knew he had them. I never touched them except when I was wrapping the bandages round and around them. That was the closest I came to them, wrapping them up. He put his arms in the air whilst I tucked in underneath and then pinned carefully, making absolutely certain there was no chance in the course of a long day of that pin ever coming undone. That was it. Other than that, they didn't exist. Not really.

FEATURES

Colman Moody leaves the house of Edith Moore at 9 p.m. He leaves her watching the nine o'clock news. He is carrying the photograph of Josephine, aged seven. Edith Moore has given it to him in a brown envelope. There she is, Josephine Moore at the age of seven, smiling a gap-toothed smile, the first two milk teeth gone missing together. Her hair a mass of black curls. A great big happy grin. She is wearing a white blouse and white ankle socks. Black shiny shoes. A pleated dark skirt. She is standing next to the wall of the house she lived in then. 20 Aberdower Road. Edith told him all the addresses she had ever lived in. She reeled them off with the satisfaction of somebody at last able to remember something accurately. She paused dramatically at the end of each address. Colman stops under a street lamp and stares at the photograph again. He can't get away with it. Now that he's seen the little girl, he can see something feminine in his memory of his father's face that must have been there all along.

The streets are too dark, and the light too dim

for him to see the little girl clearly, but he stands and peers just the same. Waiting for something to happen. Some other image to appear behind the one that he is holding in his hand. Some transformation to occur to make sense of it all. He puts her back in her brown sleeping bag and strokes the rough manilla flat. He has a song in his head, the same song his father sang to sing him to sleep. Dreams to sell. Dreams to sell. Angus is waiting with dreams to sell. He carries the photograph gently, making sure he will not damage it.

He strolls down Braehead Road in no hurry. Edith has told him to walk to the Clock where he'll find the cab office. She said it is quicker than phoning one. He is glad of the walk, of the night air. How could his father have stopped seeing her? What a waste. Colman has had lunch and supper at the house of Edith Moore. He is certain the old woman has fattened him up. Just lifting one foot and then the other, just making the foot take a step in a straight line, just making his free arm swing back and forth is an effort. His whole body is heavy with this thick sadness. It lies across his chest, a fat sleeping dog lying by a fire, a coal fire. Some nameless person from the past of his father has been out to a bunker and shovelled that coal into a tin pail and then shovelled it into the fire. Colman walks slowly, one foot after the other. There is no lightness in his step. He needs to sleep and sleep. He can't face Sophie Stones tonight. He needs to have a drink, a malt, and drift off.

He needs to bury himself in sleep, to go down and down until he is no longer conscious of himself, until he could be somebody else dreaming of himself.

He opens his door as quietly as he can. She might be in. He doesn't want to see her. He is tense. He has to be on the red alert from now on. He tries the stupid little plastic card, disgusted at it. Whatever happened to those big keys, those ones with the huge iron balls at the end to prevent people from stealing them, or forgetting them? Shit, they were better than this plastic nonsense. Red lights and red lights. He finally gets the green light and enters his hotel room silent as a thief. What has he got to be afraid of? He darts into his room, listening out for the sounds of the Journalist. The sounds of the Hack, that's better. The Hack has got her TV on. He can hear it. He puts his on till he tracks down the same programme she's watching. *Birds of a Feather*. He turns his volume down low. His eye catches the phone blinking. It can only be the Hack on the machine. He will not listen to it.

He has to lie down. When has he ever felt like this before? If he can remember ever feeling this way before it will be a relief; he will at least know he is not going stark raving mad. He can't remember. The phone rings. He jumps. Is it cowardice that is making him worry? Is it the fact that he knows he is weak? The worst kind of coward. A coward that wants to be paid for being a coward. That must be it. Answer the phone, Colman. Tell her to go and raffle herself. If only he could go back to the house of Edith Moore, where it is safe and warm and smells of old woman, old musty woman.

It rings and rings and rings. Then the machine gets it. The machine plays its own voice then it copies hers. He listens to the copy a few minutes later, pressing the phone to his ear just in case. It has got her exactly right, the machine. Her voice is dripping. And there's something else. She's sounding a bit off-key herself, a bit worried. So the Hack is hyped up! He smiles to himself and pulls open the mini-bar. The thought occurs to him that she might guess he's in hiding and come right up to his door and rap on it. Rapid little knocks. What then?

He's made himself into a hostage. The Hack's hostage. That's what he is. He laughs softly. He knocks the fiery drink back in one smooth motion. It burns his throat then his belly. That's better. He pours another. She's paying. Let her pay. Let him clean her out.

PEOPLE: *THE OLD SCHOOL FRIEND*

In her dream last night, May Hart was the first at the scene of the crash on the M8. The whole thing happened before her eyes, the smash, squash and scream of metal till it collapsed in on itself. The monster lights of the lorry still shrieking brightness.

She would have to stop. She drove right up into the jaws of the crash and got out of her car. Her legs shook inside her trousers as if the night's fierce wind was trapped inside her bones. The girl was lying on the road face down, still alive, moaning. She moved her into the recovery position she had seen so often on the television. For a moment, in her dream, she considered her own age with total clarity. The absurdity struck her right away. She was too old to be driving, running the risk of running into this. What use was she going to be now at seventy, running for help. She sat put with the girl and took her hand. The very next moment – a young policeman is kneeling over the girl. A large tree has grown up behind him. Its huge branches waving in the accident light. It is only then that May realizes who the girl is. It is

Josephine Moore. She hasn't seen her in years. She is just wondering how come Josephine never aged when the policeman breaks in, pulling her and Josephine apart. A bunch of injection needles in his hand, pointed and thin as a hairline. 'I'm going to have to inject you. Be a good girl.' Josephine struggles, wriggling and squirming on the motorway, crawling across the M8 like an injured animal. The policeman rages. His uniform lit up by the lorry's lights. 'I said be a good girl,' he booms. 'Be a good girl!' he shouts at the top of his voice. For a moment in her dream she considers getting the policeman's baton out and knocking him over the head with it. 'I know her,' she tells the policeman. 'She went to school with me.' He looks at her as if she is mad. 'I think you're a bit confused. Wait and I'll tell the ambulance man to sedate you,' he orders.

This morning May Hart realized it was talking to that woman that was giving her these nightmares. Josephine Moore has died every night for four nights on the trot. She is always eleven years old. In only one of her dreams was May Hart young with her, but that was the worst dream of the lot. She can't even remember it now, it was so terrifying.

What did she tell her of any significance? Five days ago, on a Tuesday morning Sophie Stones arrived at 9 Milk Street, Greenock, having phoned May beforehand to explain that she was writing (an article? a book? May forgets which, the call

273

was a surprise) about her old school pal, Josephine Moore. Of course May remembered her. No, she hadn't heard of her death. She hadn't heard of her for years. She just seemed to disappear from Greenock. That was it. The journalist said nothing more. Oh, except that Josephine had become a famous trumpet player. 'Is that so?' May had said, amazed and a bit nonplussed, not being interested much in music herself. 'I wouldn't know, I'm afraid,' she'd said. 'I'm not very up on the music world.'

May got out her one copy of the old school photograph as promised. She could not remember everyone's names now, but she always remembered Josephine. She was the only coloured one in the class. A very pretty girl. Beautiful teeth. Lovely smile.

The morning of the journalist, May got up early, seven-thirty, washed, dressed, black and white checked trousers, green shirt. Not bad for seventy, she thought to herself. Wearing well. The mirror spied one or two weaknesses. A couple of veins were coming through her skin like tiny red roots. She got out her hot curling brush to give her hair a bit of body on the top. She scooshed some hairspray to keep it in place. A soft spray – she loathed those hairsprays that made your hair look petrified. She rubbed some moisturizer into her cheeks. She squirted on some of the perfume that her son had bought her from the duty free. She smelt expensive. She rubbed some foundation cream over the

274

veins. Put on some of the lipstick her daughter had given her in a Christmas stocking. The thought of talking about her childhood was filling her with nostalgia. That early in the morning the past was already bringing about some sort of allergic reaction; she started to sneeze just as she remembered the time she and Josephine had had a schoolgirl crush. She was not going to mention that to this journalist.

She examined her teeth in the mirror, clenching them together and tutting in between the two rows. The top row of teeth were her own. She was more proud of hanging on to them than she was of hanging on to her savings. Many's the young dentist who has tried to coerce her into parting with them. The middle two slightly overlap to form a tiny cross, that she hated as a young woman; now she felt a daft affection for that quirky over-lapping. At regular points in her life she toyed with getting them straightened out but decided it would take away some of her character. You are your teeth, she told herself. More than anything else, more than you are your body, or the food you eat, or the job you do, you are your teeth. Life is just a journey from milk teeth to false teeth with fill-ings and crowns thrown in between for relief. From the wondrous tooth fairy to the plague of ulcers sprouting underneath the badly fitted plate. The false teeth, planted in her mouth as evidence. She remembered the traumatic day the rich family of teeth moved into the bottom part of her house.

They were sly impostors, more suave and glitzy than her real top lot. Those silly sparkling teeth, all ready for the ball, made May realize that her husband didn't love her. Not properly. He was the one who was behind the move for false teeth because he had a set himself. He was jealous, that's what she thought, jealous watching her innocently munching and crunching on a red apple.

Looking back on that day through the fug of anaesthetic, billowing like a white skirt in the wind, she realized that it was the true turning point of her life. Without her bottom row in place, she was vulnerable, less articulate, less surefooted. It was true: her teeth going changed the way she walked. You are your teeth.

When she let the journalist into her home, she noticed the young woman had horrible teeth in one so young. They were too large for her mouth and one of them was slightly discoloured. It actually made May think twice about talking to her. What would Josephine have thought of this young woman writing a book about her? She did not look the part. She looked all wrong. Sleek and sophisticated, wearing designer clothes and smile and exuding false charm. The older she has become, the more adept she is at picking out falseness in people. It is too late to turn back. Strange though, the nasty feeling she already had. The sense that something was about to happen.

Sophie Stones seized the school photograph and peered into that old time for what seemed an age.

It made May look again at it herself and remember things. Rhona Elliot was red-eyed and crying. She never did like school. Kathleen Baxter already looked like an old woman. Aileen Forbes died of an epileptic fit. Names started returning to her. She could hear Miss Scrivner bark her name out, 'May Hart.' Everyone was called the name on the register. At least half the people in her class were not known by those names. Some of them weren't even similar. They all had two personalities. She was just reconstructing that corner of the play-ground where she, Josie and Kathy Baxter used to hang out, when she heard Sophie say, 'Amazing, amazing!' 'I know, how we age!' May said. 'It sounds daft, but it's true. You never think it's going to happen to you. When you are young, you are invincible.' Sophie Stones hesitated as if she was going to contradict her. 'You wait. You'll see,' May said confidently.

'So what was she like?' Sophie asked her still staring, bewitched at the photograph.

'Oh, great fun. Josie was great fun.'

'A bit of a tomboy?'

'No. Not at all.'

'Where were her parents from?'

'Well, that was a bit of a scandal. Her mother was from Glasgow, but her father was a black man.'

'Yes, but where was he from?'

'The West Indies.'

'The West Indies?'

'So they said.'

'Yes, but where about?'

May shrugged and laughed. 'How am I to know that? He'd been here for a long time as I remember. Even if I'd been told the name, I wouldn't remember. I've always been hopeless at names. He died when Josephine was quite young, eleven or so.'

'He died!' Sophie Stones almost shrieked. 'He died! My God! Of course!'

'Is this all for the article?' May Hart asked anxiously.

'Book,' Sophie corrected. 'I'm writing a full length book.'

'And you need to know all that, do you?' May asked her. 'Very interesting, isn't it?'

Sophie Stones smiled a creamy smile. 'Actually, May' – she snapped open her brown leather brief-case – 'it's more interesting than you think. Take a look at these.' She handed May some photographs of a male jazz musician, handsome, tall man in dark suits, patterned ties. Saxophone in hand.

'Is that one of the men Josephine played with? Is that a sax?'

'No, it's a trumpet,' Sophie said.

'Well, there you go, I told you I was ignorant about music.' May laughed.

'And that's not a fellow musician – that's her.'

'You're having me on,' May said, still laughing. 'What's she dressed up as a man for?' May looked closer at one of the pictures. Underneath the man's

278

face, she could see the girl she remembered. Josie was there all right in those eyes. Actually, if she just looked at the face, Josie hadn't changed a bit.

May sat back in her armchair. Josie looked so handsome playing that trumpet! As she stared transfixed at the photograph all the old love came spilling back. There's no love like the love you have as girls. Not the love she felt for her husband, or any subsequent lover. No love to match that burning, feverish loyalty, that hysterical devotion, that total obsessiveness. As a girl, May Hart would have died for Josie. She loved everything about her. Her hair. Her lips. How her skirt hung just above her knees. Her funny high laugh. The way she grabbed at you and touched you when she was talking to you. May even loved Josephine Moore's silence. She had a way of being silent that was just perfect! In fact she loved their silences best of all, those shy, silly, moving silences which would only be broken by girlish embarrassment and giggles. Looking at Josie all dressed up as a man, May realized that she'd missed her all her life. Didn't she have style! Look at that suit! Her Bert never looked like that in a suit. She was moved to tears. Sophie Stones was startled. She was later to write, 'May Hart was so upset at the decep-tion of her old schoolfriend that she burst into tears,' in her MOODY notebook.

May Hart was off. Sixty odd years collapsed behind her. Josie and she were in the woods at the back of St Mary's borstal school where all the bad

279

children's fingers were broken by the belt, running to their den. They found the exact opening underneath all the bush. Broken conkers were lying everywhere, the sudden whiteness of their insides, like split pears. Josie and May found some fine unbroken, unsplit conkers, the colour of a beautiful brown horse. They rubbed the conkers on each other's jumpers till they shone. Beauties. They pierced them with their metal knitting needle that they hid in their school bag at this time of year. The string made it through the tunnel and came out laughing at the other end. They pierced each other's thumbs whilst they were at it. Blood sisters. Then Josie leaned forward and said to May, 'Have you ever tried kissing? Shall we practise so that we're good kissers when we're grown up?' They kissed a bit. May liked it but she pulled away. 'Are we doing something wrong, Josie?' 'No, we're just practising.'

'It's a bit of a shock, I know,' Sophie Stones was saying. 'Do you know even her son didn't know she was a woman?' May looked straight into Sophie Stones's mouth. Her bad tooth stared back at May like a criminal. She had to get her out of her house. 'Do you think I could keep one of these pictures?' she asked. 'For old time's sake.'

May watched the journalist get into the taxi. The journalist never waved. She knew she wouldn't wave. She had to watch to be sure that her judgement was correct. Sophie Stones was not the type to wave to someone after she left. No, no, no. She was staring straight ahead in the black cab, cool as you please. A sick feeling rose up in May's stomach. What had she done to her wonderful Josephine? Had she harmed her in any way? She would never, never harm Josie for all the world. She picked up the cup that the journalist had drunk from. Lipstick stuck to the edges. She gave it a good clean. Then she scrubbed it some more. Then she threw the cup on the floor and watched the pieces smash. When she had asked the journalist how Josephine had managed to have a son, living her life as a man, the journalist had said, Josephine married a woman and they adopted a son. When she asked her what this woman looked like the journalist had made May Hart deeply unhappy by replying, 'Beautiful. Really quite stunning. I've got a photograph of her here that her son gave to me, if you'd like to see it.'

'No, that's all right. I'd rather not,' May said. What did she want to see a picture of Josephine Moore's wife for? It was absurd. May took the photograph the journalist had given her. Josephine was wearing an elegant suit: her lovely lips were blowing her trumpet.

EDITORIAL

What happened to Josephine Moore? Look at this photograph. There she is, bright as a button, chocolate brown eyes. The picture is grainy and if it had a sound it would crackle and spit. There she is. Standing next to her house on a dark stone street. She is holding the hand of a much younger Edith Moore. Her smile is her best smile, you can tell. The best smile for the discerning eye of the camera. It is not every day her picture was taken. She is wearing a pleated skirt. Her knees are bare, but she has on white ankle socks. A white blouse. No matter how long you stare at the photograph, the clothes she is wearing will not change. They are locked in their own time, with their own stitches. But every time you look at the little girl's face, you will see something different in it. The first time there is the wide smile. The second time there is something about the eyes that draw you. The eyes of a girl who knows she is going to be somebody special. Is that possible? Or are you seeing things? No, there it is that look. That look that is years ahead of its time, waiting. Bright and burning. Does she look at all tomboyish with that confident sparkle in her eye, that wild look? No. No, that couldn't be said. She looks just like a little girl. A happy little girl. She is holding her mother's hand, not tightly. The hands rest in each other. One hand is the other's cradle. Look at this photograph. Look at it again. And again. This is Josephine Moore when she was seven years old. The woman next to her, holding her hand, is her mother, Edith Moore. This photograph was taken in Greenock, the small Scottish town where Josephine Moore grew up.

GOOD HOTELS

He's run out of malt. He picks up the phone and speaks in a low voice. He asks for half a bottle of malt. 'What kind of malts have you got?' He stands at his door listening for the room service man. When he hears his step approach he opens the door, bringing his fingers to his lips, telling the man to keep quiet. He signs the room service man's board and whispers something about his baby being asleep. He closes his door, gently. It takes him another two whiskies to pluck up the courage. He will go to her door. He will tell her he's splitting. No contract signed anyway. No fucking deal.

His heart is beating fast now. Fast enough for him to think he can smell his own blood. Got to have it out. This book is starting to eat away at him. Imagine this photograph of his father as a little girl in a book with sinister captions. His father keeps coming back to him. He won't stop it. He won't let him alone. Coorie in, coorie in, he says and tucks him into his bed. He likes the sounds of the words his father makes and his father likes them too. The sounds of the words and the snug warmth of his covers. Coorie in, he says. Coorie in. He knocks on Number 308 loud enough for her to hear over her blaring TV.

THE STARS THIS WEEK

Tonight has an edge to it, as if the darkness itself was anxious. The moon is out already. The moon is out there moving through the quick swirling clouds, in and out of the waves. Appearing one minute, bright and glorious, and disappearing the next. A full moon tonight. The stars glint down at her. She is not long for this world, she tells herself. Maybe it's the last time the stars at night will brighten up her night.

She comes in from her doorstep, from looking right up into the wide night sky, from watching the moon being chased by advancing clouds. Oh, it's a wily one, the moon. It can always get away. She closes her door and locks it. Puts on her chain. She double checks everything is as it should be.

Edith Moore sighs as she puts the kettle on. Listening out for any strange noises in the night. It might be a sheltered house, but sometimes that can attract bad yins that know there are only elderly folks and a lazy warden. The old Larch folk are sitting ducks.

Josephine, Josephine. She takes off her slippers first, then her skirt, folding it on the back of her

286

bedroom chair. She slips out of her slip. She pulls her tights off and straightens them out, putting her fingers into the empty foot and pulling them back up. They'll do another day. She pulls off her bloomers, bending to get them off her feet. Bending is painful now. Her back is affected by arthritis and so are her hips. She pulls her cotton nightdress over her head and puts her dressing gown on. She goes into her bathroom and rinses out her pants. Last thing at night, she always rinses out her pants. You can't start another day with dirty pants in the house. Hanging her pants over the radiator, she wonders why the heating is still on. She was sure she turned it down. The kettle whistles. She makes herself a good cup of tea, a tiny splash of milk. She likes her tea piping hot. Not too strong. She takes her tea through to her bedroom turning off all the lights as she goes. She sits up in her bed and sups her tea. She can't read tonight. She can't even open her book. There are no sounds except the noise of the heating system, burping and gargling into the night.

GOOD HOTELS

'I don't believe you!' Sophie Stones says shrilly. They are sitting in the second-floor bar of the hotel. In the corner. On the leather couch. They are amongst the last people up. It is one in the morning. Colman is knocking back a Lagavulin. Sophie has a cognac.

'How can you renege on our agreement like this?'

'It's my morals. I can't do it.'

'You? You've got morals?'

'I've got more morals than you've had hot dinners,' Colman says drunkenly. 'You wouldn't know a moral if it slapped you in the face,' he says, trying for something better.

'I don't see what is immoral about doing this book,' Sophie says, and burps.

'Yeah, right. That's your problem.'

'Who do you think you are?' Sophie hisses, furious, drunk and feeling sadly sexual.

'Who do I think I am? I am Colman Moody, the son of Joss Moody, the famous trumpet player. He'll always be daddy to me. I'm not stopping now just because there's been a turn-up for the books.'

'A turn-up for the books? You're pissed as a newt. You must be out of your mind. We're both rat-arsed. Let's not talk any more. Cole. The book wouldn't do your father any harm. One, he's dead and two . . .'

'I thought you said we shouldn't talk any more.'

'Two, it will help people remember him. It is only the truth. You're not going to make things up.'

'How can I take that whole suitcase of letters from Edith Moore and put them in a book?'

'You didn't mention a whole suitcase? Really?'

'See, there you go again. No morals. No fucking morals.'

'Who are you to accuse me? It's not fair, Cole. Don't be unkind.'

'Stop calling me Cole, that's what my pals call me. You're not a pal.'

Edith Moore. Edith Moore is in front of him at the seaside, holding the hand of a small girl, his father. The girl has a mass of curly black hair, like himself. She is deaf. The girl takes a liking to him and starts to play with him. Then she leads him down to the basement. They are suddenly in a rich house. All the time, they are speaking in sign. Suddenly the whole place starts to fill with water. Water leaking in from everywhere. Colman puts the deaf, curly-haired girl on his back. He is going to have to save her from drowning.

He climbs stairs, frantic. Spiral stairs leading up to

the webbed feet. Spiral stairs that crumble underneath him. He takes two semi-circle steps at a time. He has got a little girl's life on his back. He has to save her. Has to save her. Has to.

He wakes up sweating. He is lying in bed next to Sophie Stones! Fuck, how did that happen? He can't remember anything. The last thing he remembers is the bar. His watch lights up in the dark. It is 4.00. He gets up quietly and picks his stuff up from the floor. His silk boxer shorts, his trousers, his shirt. He stuffs the lot under his arm and creeps to room 310. But he hasn't got his fucking card. He is standing outside in the corridor, starkers. Totally ridiculously naked. He puts his hand over himself to cover himself, protectively. Christ, he can't stand in the buff like this for the rest of the night. His clothes! Thank God he brought his clothes out. There they are lying next to his door in a bundle. He must have dropped them. He picks up his trousers and rummages through the pockets for the card. Nothing there. He pulls his trousers on in a hurry. Shit. Nothing for it but to face reception at four in the fucking morning and ask for another key.

EDITORIAL

What does the ghost writer do if the ghost gets cold feet? If the ghost gets the ghouls, the spooks, the heebie geebies. What does the ghost writer do when the ghost is no longer interested in the material? Does that make the ghost writer redundant? How does a ghost writer convince a ghost that the subject is worthwhile?

Fact: ghost writers often fall in love with their ghosts.

Fact: like biographers, they get haunted by their material. Very soon they are incapable of keeping a clear boundary between their life and the life of their subject. Many ghost writers believe they are the real authority on their subject and not the ghost themselves. They tend to get irritable if their subject disagrees with them.

INTERIOR

It dawned on me falling asleep drunk last night, just as I was falling asleep with Colman curled up beside me. It turned her on. Dressing up as a bloke and blowing that horn turned her on. There has been too much talk about Joss Moody just wanting to play the trumpet. There have been articles about how there were no women jazz musicians in the 1950s. There has been some sympathetic murmurings. Some people who are very understanding.

But if you told those people that it was nothing to do with the trumpet, if you told those people that it was fuck all to do with the trumpet, what would they say to that? Would they still offer understanding? She liked wearing those bandages, didn't she? She liked the big cover up. Going about the place taking everybody in. Going to the Gents. She got a buzz going to the Gents, didn't she? Slicking down her hair. Getting a new man's shirt and taking out the pins, the tiny pins. Shaving. Working up the lather.

Most of all, she liked the power. The power: the way women treated her, the way men treated her.

Walking down the street with that walk that she must have practised. I've got her on video. She studied that walk all right. She didn't just wake up one day and decide to be a man. She must have practised first. She must have given it a lot of thought. It can't have been easy for her, hiding like that. Stressful. Whenever I'm hiding something, I find it raises the anxiety levels. My heart beats quick with deceit. She moved town, didn't she? She moved away from Greenock then she became a man. Had to find a city, Glasgow, and then a bigger city, London. She couldn't risk staying in touch with her own mother, not for long. When was the last time Edith Moore saw her daughter? I hope Colman thought to ask that. She's studied that walk. That cool look. Yeah, she liked playing the trumpet all right, but there was more to it than that. She liked being a man. Pure and simple.

The public might hate perverts, but they love reading about them. Why? Because everybody has a bit of perversion in them. Every person goes about their life with a bit of perversion that is unadmittable, secretive, loathed. I know this. I have my own skeletons in the cupboard. So does Sarah, although she'd never admit it. There are some things families never talk about.

When I wake at 7.10, Colman is gone. I never even heard him leaving. I get up and look around the devastated room. The bottles and the glasses and my clothes fanatically folded on the chair, though I have no memory of folding them. There's a note on the dresser. 'No can do. Sorry, mate, Colman.' I grab it and screw it into a ball, a tight paper ball. I aim it at the waste paper basket. Bastard. Fucking bastard.

I turn the tap on in the bathroom. *Mate*. He is trying to humiliate me. He knows he can't turn back now. There's too much at stake. I'd be a laughing stock. I've told everybody about this book. I'll sort him out later on. It was just the drink. Just the drink talking. I shouldn't have allowed us to drink so much. I wanted him to talk, not walk. He's probably still asleep next door. Better let him sleep it off.

> I found out that my father was not a man but a woman ten weeks ago when I went to the funeral parlour in North London where his body was laid out. If I were to say I was astonished, that would not be strong enough language. I was in total shock. I felt betrayed. I couldn't actually believe it. But I had to believe it. There were the parts of a woman's body for all to see. On the person who I thought of as my father, the breasts and pubic hair looked disgusting. Freakish. He might as well have turned into an albino. That would have been less shocking. His pubic hair and breasts looked grotesque, monstrous. I was

so shocked by this and by my own reactions that I decided to write a book.

I thought that if I wrote a book about it, it might help other people. I know that not many people will ever find themselves in my position (count yourself lucky) but on the other hand unusual things happen to many people and anybody that has had anything freakish happen to them will relate to this book. I had to write this book so that I could understand my father and so that I could understand myself.

I look over what I've written. It is only a rough, but I'm quite pleased with the effect. Good idea to say 'he', that's what Cole does. I can touch it up later, after breakfast, here and there, change a word or two. Maybe take out that (count yourself lucky). Colman is bound to see from this that I'm not going to write the usual hack book, that I'm not The Ghost Writer From Hell. I have my sensitivities too. He will probably be flattered by how well Sophie understands him. I've got him under my skin. Isn't that a jazz song? That could be the title. Yes! I do my triumphant fist. Especially now, if the whole book is written as Colman. *Under My Skin*. Utterly brilliant. I will propose it to him. Later, after a bottle of good wine and a good dinner. We could try that Thai tonight. He might be surprised I'm still speaking to him. I'll miss Colman when we finish this book. Silly Cole and his stupid note!

HOUSE AND HOME

The seagulls are flying in the shape of a letter from the alphabet. V. One seagull is a rebel and is going off the other way. My eyes follow it. The sky is bleached. It is windy. I walk down to Kepper by the coastal path, the sea below me. I have grown old with this sea in my life. The wind is the sea's wild dancing partner. It bites my face, scratches the back of my neck. I remember taking Colman's small hand and holding on to it tightly, walking down this same path into the village. I remember always ending up carrying his fishing net. I wonder if he remembers any of that?

When the papers first started printing their terrible lies I felt faint. I was horrified at what I read. I imagined every person I knew reading those headlines. I imagined Joss reading them. For that first three days, I felt my whole life was ruined. Not just by Joss's death, but by the reporting of his death. But now, the newspaper articles have moved on like crows in search of other carrion and I have become yesterday's news. If Colman does this book, it will all flare up again. I can't take that. I have to do what I have to do. I have written to Colman telling him if he does this book, I will never see him again. I have written to her too, Sophie Stones, to tell her if she proceeds with this book, I will be contacting my lawyers. What would your parents think of you doing a book like this against people's will, surely they wouldn't approve, I wrote. I thought if she has had any upbringing at all, that will trouble her. I have written the hotel in Glasgow's address on the two white envelopes.

'How are you, Mrs Moody?' Mrs MacGonigal asks me in the post office.

'I'm fine,' I say. 'And you?' I slide my letters under the hatch.

I got a lovely letter this morning, forwarded on by our secretary. A wonderful letter, from a group of women jazz musicians that want to form a band. They want to call it The Joss Moody Memorial Band. It has given me hope. I am not sure whether Joss would actually have liked the idea or not. But I like it.

TRAVEL: *THE COAST ROAD*

The local bus follows the old coastal road round to Lair. The sea on the right of him. He sits by the window, staring out. It's been so long since he's been down this road. The hills in the distance; he recognizes the shapes. The Giant's Forehead, the Long Finger, the Sleeping Hare. This is the third bus he has been on today. From Buchanan Bus Station Glasgow to St Andrews, from St Andrews to Pittenweem, from Pittenweem to Kepper.

In St Andrews, he had an hour's wait for the next bus. He phoned Bruce Savage, the butcher. 'Ah, Colman, Colman, how are you?' Bruce said. 'Sorry to hear about your dad.'

He was the first person to say that to Colman, that simply. It startled him. 'Can you give my mother a message?' Colman asked him. 'Can you tell her I'm coming to see her on my own. My bus gets in at four-twenty.'

'Rightio, no problem,' Bruce said.

'Thanks, make sure you tell her I'll be on my own, will you?'

'On your own. I've got the message,' Bruce said,

laughing. 'What's happened? Has she broken your heart then?'

The bus rounds a high tight bend, he is on the other side of the harbour. He can see Kepper in the distance. His face, close to the bus window. The same old fishing harbour where he spent many many hours as a boy. His father and him and Angus on the old rowing boat. Waiting for the line to bite and tug, opening his tin of maggots, or his tin of fresh bait, attaching floats and flies to his line, choosing hooks. Reeling in the odd sensation and battering it with his mallet. The fish sometimes jumped out of his hand and flapped about the boat, even after it had died. It always startled him, that after-shudder of fish. Sitting in silence, him and Angus and his father. Keeping quiet for the fish, to attract the big catch. The special silence of fishermen. He can see his father now, holding up the three pounder by its tail, grinning from ear to ear. 'I've pulled it off,' his father says.

He gets out his father's letter. 'To be opened after my death.' He takes a deep breath. He is ready for it. Whatever it is, he's up for it. He opens it carefully. It is a long letter. Must have taken him some time to write.

LAST WORD

You wanted the story of my father, remember? I told you his story could be the story of any black man who came from Africa to Scotland. His story, I told you, was the diaspora. Every story runs into the same river and the same river runs into the sea. But I've changed my mind, now that I'm dying. It is not just fever. I am not just sweating. I'm holding a candle to myself. I can see him, because he told me the story, as clearly as if I was there.

My father came off a boat right enough, right into a broth of dense fog; the local people called it a 'real pea souper'. He had never seen fog before. The air was damp and eerie on his skin and he was freezing. Ghost country. The people and the weather shrouded in uncertainty. Shadow people, he thought, insubstantial, no colour. He was a young boy full of fears. Life, then, he said, was something that happened to him. Other people pulled the thin strings and he moved his limbs. This new country was a wet ghost, cold ingers searching his cheeks for warmth. It was as if he walked off that ship into nothing,

300

as if the strange grey air might gulp him down, whole.

This was at the turn of the century. At the turn of the century you can see the old people turn back and the young people whirl and twirl forward, he said. When the century turns, everybody turns like people in a progressive reel dance. Some turn over a new leaf, some turn a blind eye, a deaf ear, some turn the long barn tables, some slip back, sliding towards the old tongue. When the pendulum of the old clock's big hand moves forward, somebody always turns it back. Somebody who resents progress or is irritated by it or decides all change is false. Somebody who felt that the hour for the upturning of his glass was at hand. When the century turns, some people itch to betray, to desert, to escape. The turncoats walk away slowly towards the turn of the century in their long black coats. The new century arrives like a wild thing in a storm, turning up at the shore with a wet face.

When my father first arrived in Scotland at the turn of the century, the long-standing people stood huddled together in long dark coats with their long pale faces. They stood against the rock wall of the port; they seemed as if they were growing out of the rock. Standing fast, they barely moved. They were the stock-still people, chiselled into the crag. The big ship in front of them, moored and gigantic. My father looked back at it. Strange how newly arrived ships static on the sea look so unreal. He could barely believe the great vessel had actually brought him here. It looked like an enormous fiction, the letters written in italic at its side like the title of its epic narrative, HMS *Spiteful*. The closer he walked towards the people waiting for the passengers to spill onto the port, the more unreal they became. The white skin was the translucent skin of a ghost. Those people looked as if they would never find who they were waiting for; the fallen and the lost, blowing on their hands to try to bring themselves to life. They had been standing there waiting for ever with their bloodless cheeks in their secretive weather. Those people, my father used to joke, *were* the last century.

Seeing them through the fog, catching a glimpse of a hand or a boot, or a hat or a shoulder, catching somebody wipe their face with their fist through the wraith mist, my father felt as if he too was disembodied. His own body became broken up by the fog; his left arm missing, his left shoe. Close up, people would rear up and reveal something real. He never forgot that first welcome. If he closed his eyes, he told me, he could still see it. Odd that his memory would trail back time and time again to recapture mist, fog, lack of substance. Memory is a strange thing, he said to me more than once. It will catch what you would think it couldn't catch, the slippery, the runaway, the taste of wet air. But he couldn't remember what he wanted to remember. He would read many books to see if they might remind him of what he wanted to remember: the hot dust on the red road, the jacaranda tree, his mother's hot breath on his cheek. The trouble with the past, my father said, is that you no longer know what you could be remembering. My own country is lost to me now, more or less all of it, drowned at sea in the dead of a dark, dark night. Sometimes, he said, leaning close to me like he was telling me a ghost story, sometimes you think you hear your own country wailing in the wind, just before the drowning. It will always haunt me, he said, my country, my own one.

My father turned up in Scotland. Fate is a beautiful and terrible thing. When my father was six, his father persuaded a Scottish captain of a ship to take him back to Scotland and give him some kind of education. When the ship arrived into Greenock, next to Port Glasgow, Robert Duncan-Brae was there to meet it. He knew the captain and the crew of HMS *Spiteful* and offered to take my father and give him a home. Life, he told me, was like a fork of lightning. He could see exactly where one decision violently parted company with another and a new future flared up before him.

It was the first time my father had ever been in a horse and carriage. He couldn't make the horse out at first. It was like a creature of his imagination, half-hidden in the fog; he would never forget the sound of it moving from hoof to hoof, impatiently waiting to be off, knocking on the cobbled road. He heard the horse shake its breath out onto the street and lift its huge head up towards the Gods. The horse had reins around its face which the man at the top of the horse kept pulling. They were a distinguished family, those Duncan-Braes. Mr Duncan-Brae helped my father up the steps to the carriage and my father fell asleep to the sound of the horse's hoof-beat on the road. It was like percussion. It was like music he already knew.

When he got to the big house, he was given a bowl of porridge. It looked like the fog with lumps in it. He was hungry. He swallowed it down with a spoon. It had no flavour at all. He shovelled it down him. He was put in a bed and allowed to sleep for a very long time. The Duncan-Braes were not unkind to my father. But he missed his mother, his country, his mother-country. My father had a wonderful singing voice and could sing from memory just about any folk song I wanted. Every time he sang a Scottish folk song, he'd have this far-away look on his face. *Heil Ya Ho, boys, Let her go, boys, Swing her head round, And all together.*

I've never heard of a double-barrel-named family that was short of a bob or two. My father became the Duncan-Braes' servant. He polished Mr Duncan-Brae's shoes till he could see his own dark face. He polished the silver, the dark wood, the hard kitchen floor. He dusted the many books in Mr Duncan-Brae's library. He taught himself to read. He loved the inside world of books, he luxuriated in language, always making a stab at a new word, even if he got it wrong. He remembered saying for ages, 'That is a well accomplishment.' The cook didn't like his fancy black tongue. It made her seethe with inferiority, he said. Actually, it frightened her. Who was he to go about the kitchen with his sharp curved words, glinting about the place like her carving knives. He got fed up with being a servant. The cook and him didn't get on. When he was eighteen, he told Mrs Duncan-Brae that he wanted away.

'Missus, I'd like to be a painter,' he said. On the long journey over to Scotland on the ship, he had painted a couple of cabin doors and loved it. So he left the Duncan-Braes and became apprenticed to a Dundee house painter, earning a plausible living, practising his trade. Someone painted a picture of my father which I've left for you amongst the bits and pieces. The picture's called Mumbo Jumbo which has made me more angry than anything I can remember. He's not given a name. Even the name he was given, John Moore, was not his original name.

That's the thing with us: we keep changing names. We've all got that in common. We've all changed names, you, me, my father. All for different reasons. Maybe one day you'll understand mine.

When I was eleven, he died, my father. I remember my mother's pinched face. Her terrible hush. I remember the awful quiet in our house without him. The dreadful dream-like quality the whole thing had. How I kept expecting for months to wake up and find him real again. I remember the sadness in my mother's baking; once I caught her weeping into her dough. She never got over it. I never got over it. We were both changed for ever by the death of John Moore. There was no one to look at me like he did, with shining, adoring eyes, no one to clap in rhythm when I danced and sang. My mother's love was sensible, but different. Not like him. I missed holding his black hand in the street. Looking at it, comparing it to my own. I was on my own then. Looking at my own hand, trying to remember my father's lines. They were darker than mine, his lifeline, his heart.

Maybe you will understand, maybe you won't. I knew you'd come here. I knew you would come looking for stuff. I've left it all for you, my letters, photographs, records, documents, certificates. It is all here. Mine and your own. I sat down here this morning all set to destroy all of this. Burn the lot. I stopped myself. If I do that I'd literally be burning myself. I couldn't do that to myself, to my music. But most of all, I couldn't do it to you. I thought to myself, who could make sense of all this? Then I thought of you. I am leaving myself to you. Everything I have got. All the letters I have kept hidden. I've discovered a strange thing that it is probably only possible to discover when you are dying – so don't try it! – I've discovered that the future is something else entirely. That our worries are too wee. It is quite simple: all of this is my past, this is the sum of my parts; you are my future. I will be your son now in a strange way. You will be my father telling or not telling my story. (I wasn't born yesterday.) The thought of you going through all of this would have made me ill a few years ago. You will understand or you won't. You will keep me or lose me. You will hate me or love me. You will change me or hold me dear. You will do either or both for years. But I am going. I am off. My own father is back by the bed here singing. The present is just a loop stitch. *Heil Ya Ho, boys, Let her go, boys.*

Can you remember sitting on my shoulders? Remember sitting on my shoulders. Remember playing my trumpet. Do you remember fishing on the old boat with Angus? I'm being silly: remember what you like. I've told you everything. My father came off a boat right enough.

SHARES

The woman walked down the hill and into the harbour. The bus had arrived already. She walked quicker. Just as she turned the bend, where the fishing boats pondered on the water, she saw him. He was walking towards her. He moved so like his father. A bird startled her by flying close to her head. It seemed the bird had come right out of her. She watched it soar right up into the sky, its wings dipping, faltering and rising again, heard it calling and scatting in the wind.